WITCH ON SECOND

The Jinx Hamilton Series - Book 5

JULIETTE HARPER

Prologue

The night I said goodbye to my friend Myrtle, I wound up talking to a stick.

Now, hold on before you judge me. In my world, you can't take a statement like that and assign it a face value of "crazy" without hearing the explanation first.

I'll tell you more about Myrtle here in a bit. Right now, concentrate on the fact that she was my friend and I had no way of knowing if I would ever see her again.

The rest of my family—the people I'm related to by blood and by choice—walked me home. When I announced I was going straight to bed, my mother and my bestie, Tori, exchanged worried looks, but they didn't try to stop me.

Instead, they both hugged and held me, whispering in my ear that they loved me, and then they watched me start up the stairs alone.

My new "ex" boyfriend, Chase, wanted to say something. The expression on my face shut that down fast. He closed his mouth and looked at the floor instead. We had been officially "over" for less than six hours. In good Dixie Chick fashion, I was not ready to make nice yet.

Mom and Tori must have thought I was out of earshot when I disappeared into the darkness at the top of the stairs. I heard Tori say, "Are you sure we shouldn't go after her?"

"I'm sure," Mom said. "When she's hurting like this, Jinx has to get off on her own. She'll need us more in a few days."

I hadn't intended to engage in blatant eavesdropping, but then I heard Chase ask, "Is there anything you think I can do?"

If you've never had the chance to hear your mama take up for you when she thought you weren't listening, you've missed one of life's great experiences.

As I lingered quietly in the shadows above them, Mom answered him in a clipped tone. "I think you've done quite enough."

"Kelly," Chase pleaded, "please try to understand."

"Don't you 'please' me, Chase McGregor. Breaking up with my girl would have been bad enough, but doing it today of all days is inexcusable. Frankly, I don't want to be talking to you right now."

After that, all I heard was the sound of Chase's boots walking away. Smiling through my tears, I went upstairs to be with my cats—all four of them—and broke down completely.

At the end of that crying jag, they had wet fur, and my sinuses were so clogged up I could barely breathe. I knew if I didn't get a handle on my emotions, I'd wake up to the worst post-cry hangover ever.

I wandered toward my bedroom, only to stop at the doorway. Dim light filled the room. Had I left a lamp on?

It took me several seconds to realize the glow came from the raw quartz embedded in the head of a walking staff called Dílestos. I crossed to the bed, sat down, and reached for the polished piece of oak whose name means "steadfast and loyal."

At my touch, the quartz brightened, and the pulsations thrummed with a slow rhythm I found comforting. As the vise grip on my heart loosened a fraction, Dílestos began to hum.

I closed my eyes and drank in the low, soothing melody. When I opened them again, I discovered the cats were now with me on the bed, staring at the crystal with hypnotized, golden eyes. The combined rumble of their purring struck a warm undertone to the staff's gentle melody.

My next door business neighbor and fellow witch, Amity Prescott, gave me the staff the first time I went to Shevington. She told me all the women in my line carried Dílestos. The Mother Tree originally gave the staff to my Cherokee ancestor Knasgowa.

It suddenly occurred to me that I'd never thought to ask why the Tree shared a part of herself, an idea that instantly ignited a second realization. Myrtle had merged her spirit into the Mother Tree. Could she be trying to speak to me through Dílestos?

"Is that you, Myrtle?" I asked hopefully.

Through the maelstrom in my mind, a lyrical voice answered, "The aos si now resides with the Mother Oak. Just as I can never be truly separated from my source, she whom you know as Myrtle is ever with you."

That wasn't the direct communication I wanted, but the words still comforted me. "Have I neglected you, Dílestos?"

After that first trip to Shevington, I leaned the staff against the wall beside my bed. The idea of interacting with it again literally never came to my mind until that night. Now I understand the delay wasn't my being neglectful; there was a larger plan afoot.

"Our time is as it should be," Dílestos answered. "All comes in the appointed order."

"How do you know what happened today?"

"I felt the spirit of the aos si flow into the blood of my mother."

"Does that have anything to do with why you decided to talk to me tonight?"

Under my hand, the wood warmed. "Tonight you had need of my company. You must rest. Your tears cannot undo what was done this day."

Basically, an enchanted stick told me to go to bed. Ask my mother. I was never good about the bedtime thing.

"I shouldn't have been so selfish," I said, ignoring the admonition to rest. "I've been lazy riding my bike to the portal instead of walking with you so you could see your mother."

To my surprise, Dílestos laughed. "All who journey seek to reduce their steps."

Even though my eyes were starting to grow heavy, I stubbornly kept asking questions. "Why did your mother give you to Knasgowa?"

"For the One, I create the way to the many."

"That makes absolutely no sense," I yawned, dimly aware that the staff's humming was responsible for my growing lethargy.

"Your time of joining nears. Then you will know."

Still holding the staff, I stretched out on the bed. My cats instantly surrounded me, their purring sending me tumbling farther toward unconsciousness. "Can't anyone just answer a simple question?" I mumbled.

"What is plain to the ear of one seems but gibberish to the ear of another," Dílestos said softly.

"Did you just call me clueless?"

"You are not without a clue, only lacking some. Tonight you are sad and tired. Sleep."

I think I said something about that being the story of my life. I really don't remember—but I do remember what Dílestos said right before my exhaustion claimed me.

"The story of your life is only now beginning to be told as long ago it was written."

Chapter One

As I shifted to get more comfortable, my hand brushed the frigid granite beneath me. If Tori hadn't thought to bring two stadium chairs to the cemetery, sitting on the stone bench would have chilled me to the bone.

Normally at the end of October in Briar Hollow, North Carolina the low temperatures hover in the forties. That Thursday night, about a week before Halloween, it was almost freezing. By noon the next day we'd be back in the sixties, but at that moment, I would have given anything to be in front of a fireplace.

Okay. I guess I might as well be honest with you. Most of the chill I felt that night came from inside my soul.

I could opt for the simple explanation, "My boyfriend broke up with me," and leave it at that. Everybody gets why a woman would feel down over being dumped, right?

Unfortunately Chase and I run neighboring businesses, we live in apartments over our stores, and the men in his family are sworn to protect the women in mine. Avoiding him wasn't an option.

Our relationship ran straight into a massive wall of intolerance. Werecats are only supposed to get together with other werecats. Things go bad when they don't.

How bad, you ask? They crank out certifiably crazy kids who can't shift into feline form and who take out their frustration on the rest of us in murderous ways.

We spent the last weeks of that summer dealing with a guy named Malcolm Ferguson whose whole family nurses a decades-old grudge with the McGregors. The feud started when a werecat, Jeremiah Pike, married a human. Then, competing real estate claims kicked in.

You may not like your homeowner's association, but I'm betting they don't hire a hit men when you plant a rose bush in the wrong place.

Well, on second thought, maybe they do. From what I can tell, HOAs are in league with the devil. Werecats, however, are not, but they do get their backs up over territory.

Malcolm is dead, but he's not the last of the Pike descendants. That problem might be temporarily shoved to the back burner, but I have a sneaking suspicion it will boil over again.

As if all of that weren't enough, Chase and I faced an added wrinkle—the incompatibility of witch/werecat magic. We would never have been able to have kids at all, crazy or otherwise.

I coped with our situation and everything else that landed on my head that summer with the help of a dear friend.

No, I don't mean Tori, although she's never left my side. My friend and mentor was an ancient fae spirit, the aos si. We called her Myrtle.

If I'd lost Myrtle to death, I might have been able to make peace with the transition. You know, the five stages of grief—denial, anger, bargaining, depression, and acceptance.

But Myrtle didn't die. She merged her essence inside an ancient tree to recuperate from exposure to a toxic magical artifact.

Is she coming back when she gets well? I don't know.

My world runs short on easy, straight answers. That used to scare me. Now, I rely on focus and discipline to keep confusion at bay.

So, yes, in those first weeks of fall, sadness dogged my every step, but anger and determination walked side by side with the melancholy.

None of the other people in my life left me. Tori was right downstairs in her micro apartment, greeting me every morning with a goofy grin and a perfect latte.

My loveable Aunt Fiona, who gave me the store and my magic, invited me daily to come to her cottage in Shevington and learn herbology, her speciality.

Darby, our resident brownie, in collusion with my southern mother, opted for the food solution, cooking sumptuous meals for us around the clock.

Rodney, the black-and-white domestic rat with the mind of a genius who lives in the storeroom, spent most of his time curled around my neck. Rodney wanted to come to the cemetery that night, but I insisted that he stay back at the store.

In response, the little guy stomped his foot and let out with a string of chattering protests. I was having none of it. "There are things out there that would see you as an hors d'oeuvre. I can't lose one more person, Rodney."

Sympathetic tears filled his eyes. He patted the back of my hand with his tiny paw and nodded in reluctant acquiescence.

Don't get me wrong, wonderful people love me. Some of them have four legs, and some of them are, technically, dead like Colonel Beauregard T. Longworth, late of the Army of Northern Virginia, deceased since 1864.

Beau was the reason I was sitting on a graveyard bench that night. Were we there to complete some arcane ritual? To chant an incantation to raise the dead?

Nope. Been there, done that, got the t-shirt.

We were there to play baseball.

Well, *he* was there to play baseball. I was there to get cheered up.

A few nights earlier, sitting by the ever-present fire in our basement lair, Beau taught me a new word—animus. There's a simple definition—hating or disliking something. But the more metaphysical meaning is "basic attitude or governing spirit."

To help Beau get caught up with the last 150 years or so, Tori recently gave him an iPad. He absolutely loves the thing, spending hours online reading and watching YouTube videos.

When Beau asked me if I knew what "animus" meant, he handed me the tablet so I could read the definition.

I returned the device with a limp, potentially surly question. "So, what's your point?"

With infinite patience, Beau said, "Over these past few months Myrtle became your personal animus. Dear Jinx, you must now find true north for yourself."

The petulant child in me wanted to declare, "Can't make me!" Thankfully, that didn't happen. He was right.

In addition to being my friend and mentor, I believed Myrtle to be the animating spirit of the fairy mound on which our store sits. In her absence, for me at least, our home seemed hollow and less magical.

Everyone else found a way to pick up and go on like Myrtle wanted us to do—really pretty much *ordered* us to do.

Me? Not so much.

Maybe if Chase hadn't broken up with me the morning Myrtle announced she was leaving, I would have coped better—or maybe I wouldn't have.

Either way, Beau nailed it. Myrtle *was* my true north. Without her, the needle of my internal compass circled aimlessly.

But for his part, Beau was fulfilling his promise to Myrtle to take care of me—by studying magic, by sitting with me next to the fire, by taking long walks with me high in the mountains, and by organizing a baseball game.

Beau knows when to talk and when to be quiet—and he knows when to go for the laugh. That night in the cemetery, there was no way I couldn't smile at the two teams warming up amid the tombstones. It was ludicrous, improbable, and kind of wonderful.

The major league season might be over, but we were definitely in the minors—the post-mortem minors—and about to witness the opening game of the newly formed Briar Hollow Spectral Sports League.

As I watched, Tori lifted the Amulet of the Phoenix over Beau's head, struggling to ease it past the bill of his cap. Beau, who typically goes about in white shirts, dapper vests, and tall black boots was decked out in full baseball uniform.

He was also juggling an impressive armload of bats, gloves, and balls. In the absence of the amulet whatever Beau is wearing or holding goes back into the ectoplasmic state with him. That was the only way he could outfit the players on the Dead Sox, his team, and their opponents, the Deceased Dodgers.

While Beau distributed the equipment, Tori walked over and handed me the amulet for safe keeping. As the official umpire, she dressed in thematic black, complete with a cap emblazoned with the words, "Whether I'm right or wrong, I'm right.—The Ump"

As I took the amulet from her, I said, "Tell me again why the mom's can't be here tonight?"

"Beats me. They said they had a meeting."

"Irma's pre-SpookCon Committee meeting?"

"No. If I had to guess, I'd say they made up an obligation to get out of the game and Irma's meeting?"

"Well, it is hard to expect much out of this bunch."

The motley assortment of players included two farm women

in long gingham dresses wandering toward the infield and a departed hairdresser with a beehive positioned at first base.

"You never know," Tori said cheerfully, plopping down beside me. "Everyone has hidden talents, even Duke."

I followed her gaze toward home plate, a flat grave marker bearing the oddly cheerful inscription, "Here lies Jed, better off dead." There, a pale, wispy coon hound sat in a state of agitated attention.

"Duke is playing?"

"You bet," Tori replied. "He's the catcher, a real natural."

"Uh-huh, and what if he needs to actually *throw* the ball?"

Tori shrugged. "Beau assures me Duke can handle it. Go with the flow, Jinksy. Prepare to be surprised."

Her words proved to be prophetic. As we watched, Duke made a flying leap to catch a ball thrown in his direction. The ghost hound gyrated in mid-air, spinning faster and faster until his tail stood straight out like a propeller. When he built up enough momentum, he let fly with the ball, which sailed right on target back to the pitcher.

Now, let's talk about the pitcher.

I thought he was another deceased farmer laid to rest in a threadbare suit until he started pelting fastballs at a ghost named Jeff, who, incongruously, was dressed in his Briar Hollow High football uniform.

"Who the heck is the pitcher?" I asked Tori. "I don't remember seeing him here before."

"Hiram Folger," Tori said. "He pitched one season for the Durham Bulls when they were a Class D minor league team in 1913."

"Why just one season?"

"His father died," Tori said, "so Hiram came home to work the family farm. I think he could have made the majors if he'd kept playing."

Hiram let loose with a ball that hit Jeff's glove with such force, it sailed through the foggy remnants of the well-oiled leather and Jeff's chest before coming to rest against a tombstone behind him.

"No kidding," I said appreciatively. "How are you going to call a play like that?"

"Danged if I know," Tori said. "I'm pretty much making everything up as I go along. You know, opting for the supplemental rules in light of everyone's deficits."

The situation certainly called for flexible officiating since being non-corporeal definitely qualifies as a handicap.

"Is Beau excited?"

"Try over the moon. He's been dying to play for months, no pun intended."

After watching baseball movies with Tori and reading everything he could get his hands on, Beau longed to actually play baseball with the kind of passion known only to the converted.

For a while he made do pitching a ball back and forth in the alley with Chase. Then Tori took him to the public batting cages in a nearby town, but neither of those activities could take the place of the real thing.

Since the only people Beau knows outside of the store are the spirits at the cemetery, he organized the two teams and arranged the game. He was going for a triple. Enrich their afterlife, feed his obsession, and make me smile.

Jeff jumped at the chance to captain the Deceased Dodgers even though he would have preferred the ghosts learn football. Given the dearth of sporting activities on the other side however, he was willing to take what he could get.

After a lengthy planning session, Beau and Jeff agreed on specific tombstones to serve as the bases and selected a raised grave covered in cement set with sea shells for the pitcher's mound. The current occupant, a dentist who drilled his last tooth sometime around 1884, agreeably gave his permission.

What's with seashells, you ask? You'll find graves like that from the Victorian era all over the south, even inland. Since that night, I've looked up the meaning behind the tradition. There are a lot of theories, but I like the one that says the shells signify a safe journey to an unknown shore.

I'm not going to give you a play-by-play, but that game was a wild ride. I do want to tell you about Susie Miller, though.

When Tori and I met Susie, she was a nameless Jane Doe ghost. We were lucky enough to solve her murder and help her to find peace in her afterlife. Instead of moving on, however, she has stayed in the cemetery with the spirits she regards as her family.

Susie is now a happy member of their community, but she's still a mere whiff of a ghost. I was surprised Beau coaxed her into playing, and even more surprised when she smacked the ball Hiram sent her way with considerable authority.

As we watched and cheered, the glowing projectile, sailed toward left field allowing Susie to reach second base before one of the gingham grannies managed a credible catch.

Susie caught my eye and gave me a thumbs up, which I returned with a grin.

Looking back now, I can tell you that the next nine days in our lives would be about all kinds of seconds—second base, second chances, and yes, even second thoughts.

Chapter Two

The moon illuminated two sets of amber eyes in the shadowed woods. Chase and Festus sat together in mountain lion form watching the game. Chase kept his eyes trained on Jinx, while Festus engaged in a running diatribe about baseball.

"I don't get it," Festus said dismissively, turning his head to hock a hairball. "Where's the reward? You spend all that time and energy knocking a ball around a field for what? Numbers on a scoreboard? At least in Red Dot there are incentives."

Without glancing at his father, Chase said, "Would it hurt you to kick some dirt over that hairball?"

"Oh, for Bastet's sake," Festus replied, half-heartedly flicking a wad of leaves over the regurgitated fur. "When did you get so squeamish? The least you could do is agree with me about Red Dot. After all, it *is* the werecat national sport."

"Red Dot," Chase said, "is not a sport. It's a drinking game. The sole purpose is to get sloshed on creamed whiskey, and the *only* place Red Dot is considered a sport is the Dirty Claw."

"A bar where you'd be better off drowning your sorrows with the guys than sitting out here mooning over a woman."

Chase's whiskers twitched in irritation. "Whether Jinx is speaking to me or not, it's still my job to protect her. How about you keep your opinions to yourself and watch the game?"

"*Watch the game*," Festus mocked in a sing-song voice. "Fine. I'll watch the game if you'll explain to me whose idea it was to let a dead dog catch."

"Duke likes to catch balls."

"How very canine of him," Festus said sarcastically. I am in serious danger of either dropping dead from boredom or freezing to death. I can't even tell if they're keeping score down there."

"The Deceased Dodgers gave up two runs in the eighth," Chase said flatly. "Stop pretending you can't follow a baseball game. You took me to the 1938 World Series when I was eight years old."

Festus chuckled ruefully. "So I did. Damn shame Dizzy's arm gave out. Gehrig retired the next year. That guy down there on the pitcher's mound is good, by the way. Too bad he never made it to the show."

When Chase didn't answer, Festus went on. "Seriously, boy, why are we out here freezing our fur off? Jinx isn't in any danger that I can see."

"I'm not worried about the danger we can see," Chase snapped. "I'm worried about what we can't see. If all you're going to do is sit there and complain, go home."

In one fluid movement, the older cat pivoted and smacked his son hard across the snout with enough force to rock him backward.

"Hey!" Chase cried, curling his lips in a snarl. "What the heck was that for?"

"That," Festus said, laying his ears flat and narrowing his

eyes, "was to remind you to respect your elders, boy. I'm out here to keep you company. Show a little gratitude or next time I'll put my claws out."

Rubbing his whiskers with one paw, Chase muttered grudgingly, "Fine, fine. I'm sorry. Thanks for coming with me."

Returning his attention to the game, Festus said, "That's more like it. Can the attitude, boy. What would your mother think? Act like you had some raising."

They sat silently for a few minutes before Festus tried again. "Look, I know this is hard on you. Sooner or later Jinx *will* start talking to you."

"Yeah, I guess," Chase answered glumly, "but will that make things better or worse?"

Festus snorted. "With a woman, son, it's hard to tell."

Sounding less hostile and more uncertain, Chase asked, "Did Mom ever stop talking to you?"

"I should have been so lucky. When Jenny had enough of my crap, she told me about it in no uncertain terms."

Hesitating for a fraction of a second, Chase asked, "But she loved you, right?"

Heaving a weary sigh, Festus said, "Of course she loved me, boy. Jinx not loving you isn't the problem here. May I point out that you *are* the one who broke up with her?"

"Gee, Dad," Chase said, bitterness dripping from every word, "thanks so much for reminding me. What else was I supposed to do? Wait for the next bigoted werecat traditionalist to come along and try to kill her again?"

"It's not just a matter of tradition, and you know it."

"Says the werecat who is in love with my ex-girlfriend's mother."

Without warning, Festus struck again, cuffing Chase's head solidly with a one-two combination and coming away with fur in his claws.

In response, Chase hissed and drew his own paw back—

only to stop when his father growled deep in his throat and said, "Do you remember what I told you the last time you hissed at me? If you think you're big enough, boy, go right ahead."

Chase slowly lowered his paw, but his golden eyes blazed with barely suppressed fury.

Festus was not impressed. "Glare at me all you want, but I'll thank you to shut your ignorant mouth about Kelly Hamilton."

Hanging his head again, Chase said, "I'm sorry, Dad. I shouldn't have said that."

This time, Festus reached out and patted his son consolingly. "Don't worry about it, boy. You get your temper from me, but mostly you're like your mama. That's a good thing, Chase. You can't let this business with Jinx change who you are."

"It already has."

"Son, the bitter truth of it is that I had no more business being interested in Kelly than you had chasing after her daughter. Trust me. I know the appeal of a Ryan woman. They get under your skin. Jinx's grandmother Kathleen was the same way. They can't help being who they are any more than we can."

"I thought we could be friends."

"Don't be one of those damn fools who breaks a woman's heart and thinks he can still be her friend." Festus said. "In this instance, you will be friends again—in time. The McGregors and the Daughters of Knasgowa are linked forever. But for now, you need to quit acting like a love-struck idiot and get your mind back on business. We do have some things to tend to."

"Like what?"

"Oh," Festus deadpanned, "inconsequential stuff like Malcolm Ferguson dying with Anton Ionescu's name on his lips."

"Don't you think I realize that?" Chase said, frustration rising again in his voice. "I understand the Strigoi are a danger to Jinx, but how am I supposed to convince her of that when she doesn't *know* Ferguson said Ionescu's name before he died, plus she will hardly even *look* at me."

"What did you expect? The same day you broke up with her, she lost the aos si. The last few months have been hard on the girl. She's about reached her limit. Count yourself lucky, boy. The way her powers have been growing, I'm surprised she didn't fry your butt with a lightning bolt when you broke up with her out of the blue."

"That's exactly what she'll do when she finds out we're keeping the information about Ionescu from her."

"You can blame that on me when the time comes."

"Gladly."

"But I'm not to blame for how you handled breaking up with her," the old cat added quickly. "That is totally on you."

"There wasn't any other way to do it," Chase insisted stubbornly. "Breaking up with Jinx hurt so much, I had to get it over with, like ripping off a bandage."

"Which worked fine for you, and was plain damned awful for her. You have no right to be upset with that woman for being mad at you, boy. None. You have to admit your approach lacked finesse."

"Lacked 'finesse?'" Chase said incredulously. "If there's a good way to break up with a woman, by all means, let me in on the secret."

"Truthfully, son, I wouldn't know. I've only ever loved two women in my life; one I couldn't have and one I buried. There are worse torments than what you're suffering, so suck it up and get over yourself. You'll live through breaking up with Jinx. Having to put her in the ground is something else altogether."

Chase looked back to the figures at the far end of the

cemetery. He watched as the gossamer thin ghost named Susie hit the ball and half-ran, half-floated for first base, then second before stopping. The girl looked at Jinx and gave her a thumbs up, which Jinx returned. The exchange energized the lost spirit so much, her form settled into a more solid silver cloud that shimmered in the moonlight.

"Look at her," Chase whispered. "She can even make a ghost feel happy."

"She's special. All the Daughters of Knasgowa are special."

"What do I do, Dad?"

"You go right on loving her even though you can't have her. You make up your mind that you're privileged to still be in her life, and you do your job. Trust me, boy, it's the only way to keep your sanity in a situation like this."

"Okay," Chase answered with a note of resolve. "How do we figure out what Ionescu is planning next?"

Festus reached up with one hind leg and scratched his ear. "Well, he's already hired a hit man, so it's as plain as the fur on your face that he's willing to kill to get what he wants."

"What do you know about the Ionescus?"

"That," Festus said, "is a long story. Is there the slightest chance I can convince you to go home so I can tell you in front of a warm fire?"

Chase's eyes tracked back to the figures in the graveyard. The game appeared to be over, and from the looks of things, the Dead Sox won. "Yeah," he said, standing and stretching, "we can go back to the shop—and I think we can have a glass of single malt to go with that fire."

"Now you're talking like a McGregor!" Festus said as he followed his son into the dark woods, limping to favor his lame hip. "There's nothing you can't improve with a good Scotch."

Chapter Three

Gemma kept her eyes on the winding road while running through a list of her new SUV's amenities. "I told you about the rear view camera, right?"

"You told me, *twice*," Kelly replied, twisting in the passenger seat to look at her friend. "Why are you excited about a rear view camera? You've been backing up without one for years."

"This might be the first car I've ever owned without a dented back bumper."

With deadpan seriousness, Kelly asked, "Are you ready to give up your signature look?"

"It's not a done deal," Gemma admitted. "I still have to *remember* to use the camera."

Kelly laughed. "That would be funnier if it weren't so true. Yesterday I spent half an hour looking for my reading glasses. They were on top of my head."

"Stop!" Gemma commanded. "You're making us sound old. We're about to *contact* the dead, not join them."

Indecision filled Kelly's expression. "I know this was my bright idea, but I'm starting to have second thoughts."

"Why?"

"Mother always said you can't control who shows up at a seance. We're asking to speak with Mo, but there's no guarantee she will be the spirit that comes through."

Gemma considered the possibility. "We're doing this in Mo's cabin," she said. "It's almost exactly the way she left it. I think there's a good chance we'll be successful. Besides, our other options for the evening aren't that great."

"What do you mean?"

"We can go sit in a cold cemetery with the girls and watch ghosts play baseball or we can attend a fall festival committee meeting. Want me to turn around?"

Kelly shuddered. "Keep driving. Besides, isn't the committee meeting in the morning at the store?"

"That's the *official* meeting. Irma decided to host a *pre*-committee meeting at the grocery store tonight for anyone who wants to attend."

"And do what?"

"Beats me. I imagine the whole thing will devolve into Irma and Amity arguing about bogus hauntings again."

"Okay. You convinced me. Summoning the dead sounds better by the minute."

They drove in silence for a mile or so enjoying the fall colors lying dappled under the rays of the setting sun.

As her gaze moved over a particularly vibrant patch of red, Kelly said, "I understand why Mo never wanted to come down from her mountain. It's beautiful up here, especially this time of year. You can almost forget there's a modern world back down the road."

On cue, her cell phone went off, playing the theme from *Bewitched*.

"I think the modern world just took offense at being dissed," Gemma snorted. "Whose ringtone is that?"

"Fiona's," Kelly replied, digging in her purse for the

offending bit of technology. "She better not be trying to get out of this seance for tarot bingo at the VFW hall."

"The Veterans of Foreign Wars have a hall in Shevington?"

"No, but the Valorous Fairy Wing does. They host tarot bingo nights catered by The Dirty Claw."

"I'm probably going to be sorry I asked, but how do you play bingo with tarot cards?"

Kelly rolled her eyes. "I quit listening to the explanation when Fiona brought up hallucinogenic mushrooms."

Cutting her friend a bemused look out of the corner of her eye, Gemma said, "I'd pay good money to see Fiona stoned on shrooms."

"I told her to show up at the cabin with a clear head. She's supposed to be the older, more responsible sister."

Studying the iPhone screen, she added, "It's a text message, not a call."

"What does she have to say?"

Diving back into the bag for her glasses, Kelly peered more closely at the smartphone. "Stan's bunny had kits. Fiona will be a few minutes late because the baby shower is running long."

"You gotta love Fiona," Gemma said, as she slowed the vehicle and put on her blinker. "Getting stoned with fairies one minute, throwing parties for baby bunnies the next."

She turned left onto the dirt road and stopped. The two women stared up the lane that ascended the slope and disappeared into the deepening shadows.

"Are you *sure* you're sure about this?" Kelly asked.

"Now what are you worried about?"

"Jonas Mahoney coming after us with a 12-gauge."

"Okay," Gemma chuckled, "that's a valid concern, but I'm way ahead of you. I called Jonas and told him we'd be spending the evening at Mo's cabin."

"How can you be certain he won't wander over?"

"Jonas ran Mo a close second in the reclusivity department," Gemma said, taking her foot off the brake and easing the vehicle forward. "If he saw an unexplained light he'd investigate, but mountain folk don't go where they're not invited. He won't bother us."

Kelly's studied the wooded slope. "Is he up here all alone now?"

"Jonas is part of a dying breed. The Hillbilly Highway left a lot of old timers isolated and on their own."

"The migration north out of Appalachia happened more than 50 years ago. How old is Jonas anyway?"

"I have no idea. Mo told me he tried to leave once, but he came back. She said he didn't make a good outlander."

"Neither did she."

"No," Gemma agreed, "but she didn't go far—into town for Henry's sake and then up here again when he died. Scrap had a fit when she told him she was coming back to the old home place."

"It must be lonely for Jonas without her. They were good friends."

"He took her death hard. He keeps fresh flowers on the grave. I don't think Jonas would mind one bit if Mo showed up as a haunt."

Kelly looked crestfallen. "Now I feel awful that we're *not* inviting him to the seance so he could have a chance to see her again."

While they talked, Gemma had guided the SUV up the rough track, trying to avoid the biggest rocks. When the irregular split-rail fence encircling the cabin appeared in the headlights, she steered onto a patch of smooth ground and cut the engine.

Reaching into the center console, she took out two flashlights and handed one to Kelly. "There's no electricity."

Both women stepped out and played twin beams over the

cabin. The long, distorted shadows of an empty rocking chair angled awkwardly across the porch.

"Is it wrong to be a witch and also be creeped out by this place?" Kelly asked.

"I won't tell if you won't."

"Why wouldn't Mo have electricity?" Kelly asked as she followed Gemma through the gate. "The government started running lines into the hollers in the 1930s."

"Yes, and a lot of linemen dodged buckshot for their troubles. Mo had electricity when she and Henry lived in town, but she said light bulbs hurt her eyes. She preferred coal oil lamps. Hold your flashlight on the lock for me."

Kelly watched as Gemma pulled a worn skeleton key out of her pocket. "I'm surprised Mo had a lock at all."

"Having a lock and using it are two different things. It took half a tube of graphite to get the tumblers in this thing to turn."

"How did you ever find the key?"

"Easy. There were two of them hanging on a nail right here on the porch."

The door swung open on creaking hinges. Gemma went in first. She located the lamps and lit them with a snap of her fingers. As each wick sprang to life, the details of the interior emerged from the shadows.

Next Gemma moved to the fireplace where freshly laid wood waited. She ignited the kindling with a word of Latin.

Stepping toward the welcoming blaze, Kelly asked, "Is the ready-made fire more of Jonas's doing?"

"Yes. I think he comes in and checks on the place once or twice a week. We've only been here a handful of times since Mo died, but whenever we light a fire, the next time we come, the ashes have been shoveled and fresh wood laid out. It's almost like Jonas thinks Mo is coming home and he wants the place to be ready."

Kelly looked around the room, her eyes settling on the silent autoharp. "It's easy to imagine she might. Mo could have walked out of this room only an hour ago."

"That's what we're counting on to make this seance work."

From the front porch, Fiona called out, "Hello?" Are you girls in there?"

"We're here, Fi," Kelly answered. "Hold on. I'll come to the door with a flashlight."

"Don't be silly. I can find my way."

A glowing orb floated placidly into the room with Fiona following behind wearing a purple velour pantsuit and bright red sneakers.

Taking in the burning lamps and the fireplace, she extinguished the orb with a wave of her hand. "You should have said we were going for ambiance. Hi, you two."

"Hi," Gemma said, reaching to hug her. "Thanks for coming."

"Oh, I wouldn't miss a seance for all the tea in China. Come here, baby sister, give me a hug."

Kelly laughed and stepped into her sister's arms. "How was the trip from Shevington?"

"Easy as pie. There's a portal up the holler. We haven't used it in years, but it opened right up and I strolled on down here."

"Most people don't think walking down a mountainside in the dark qualifies as a stroll," Kelly said. "Come on. Let's sit by the fire."

Gemma brought in an extra chair from the kitchen and they arranged themselves in a loose semi-circle around the hearth.

"Alright then," Fiona said, slapping her knee. "Now does one of you want to clear up for me *why* we're doing this?"

After an awkward pause, Kelly said, "Fiona, we think that Mama and Mo knew each other."

"Of course they did," Fiona said brightly. "We all became

friends when the girls were . . . oh . . . I don't know. Maybe eight years old?"

"Why am I just now hearing about this?" Kelly asked.

"Well, dear, it's not like we were all on the best of terms back then, now were we?"

As she spoke, a chill wind blew through the room and a rolling carpet of thick fog flowed over the rough floor boards.

"Oh, good!" Fiona said. "They're here. They can tell you all about it themselves."

As the women watched, the vapor boiled up and coalesced into the forms of three seated apparitions.

The one closest to Kelly laid a thin, translucent hand lightly on her arm. "Hello, honey. Fiona's right, but the state of family relations back then wasn't entirely your fault."

A gasp from Gemma cut off Kelly's answer. "Mama? Is that you?"

Rebecca Campbell held her hands out to Gemma whose eyes widened at the unexpected contact. "You look exactly the way I remember. How is this possible? How can I touch you?"

"The three of us are pooling our energies for this visit," Rebecca said. "It will shorten our time here, but we wanted the remembrance of corporeality. *I* wanted it."

Tears filled Gemma's eyes. "I've never stopped talking to you. Do you hear me?"

"Every word. You were so little when I died. I'm sorry I wasn't there for you, baby."

"You're here now. Can I . . . can I . . . hug you?"

The spirit opened her arms and drew her daughter into a cool, otherworldly embrace. "You've been having such a hard time, Gemmy. I'm so proud of you. You did the right thing studying with Mo—and your husband is a damned idiot."

Gemma laughed, sat back, and wiped her eyes. "You have no idea. Thank you, and thank you, Mo."

The third presence patted Gemma on the knee. "Hi'dy, lil gal. I figured you wouldn't mind if I brung friends."

"Mind? I couldn't be happier. Hi, Kathleen."

"Hello, dear girl. Thank you for the way you've stood by Kelly's side all these years."

"We're Daughters of Knasgowa. That's what we do."

Fiona chimed in. "They thought they were going to have to hold hands and intone some silly incantation to get you all to come tonight. I played along for the fun of it."

Kathleen laughed. "If you feel that you must go through the formalities for this to be a legitimate visit, we can go outside and come in again."

"Mother," Kelly said sounding shocked, "you've developed a sense of humor on the other side."

"Oh, I always had one," Kathleen replied, "but I didn't choose to use it nearly enough. Sometimes you have to die to understand the mistake of taking life too seriously, a problem your sister has never had."

"I certainly try not to," Fiona agreed, "but it's a whole lot easier staying in a light frame of mind living in Shevington than it was here. The Human Realm can be so unnecessarily complicated."

Mo made a tsking sound. "It don't have to be all complicated if people didn't go trying to rise above their raising. After my man died, I came back up here to the holler to get away from that kind of flatlander foolishness. What can we do fer you girls?"

"They want to know about the deal we made when Jinx and Tori were children," Fiona said. "I could have explained, but I thought it would be so much easier if were all together."

Kathleen and Rebecca exchanged ghostly smiles.

"Okay," Gemma said. "I know that look. Kel and I do it and so do the girls. What's up?"

"We've been waiting for an opportunity to resolve some

things for you," Kathleen said. "Rebecca, do you want to go first?"

Still holding her daughter's hand, Rebecca said, "You've both believed that by halting your practice of magic you disrupted Knasgowa's line, but that's not true. The interruption started when I died and left Kathleen alone. That Daughters are meant to work in pairs, but without me, Kathleen was forced to evolve in a different way."

"I became too much of a solitary," Kathleen said. "That attitude harmed my ability to guide you, Kelly. After Connor was sent away, you understandably distanced yourself from the world of the Fae. I should have told you before I died that with Myrtle's help, I came to understand your decision to raise Jinx in ignorance of her magic."

Kelly's jaw dropped. "You did?"

"We both did," Fiona said cheerfully. "Not that it was easy, of course, but with Mo preparing Tori to have a receptive mind and Myrtle assuring us the girls share a special purpose, we had to let the natural order have its way."

Gemma frowned. "I hate to be the skeptic in the group, but there's something that has always bothered me. Jinx and Tori weren't like other Fae children. It wasn't just that we didn't practice magic around them. They never accidentally used their powers. You did something to them, didn't you?"

"Me?" Fiona said. "Heavens no. That was Myrtle. She sort of put the girls' abilities on hold and told us how to start their development again when Jinx asked for her magic."

"How did Myrtle know Jinx would ask?"

Fiona looked confused. "She's Myrtle."

Kelly looked at Gemma and shrugged. "You have to give her that."

"I suppose so," Gemma agreed. "Mo, how did you get mixed up in all this?"

Mo chuckled. "I caught on that your mama and your sister was witches, and came down to town to have a talk with them."

"That's when we came to an arrangement," Kathleen said.

"What kind of arrangement?" Kelly asked.

"We agreed that Mo would teach Tori mountain magic so she would be ready when Jinx came into her powers. Jinx, however, was never to be exposed to any of that teaching."

Gemma looked at Mo. "What did you get out of the deal?"

"A forgetting spell on my boy," Mo said. "Kathleen made it so Scrap never saw what we was doing down in your basement. I didn't count on what would happen if he found out. I'm sorry about how he's been acting, honey. His pa raised him to do better by his family. I'd like to tell you that boy of mine is done being a jackass, but it ain't so."

"Color me surprised," Gemma muttered. Then, when Kelly fell back heavily in her chair, she asked her friend, "Hey, are you all right over there?"

"Yes. Just trying to assimilate that I've spent 30 years thinking I'm a bad mother for nothing."

"I wish the guilt aspect of the plan could have been avoided," Kathleen said, "more than you can possibly know. None of what has happened was your fault. Destinies were at play beyond our control."

Throwing up her hands, Kelly said, "There's that damned word again. I think I hate it as much as Jinx does."

To her surprise, Rebecca echoed her frustration. "I don't like the idea of destiny either. It implies a lack of choice. The older you get, either here or in our plane, you realize that all destiny is built on a foundation of choices."

"Everybody gets set down on a path," Mo agreed. "Some folks got to make big choices, and others got to live small. Ain't none of us in this room small kind of women. If'n we was, them that's on the side of evil would win."

Kelly eyed her keenly. "Something is coming, isn't it?"

"Yes," Kathleen said. "You wanted to speak with us because in Myrtle's absence you fear you do not know how to be there for your daughters."

"We've never been without the advice and counsel of the aos si," Gemma said. "Is it wrong to be concerned?"

"Not at all," Kathleen said, her form starting to waver, "but our time here grows short and there is little we can say for fear of disrupting what must be."

Leaning forward urgently, Kelly said, "Tell us what you can. Please."

The wind began to rise in the room. Rebecca caught Gemma's gaze and held it. "Never forget that I love you, Gemmy. We will see one another again."

Kathleen tried to take Kelly's hand, but the pale outline of her spectral fingers dissolved. "You are to blame for nothing, daughter," she said, her voice distant and hollow. "You have found your courage, and you will use it at the right time."

"*No!*" Kelly said. "You can't go without telling us more than that."

Her entreaty came too late. Kathleen and Rebecca were gone, leaving only Mo sitting in the wavering light of the fire. As the old woman's body dissipated into fine mist her final words hung in the air.

"There's a storm a'coming. Walk into the wind. Don't be afraid to call down the lightning."

Chapter Four

The first thing I did when I came downstairs was tear the old sheet off the wall calendar in the espresso bar. Then Tori and I sat down with lattes and bear claw pastries. It was Friday, October 23, 2015.

The clock above the calendar read six a.m., an unholy hour given how late we'd stayed up at the baseball game. The early start wasn't our idea, but we couldn't get out of it. In about an hour, the members of The Briar Hollow Town Square Business and Paranormal Association's fall festival steering committee would walk through the front door.

Tori and I "donated" the espresso bar for the meeting after the co-chairs, George and Irma, who run the corner grocery, pointed out we have the most available seating. Technically, that's not true. Pete, the owner of the Stone Hearth pizzeria, could have handled three times the number we expected, but I didn't want the meeting to be held there.

Although I had no proof, I believed Pete had been involved with Malcolm Ferguson, a theory Chase soundly opposed. We'd argued about it before we broke up. Now it wasn't any of

Chase McGregor's business what I was thinking about anything.

He'd made a few half-hearted attempts to talk to me about the ongoing danger of not knowing if Ferguson was working alone or was a claw for hire. Frankly, I was barely civil during those exchanges. Chase could go on all he wanted to about his "responsibility" to take care of me. For Mr. McGregor's information, I could take care of myself.

Yeah. When I wasn't crying my eyes out, I wasn't exactly in a "constructive" frame of mind. Since Chase would be at the meeting however, I resolved to behave in front of witnesses, particularly those of the non-magical variety.

Irma wanted to ensure there were no loose ends before the Saturday night street dance that would officially open the "First Annual Briar Hollow Paranormal Halloween Fall Festival," or as Tori lovingly called it, "SpookCon1." She was so worried that the night before while we were at the cemetery she held a pre-committee meeting and was highly distressed we couldn't be there.

Leaf peeping season was winding down, but there were more tourists in town than usual. All around the square, store windows sported otherworldly decorations. When we got in last night, we saw a smattering of ghost hunters with cameras trained on the Confederate monument.

"Oh, dear," Beau said, "I hope I haven't disappointed them. Do you think I should change into my uniform and make an appearance?"

"No," I said. "If you show up like an on-demand haunt they'll start thinking you're a hoax. I'm already worried someone is going to recognize you."

Beau feels obligated to help our community. For weeks he'd been appearing at the foot of the Confederate monument to stimulate the paranormal tourist trade. When he first assumed a corporeal form we told people Beau was my uncle from

Tennessee. Then Beau expressed an interest in working on the festival committee, arguing he could bring "added value" to the event. Beau wanted to organize timed materializations by the cemetery ghosts at key times during the week.

George and Irma had developed a mostly bogus list of haunted sites in Briar Hollow. Under Beau's direction, each location could become a guaranteed ghost goldmine. That meant we had to up the ante on our cover story and reveal that our Beau descended from "the" Colonel Beauregard T. Longworth who died in the foothills outside of town in 1864.

Once Beau began making his spectral appearances, Linda Albert, the town librarian and head of the historical association, began looking into the possible identity of the soldierly apparition. She found an account written by James McGregor, Chase's grandfather, detailing the day Union soldiers ambushed Beau's cavalry unit.

The Yankees wiped out the entire Confederate troop. James found Beau's body and identified him from the inscription in his pocket watch. Realizing he was a brother Mason, James, who was the Worshipful Master of the local lodge, arranged for Beau to be buried with full Masonic rites.

Linda wrote the story up for the *Briar Hollow Banner*, surmising the late Colonel Longworth was the Confederate ghost on the courthouse lawn. She managed to locate a photo taken of Beau in 1860, which raised the real danger that she might recognize my "uncle."

When the paper came out, Beau stared a long time at his image on the front page. Finally, I said, "Hey, you okay?"

"Yes," he answered, his eyes still on the picture. "I was remembering the idealism with which I entered the conflict you call the Civil War. There is great truth in saying it was a rich man's war and a poor man's fight. We should not have been so obdurate in our dealings with the North, especially in the matter of the Negro slaves."

"You told me you freed your slaves when your father died."

"I did, and I did not support that abhorrent institution. I went to war in the name of states' rights, a political topic that would appear to still color aspects of public debate in our great nation. I fear my conflict resolved nothing in that regard. Men are always the poorer for taking to the sword in place of calm words and reasoned conversation."

"That's true," I said, "but you did look handsome in your uniform."

Beau laughed. "Uniforms are, in general, a kind enhancement to the men who wear them."

"This likeness is good enough that someone could recognize you, Beau. Stay misty, my friend."

He didn't pick up the bad beer commercial pun, but he got the idea. The next time Beau made one of his appearances, I noticed he kept his broad-brimmed Panama hat pulled low over his face.

Beau got ahead of the Linda situation by presenting himself to her at the library as an "amateur Civil War enthusiast and genealogist" with an "avid interest in assisting with the compilation of material ahead of the planned festival."

Together they assembled profiles of the local "haunted" sites, which put Beau in perfect position to orchestrate his covert band of merry spirits.

During all of this, one spirit cropped up we weren't counting on—the late Howard McAlpin, former mayor of Briar Hollow and now the bumbling courthouse haunt.

After the mass resurrection at the cemetery Howie moved back into his old office, which, coincidentally, was also the scene of his death. Depending on who tells the story, Howie either fell into the protruding bill of a brass swordfish and killed himself, or the real winner stabbed him in revenge for being cheated out of his angling glory.

Version number two is the truth. When the mayor's office

made the list of local ghost-infestations, Howie decided to take full advantage of the festival to re-establish his reputation.

A sizable amount of jealousy threaded through his enthusiasm for the festival. After months of practice, Howie can still only materialize from the waist down. Aunt Fiona says that's perfect since in life he was the trailing end of a north bound horse.

Beau's carefully crafted manifestations at the monument irked Howie to no end, so none of us bought the mayor's declarations of "a feeling of post-mortem responsibility for the economic future of our fair city."

As Tori and I sat talking over our coffee that Friday morning, I heard Beau's boots on the basement stairs. He came into the espresso bar still beaming from his team's victory the night before.

"All hail the conquering hero!" Tori called out. "Would Caesar care for coffee?"

In response, Beau inclined his head deferentially and said, "Ah, yes, thank you. But as to the conquest, Miss Tori, I would recall to you the words of the Auriga."

"The who?" Tori asked as she reached for a mug.

"The slave with the status of a gladiator who held the laurel crown over the head of a triumphant general," Beau replied, "while whispering repeatedly *memento homo*."

"Meaning?"

Before Beau could reply, I said, "Remember you are only a man."

Tori let out a low whistle as she put Beau's coffee down on the table and reclaimed her chair. "Listen to you, Latin Girl."

The smile on Beau's face broadened. "Miss Jinx is proving to be an adept student."

Burying yourself in your work to forget that your heart is breaking will do that for a girl.

But I didn't say that. Just a tip. Making your friends feel

awful isn't fair. Misery may love company, but trust me, the company isn't in love with the misery.

Instead, I bobbed a sort of sitting curtsy and said, "Thank you, kind sir."

Tori coughed in her hand to hide the words "suck up," which made us all laugh.

Just then we heard a rap on the front door. George and Irma were early. Pasting a smile on my face and muttering "show time" under my breath, I let them in.

Irma clutched a huge portfolio overflowing with notes, flyers, and miscellaneous papers while George balanced a wobbling column of doughnut boxes in his beefy arms.

"Just put those down on one of the tables," I told him. "We're planning on putting out coffee carafes and letting people serve themselves."

George headed straight for the table holding the ornately carved musical chess set, the evil fox in our magical hen house.

When he tried to move the cursed board it wouldn't budge. "What the heck is wrong with this thing?" he asked.

"Oh," I said lightly, "that's my fault. When I varnished the table, I put the chess set down too soon. It's stuck solid. We work around it. Don't worry about it, just use another table."

"Nonsense," he said, reaching into his pocket. "A little work with a knife should get it loose."

Great. Glancing around quickly, I saw that Irma had deposited her portfolio on the counter and was talking to Tori and Beau with her back turned to me. The instant George bent to examine the chessboard, I lifted the portfolio into the air with a flick of my hand.

Tori's eyebrows shot up, but she didn't say anything. Bringing the portfolio a couple of feet away from the counter, I flipped it over, raining papers, several pencils, a calculator, and one of Irma's paperback "historical" romance novels onto the floor.

"Oh, my gracious!" Irma cried, wheeling around and clutching her chest with one hand. "How on earth did that happen?"

Stepping smoothly into the breach, Tori said, "Oh, I am so sorry! I used some new polish on the counter yesterday, and it's slick as glass. Let me help you."

"George," Irma ordered, "leave that silly chessboard alone and help me find my colored pencils. All of my notes are color coded. I can't afford to lose a single pencil."

Obediently, George closed his knife and got down on his hands and knees to search for the scattered pencils. I used the opportunity to shift the doughnut boxes to another surface while shoving the chessboard table back against the shelves.

People started coming in, touching off a flurry of greetings and doughnut grabbing. Our next door neighbor, art store owner Amity Prescott, was the first to arrive, followed by Aggie who runs the dress shop two doors down. Linda and Pete were right behind them along with the rest of the committee members—including Chase.

He was carrying a coffee cup and looked distinctly uncomfortable as he took a seat in the back. For an instant I felt sorry for him, but then a surge of anger canceled out my longing to go over and put my arms around him. When our eyes met, I gave in enough to offer him a nod, which he awkwardly returned.

"Is it my imagination," Tori whispered, handing me two carafes of coffee, "or did the temperature drop twenty degrees in here?"

I accepted the containers without acknowledging her comment. "Are these regular or decaf?"

"Regular." Tori said. "The one with the arsenic for Chase isn't ready yet."

"Very funny. If you'll notice, he brought his own."

"Smart man."

Irma called the meeting to order and reminded everyone of the need to emphasize the number of "potential" hauntings in Briar Hollow. "We need to stress *quantity*," she said stoutly.

"Over *quality*?" Amity asked acerbically. "I still want to know what you're going to tell people when no ghosts show up."

The rest of the committee members shifted nervously. This was a conversation that had been going on for weeks with no resolution.

Setting her mouth in a firm line and drawing herself up to her full five feet, Irma said, "Now, Amity, we went over this at length last evening. I'm not asking anyone to *lie*. Just play up the *potential* of each location. Honestly, haven't you ever watched *Ghost Hunters*? Half the time they wander around in the dark and talk about creaking floorboards. At least we have my Twinkie video."

Ah, yes. "The" *Twinkie* video, also captured during my accidental raising of the dead. Apparently, somebody in the afterlife was itching for chocolate and fake cream. Irma's security camera caught the levitating Twinkie box, which the hungry ghost deposited on her front counter in an honest effort to pay.

In honor of the festival, George and Irma had installed a big screen TV in their front window playing the Twinkie video on a continuous loop. They also laid in triple their usual stock of Twinkies, in case the video inspired patrons to binge on junk food.

At the mention of the video, Amity made a face. "Irma, if I have to watch that silly video one more time . . . ."

Linda, hoping to forestall yet another confrontation between Irma and Amity, skillfully interrupted. "I'm happy to report the festival website is up and running, and we're ready to host any evidence participants gather. We can handle audio, video, and still photographs."

That information distracted Amity, who was hosting a

week-long paranormal photo contest with entries displayed in her store window. The winner would take home a brand new digital camera complete with infrared lenses for low-light ghost shoots.

"You've posted the photo contest rules?" she asked briskly.

"Yes," Linda assured her, "and they're prominently placed on the site."

"You've made it clear we're not accepting any of that orb nonsense?"

"Crystal clear."

"It's going to take a lot more than dust in the air to convince me that ghosts exist," Amity went on. "Tourist money or not, this paranormal business is ridiculous."

Tori and I could barely keep from bursting out laughing at the vehemence of Amity's declarations, especially since she was sitting right beside Beau. Amity is a fellow witch and sees ghosts on a regular basis. Because of that, she took it upon herself to be the requisite skeptic on the committee. I have to say that in the company of the group, she fulfilled the role with gusto.

In private, however, she and Beau spent hours watching paranormal television so they could coach the graveyard spirits on how much energy to put into their materializations. We wanted people to be able to take intriguing photos, but not perfect enough the organizers would be labeled hucksters—which they were, in a benign way.

The conversation moved on to a discussion about the Halloween costume contest to be held the following Saturday. Aggie was in charge of that event, and, good fan of *The Walking Dead* that she is, insisted the advertisements include the words, "walker make-up strongly encouraged."

She made a compelling argument for winning over the "zombie apocalypse crowd." The group agreed if all went as planned and the festival became a yearly event, we'd dedicate a full day to zombie-themed events.

George asked what would happen to the zombie apocalypse if the television show was canceled. Aggie informed him solemnly, if somewhat oxymoronically, that *The Walking Dead* will never die.

Next, we ran down the list of carnival attractions, which included face painting, fortune telling, and pumpkin carving among other tried and true stalwarts like the ring toss and the balloon/dart throw. There would be a dunking booth and even a good, old-fashioned cake walk.

Sheriff John Johnson planned to block off the west side of the square at 6 o'clock so the band could set up to start playing at seven. All the stores on the square were staying open. There would be no shortage of food from pizza at Pete's to barbecue by the plate courtesy of the historical association.

We advertised the festival as "family friendly," but the adults could buy beer in a closed-in area near the dance floor under the watchful eye of Johnson and his deputies.

Sunday afternoon Linda would chair a ghost tour seminar at the library before the first scheduled haunted outings that night. The committee agreed to meet Monday morning to take stock of the weekend and discuss any needed adjustments ahead of the culminating event, a two-day carnival starting Friday and ending on Halloween itself the next night.

Lawrence Anderson, the publisher of the *Banner*, raised his hand when Irma called for questions. "Lots of folks have decided to decorate their yards for Halloween. You know, the holiday is getting almost as popular as Christmas when it comes to putting up lights and stuff. You all think it's too late to announce a yard display contest?"

The group promptly voted on his informal motion, which passed by acclamation. The *Banner* comes out on Tuesday, so

Lawrence agreed to publish an advertisement for the contest at no charge.

One of the ladies from the Briar Hollow Garden and Beautification Committee volunteered the group's officers to serve as judges. Tori offered to come up with some kind of trophy to be handed out during the final street dance.

I piped up and said we'd also give the top three contestants free coffee for a month.

"A month?" Tori muttered under her breath as applause circled the room.

"We'll make it back on pastries," I said out of the corner of my mostly fake smile.

Irma wrapped up the meeting before 8 o'clock. I was grateful to see everyone filter out quickly to open up their own stores, and not so thrilled that Chase lingered.

Beau excused himself, and Tori got busy cleaning up the espresso bar. Chase shifted restlessly from one foot to the other and then said tentatively, "Good meeting."

"It was," I replied flatly.

"Uh, I'm going up to the Valley this morning, may I go through the basement?"

"You can get to the basement from your store."

A blush crept over Chase's cheeks. "Does it really have to be this way between us, Jinx?"

Behind his back, Tori caught my eye and gave me the "yeah, you are kinda being a bitch" look.

Okay, fine.

"Sorry," I said. "I didn't get much sleep last night. It was the opening game of Beau's new spectral baseball league out at the cemetery."

"How did it go?"

"His team won. Be sure and congratulate him when you go through the lair."

"I will," Chase said, "and thank you."

He crossed the floor with long strides and opened the basement door, closing it quietly behind himself. We listened as his footsteps receded.

"So," Tori said brightly, "hate to break this to you, Jinksy, but I'm not seeing the Miss Congeniality crown in your future."

Chapter Five

Chase walked slowly through the stacks in the basement archive. He could have used one of the bikes parked in the lair to cut his travel time to the Shevington portal, but he wanted time to think.

Jinx's behavior hurt. Even though Festus swore no woman could stay mad at a man forever, Chase had his doubts. He wasn't proud of delivering the news about the break up as a brutal *fait accompli*. He should have talked things over with Jinx. But if he had tried that approach, Chase knew he wouldn't have been able to go through with it.

When he and Festus arrived home the night before, Chase changed into human form while his father shrank down to his usual ginger cat self. As Festus warmed himself in front of the fireplace in their apartment, Chase poured a glass of Laphroaig single malt and distributed a dram in a bowl for Festus.

"*Slàinte*," Chase toasted, raising his glass.

"*Do dheagh shlàinte*," Festus answered, inclining his head before sipping the whisky and closing his eyes in satisfied appreciation. "Like mother's milk."

"Only if Grandma nursed you on hundred proof."

"My mother may have looked like a sweet little slip of a werecat," Festus said proudly, "but that woman could hold her whisky."

In spite of his mood, Chase laughed. "Okay, Dad, you've got your fire and your single malt. We need to talk Strigoi."

"That we do," Festus said, licking his lips. "Look in your DropBox account."

"What for?"

"I had Merle, Earl, and Furl use the Registry computers to do a little digging for us. Furl emailed me the report, and I saved it to Dropbox."

Laughing, Chase asked, "Do you suppose Steve Jobs realized the iPad would become the feline computer of choice?"

"Doubtful. The humans are already worried cats are a higher life form. They're more comfortable believing the only thing we care about is that ridiculous koi pond app."

"What's the name of the file?" Chase asked, tapping at the screen of his tablet.

"StrigScum dot PDF."

Arching an eyebrow, Chase said, "Nice with the tolerance there, Dad. Would you mind telling me what the International Registry for Shapeshifters has to do with the Strigoi?"

"Nothing. Furl used their computers to hack the IBIS database."

Chase's head snapped up. "Tell me you did not just use the word 'hack' in connection with the International Bureau of Indefinite Species."

"Oh, please," Festus scoffed with a dismissive wave of his paw. "Those IBIS boys are too busy chasing down chupacabra rumors to pay attention to who might be looking at their computers. They only use the fool things to control the flow of fake information the humans get on the Internet."

"Fine, but if we get caught, I'm throwing you and Furl under the bus."

"Furl who?" Festus asked innocently.

Shaking his head, Chase opened the PDF. He scanned the page and frowned. "What am I looking at here?" And why go to IBIS in the first place?"

"That's every bit of information IBIS has gathered about the Strigoi since the bureau's founder began researching them. They're classed as an indefinite species because Strigoi come in two flavors: living and dead."

"Which one is Anton Ionescu?"

"Living."

As he swiped to the next screen, Chase started to ask, "Is that good or..." Instead, he froze mid-gesture and croaked, "*Benjamin Franklin* founded IBIS?"

"Not per se," Festus answered, complacently returning to his whisky, "but his secret research papers form the core of the Bureau's original database. Damned Brits made off with the files after the American Revolution. Barely left poor ole Ben with his kite string."

"So that's why IBIS is based in London. I always wondered about that. How long is this report anyway?"

"Couple of hundred pages," Festus yawned. "I'm gonna take a nap while you do your homework. Wake me up if you need anything. Try not to need anything."

Chase passed the deep hours of the night listening to the complacent rhythm of his father's snoring. The contents of the report transported him far away from his comfortable chair in Briar Hollow to the highest reaches of the Carpathian Mountains in Transylvania.

The tale was not one filled with typical vampires. Instead, Chase learned that Anton Ionescu and his clan descended from a common ancestor, a human cursed by a witch to become a *Strigoi viu*.

Consulting a Romanian-to-English translation engine, Chase discovered the term meant "undead alive," as opposed to "*Strigoi mort*" or "undead dead. Bram Stoker based *Dracula* on the latter.

The *Strigoi mort* reputedly rose from their graves and returned to their homes and families. They slowly drained the life force from their loved ones until they, too, expired. The creatures existed in an ambiguous space between the human and the demonic.

The *Strigoi viu* possessed both the power of invisibility and the hunger to drain the life essence of those around them. They could, however, choose their victims, unlike the *Strigoi mort* who affected everyone in their vicinity equally.

As to the matter of invisibility, Furl inserted a comment in the PDF. "All accounts suggest that rather than becoming actually invisible, the *Strigoi viu* cloud the minds of those around them so that they are not observed."

In the old homeland, under the auspices of the Romanian Orthodox Church, the distinction between living and dead Strigoi didn't matter much. Both were condemned as unnatural creatures in league with the devil and hunted with equal religious avidity.

One priest, however, was troubled by the free will enjoyed by the *Strigoi viu*. Father Samuel Damian reasoned that if the "undead alive" could choose to drain energy from their victims, they could choose *not* to do so if presented with an alternative food source.

In 1748, Damian came to America ostensibly to meet with Benjamin Franklin to confer on electrical experimentation. Furl helpfully included a scan of an advertisement from the *South Carolina Gazette* announcing a planned electrical demonstration by Damian for the general public.

IBIS possessed correspondence between Damian and Franklin spanning the period 1753 to 1755. The men conversed in Latin. Together, they developed a method to feed the *Strigoi vui* electricity, allowing them to settle peacefully in what was then the remote region of North Carolina surrounding Briar Hollow.

Franklin's work with Damian fueled his growing interest in the paranormal and cryptozoology, touching off a wealth of clandestine research. Following his death, other scientists, human and Fae alike, including a number of notable alchemists, continued Franklin's efforts to catalog and understand esoteric species. In time, they formed the International Bureau of Indefinite Species both to protect the creatures they studied and the humans who crossed paths with them.

The last page of the report was a personal note from Furl to Festus. "Hey, you old drunk. Here's what I found out from our werecat operatives in Romania. This Ionescu guy is the head of the clan. If he cursed Kelly, everyone in the family is honor bound to enforce the terms. If you've got one Ionescu coming after you, you've got them all. Plus, staying juiced up on electricity all the time makes them super sensitive to magic. Normal surveillance is a no go. Let us know what else we can do to help. Remember, Red Dot at the Dirty Claw this Wednesday."

But it was the post-script that made the hair on the back of Chase's neck stand up. "Oh, yeah," Furl wrote, "I almost forgot. I looked at Anton Ionescu's client list in Raleigh. He's Irenaeus Chesterfield's lawyer."

Chase switched the tablet off and glanced at the clock—5 a.m.. He was supposed to be next door for a festival committee meeting in two hours. Trying to sleep now would make him feel worse, so he showered and shaved before starting breakfast.

When the smell of frying bacon filled the apartment, Festus woke up and padded into the kitchen. "Morning, boy," he said companionably, jumping on the counter beside the coffee machine. "Stick one of those plastic thingies in the machine for me, will you?"

Chase obligingly loaded a brewing cup and positioned a broad, shallow mug under the spigot, leaving Festus to punch the button and watch the dark liquid trickle downward.

When the machine finished, Chase moved the full mug onto the counter and lightened the coffee with a splash of cream. After Festus had lapped up a few swallows, he said, "You're talkative this morning, boy."

"How do you want your eggs?"

"Scrambled. I assume you read the report."

"Yes," Chase said, breaking three eggs into a bowl and whisking them.

"That last line is a killer, huh?"

"Nice choice of words. Is there the slightest chance that it's a coincidence that Ionescu and Chesterfield know each other?"

"I guess so," Festus said, "if you believe in Santa Claus."

"The real Santa Claus was a goat-headed Bavarian demon named Krampus who chained up misbehaving children," Chase replied, shoving a plate toward his father.

"My point exactly," Festus said, snagging a piece of bacon. "I'd say when you team up a revenge-seeking Strigoi with a power-hungry Creavit wizard, the combination is about as precious and darling as Krampus."

Refilling his coffee cup, Chase leaned back against the counter. "What do you know about the curse Ionescu placed on Jinx's mother?"

"Carry this plate over to the table for me, will you?" Festus said, jumping down. "We can at least pretend to be civilized."

When they were both seated at the table—or in Festus' case, *on* the table—the old cat continued. "You know about Kelly and Gemma wanting to be cheerleaders in high school?"

Chase nodded.

"They cast a spell on two girls to make them late to school, but something happened, and the car went off the road. It was raining that day, and the roads were slick. Kelly blamed herself. That's why she gave up magic for so many years. But she gave up a whole lot more."

"Her first born."

"Yes," Festus said, pausing to chew a mouthful of eggs. "A boy. She named him Connor. Ionescu was the father of one of the dead girls and the uncle of the other one. When he found out Kelly had a baby, he wanted revenge. He cursed Kelly to be forever parted from her son, which meant Ionescu planned to drain the boy's life force."

"Until Barnaby and Myrtle intervened."

"Right. The deal was that Connor would be taken to Shevington and Kelly would never see him again."

"And she hasn't."

"Not *yet*. Either Ionescu has found out Kelly's taken up her magic again and is going back and forth to the Valley, or he's still consumed with revenge, but I think he hired Malcolm Ferguson to come after her and Jinx through us."

Chase scrubbed at his face with his hand and stared out over the mostly deserted courthouse square. "Furl says we can't get close to the Ionescu's compound up in the mountains. Now, what?"

"Now," Festus said, "you go to the Valley and talk to Ironweed."

"Ironweed? What in the world does the fairy guard have to do with all of this?"

"Sometimes Ironweed drinks with us at the Dirty Claw."

Chase shook his head. "Ironweed is an adrenaline junkie. What fairy in his right mind would drink with a bunch of werecats? He gets mistaken for a moth, and he's a goner."

"Not bloody likely," Festus snorted. "You ever notice that long thin scar on Merle's nose?"

"Yeah. What about it?"

"He decided to chase Ironweed one night, and the little bugger cut him with a combat knife. Never judge a fairy by his size."

Chase chuckled. "I would have paid good money to see that. Tell me again why I'm going to see Ironweed?"

"Gnats. You're going to talk to him about gnats."

Chapter Six

Friday presented challenges. After Chase left for the Valley, I grappled with equal parts depression and annoyance. The fact that I couldn't—or wouldn't—ask why he was going to Shevington plunged me into a blue mood. Chase's movements were no longer any of my business.

I kept repeating that to myself as I dusted things that didn't need to be dusted and rearranged displays that didn't need to be rearranged.

It's none of my business.
It's none of my business.
It's none of my business.

There was no way I intended to appear interested in anything Chase did.

No. Way.

My growing annoyance involved harboring a secret plan to sneak off to the Valley myself that night and the uncomfortable possibility my stance on Chase might be a tad hypocritical in light of that.

Bear with me for a second. Let's put my motivations aside and consider the logistics I faced executing my covert op.

I live in the same building with my best friend, a hyper-intelligent rat, an overly solicitous brownie (who can make himself literally invisible), a mini witch with a love for late night TV, and my newly corporeal ghost dad.

Getting through the lair and on my way to Shevington would require a minor miracle under the best of circumstances. In the wake of Chase's announcement, I now faced the real chance of running into my ex who would expect an explanation.

Which I wouldn't give.

Which meant I would lose my temper.

Thus taking things between us from worse to . . . more worse.

But wait, I'm not done.

Remember, that was a Friday, meaning the moms would show up around closing time for our mother/daughter, witch/alchemist, potluck/workout. As winter approached we'd started combining our magical activities with family time.

This time, however, the moms planned to spend the night. Tori and I both had responsibilities with the festival committee to get ready for the dance. We needed the extra help in the shop. Then there was the matter of the dads.

When Malcolm Ferguson kidnapped the moms, I learned that my perfectly ordinary, truck-driving, fishing-obsessed father, has known about magic all along.

While shocking, the news came as a huge relief. Any family scenario that doesn't involve complicated lies is good in my book.

Tori didn't get that lucky. Her dad, Howard "Scrap" Andrews, so christened for the lumber yard he runs, had no idea that both his wife and daughter possessed supernatural powers.

Gemma's confession of Scrap's blissful state of ignorance stunned Tori. "You studied alchemy on the sly in our basement all these years with Granny Mo and Dad didn't figure it out? How on earth did you manage that?"

"The same way I managed it with you," Gemma replied placidly. "I told you all I was putting up preserves, which I occasionally did, but with expedited cooking methods."

"I've been eating alchemically pickled peaches my whole life?"

"Eating them and loving them, so quit having a conniption. Your father is too practical by nature. He thinks in two by fours. I didn't see any reason to confuse him."

"And now?" I asked.

"Well," Gemma said, "things have changed. You two have your abilities. Kelly and I are back in the game. We need to be over here more, and it's too much trouble to keep inventing excuses. Jeff is dealing with things fine. Scrap will have to catch up whether he likes it or not."

But Scrap didn't catch up, and he didn't like it—at all.

When Gemma told her husband the truth about herself and their daughter, he took the news as a betrayal of their marriage. The line that crushed his normally stalwart wife was, "How can I be sure anything about our relationship was ever true?"

Exactly one week before the planned sleepover, Gemma sat in the lair and reviewed high—or I guess low—points of her conversation with Scrap. Her pale face and strained features betrayed how much her husband's suspicions hurt her.

When her mother finished talking, Tori ventured out onto the sea of egg shells littering the conversation and said tentatively, "I can understand why Dad thinks you lied to him."

My mother gasped. "Victoria Tallulah Andrews! Apologize to your mother this instant."

Full names. Very bad. Coming from either mother.

Tori swallowed hard, but to her credit, she didn't back down. "I'm not trying to be hurtful, Kelly, but Mom and Dad have been married for 35 years. That's a long time to find out your wife has been keeping something from you."

Mom drew herself up in preparation for a major lecture, but Gemma laid a calming hand on her arm. "Down girl. The kid is right. You can ruffle your feathers and defend me all you like, but I *have* been lying to Scrap for years. I lied to you, too. I told you I wasn't practicing magic, and that wasn't the truth."

"If you hadn't kept up your powers in secret," Mom said loyally, "we could never have faced a sorceress like Brenna Sinclair. She would have killed us both. You were doing what you thought you had to do to protect these girls and me."

Gemma nodded sadly, "Yes, but that doesn't get around the lying part."

Still treading carefully, Tori asked, "How did you and Dad leave it?"

For a fraction of a second, I thought Gemma was going to cry, but then she got a hold of herself. "I don't know. He hasn't been home all week."

Tori looked like she had been hit with one of her father's two by fours. "He hasn't been home? Where has he been?"

"Sleeping in his office at the lumber yard," Gemma answered, her lips quivering slightly.

Mom looked stricken. "Oh, Gem, why didn't you tell me?"

"Because you'd have gone charging down there to have a talk with him and I didn't think Scrap was quite up for that yet."

In spite of the seriousness of the conversation, we all laughed. Mom doesn't get mad often, but when she does, she gets mad all over.

A couple of bottles of red wine and a good bit of popcorn later, a plan evolved to have my father take Tori's dad on an overnight fishing trip. Somewhere between baiting the trot lines and drinking good bourbon, we all hoped Dad could talk some sense into Scrap and get him to come home.

We'd find out the next night when Dad either showed up for the street dance alone or with Scrap in tow. Tori had been on edge about the whole thing all week, especially since her father wouldn't take her phone calls.

When she told me that, I said, "Why isn't he talking to you?"

"Maybe he doesn't want a magical daughter either," Tori answered, her voice breaking.

Since we're both daddy's girls, I knew exactly what she was going through. I pulled her into a hug and said, "Stop that. Scrap loves you to pieces. He's just got to get used to all this."

"I hope so, Jinksy," she mumbled against my shoulder. "I hope so."

So you see, we were both preoccupied that Friday after the committee meeting. Tori by her personal family crisis, and me because I was doing some lying of my own.

Something else came to light that summer—a huge something that seemed beyond my control until an opportunity presented itself.

I have a brother named Connor whom I was not allowed to meet.

If you just had a "what the" moment, join the club. My sentiments exactly.

Here's the deal, Connor doesn't know we exist. Thanks to a curse put on my mother by a Fae being called a Strigoi, Connor was exiled to Shevington as an infant and never told about his real family.

When Mom turned up missing during the whole mess with Malcolm Ferguson, Dad blurted out the story, assuming there had to be a connection. Since we still don't know if someone hired Ferguson to come after us, I can't say Dad was right or wrong.

When the dust settled after Festus killed Ferguson, the Hamiltons held a family conference. We agreed that contacting

Connor would put him in danger. Mom and I promised Dad and Aunt Fiona we wouldn't do anything to try to contact my brother.

Confession time. I had my fingers crossed behind my back.

Are you freaking kidding me? I have a *brother* and I'm not *allowed* to meet him? So *not* how I intended to play.

Connor works for Ellis Groomsby in the Shevington stables. That Friday, Ellis and all of his staff, with the exception of Connor, would be working in the upper valley relocating saltwater life forms to the new merfolk environment.

I know this because I drink my coffee in Shevington in a corner shop not far from the stables. Go down the sloping street and turn left, you're at the fairy barracks where the Brown Mountain Guard does flight drills. Turn right, and you see the stables. The big meadow north of the city sits between the two.

The week before, I overheard a table full of workers from the stable discussing the transfer of the sea creatures. My ears perked up when he said, "Everybody's coming but Endicott."

Connor was raised by an old friend of Aunt Fiona's who posed as his grandmother. Her name was Endora Endicott. After Endora died last year Aunt Fiona moved into her cottage.

"How come Endicott gets off light?" one of the men asked.

"The unicorn mare is about to foal," his companion replied. "She's been unusually skittish during her pregnancy. Ellis can't even get near her. Endicott is the only one who can handle her. Besides, somebody has to muck out the stables."

That elicited a round of laughter as the men returned their cups and plates to the counter and walked out as a group. I left too, heading back to Briar Hollow, the wheels in my brain turning at full steam.

I knew all about the merfolk project. In the face of worsening ocean pollution, they requested and were granted sanctuary in Shevington. The only requirement was that Myrtle and Moira create a place for them to live.

Myrtle helped complete the successful design for the inland sea that would be the merfolk's new home only days before she merged her energy with the Mother Tree.

Whether the moms were underfoot or not, I had to go to Shevington that night. With Ellis out of the way, I could visit the stables without Barnaby finding out.

If someone did see me in the street and questions were asked later, I could say I was picking something up at the bookshop or the apothecary. If all went well, I would get to the Valley in time to actually stop at one of those places and then I wouldn't be technically lying.

This renegade notion of mine did not extend to some dramatic reunion with my brother where I blurted out the whole story and turned his life upside down. I only wanted to see him, to know what he looked like, and maybe to hear his voice.

For this scheme to work, timing would be everything.

In addition to getting ready for the festival, we had plenty to do with the moms. Tori and Gemma were right in the middle of a comparative study of divination methods. Crystal balls and tarot cards littered their work tables along with runes, I Ching wands, and currently, sacks of flour.

Yeah. Aleuromancy. The use of flour to foretell the future. That's how the whole fortune cookie thing got started. Who knew?

Tonight they would be trying to mix flour with water to interpret patterns in the "slurry." I figured worse case scenario, they wind up baking cookies.

Mom and I planned to conduct drills with simultaneous powers. I was learning to move an object with one hand while hitting a target with energy bolts using the other. Mom was perfecting transformation and relocation spells.

Translation: I could lift a target in the air and zap it at the same time. Mom could blink an apple out of one place and have it reappear somewhere else as an orange.

While those specific power combinations might not ever do us any practical good, the goal was to achieve control over two or more concurrent streams of magic with equal accuracy.

In my head, we'd do dinner, drills, and a movie. From past experience, I knew the moms and Tori would fall asleep, which would allow me to leave a note saying I went upstairs to be with my cats. Since time runs slower in Shevington, I could get to the Valley, meet Connor, and get back before anyone was the wiser—unless I ran into Chase.

Chapter Seven

As I unloaded the dishwasher in the espresso bar, my mind worked at full preoccupied capacity. I ran through all the possible scenarios I might have to deal with to get to Shevington, and then ran them again with different variables.

I didn't hear Tori until she delivered a good-natured hip bump accompanied by the admonition, "Hey, let it go."

Startled, I covered my incomprehension with a fairly grumpy, "Let what go?" Thankfully that put her on the wrong track about what I'd been thinking.

"Don't try to play that game with me, Jinksy," she said. "You're beating yourself up for snapping at Chase, *and* it's eating you up that you didn't ask him why he was headed to Shevington."

Neither statement was entirely untrue, so I went with it.

"Okay. Fine. Busted."

Reaching to help me put cups away, Tori said, "Look, break-ups suck. Period. Trust me, I know. Remember who you're talking to? The Queen of Lousy Relationships?"

I closed the dishwasher and leaned against the counter.

Even though I hadn't been thinking about the break-up with Chase, I felt myself going on the defensive.

"That," I said, crossing my arms over my chest, "would be the problem. We *didn't* have a lousy relationship."

"True," Tori said. She picked up the coffee pot and gave me a questioning expression. "You want some?"

"Yeah, sure."

Why not pour caffeine on top of my already anxiety-ridden secret plot?

As she filled both cups, Tori continued trying to reason with me about Chase. "Maybe the relationship wasn't bad, but you two were up against a lousy werecat taboo. The deal with Ferguson scared Chase."

That struck a chord and not a pleasant one. "Then he should have talked to me," I said, an edge of anger coming into my voice.

"Maybe he didn't know how."

"If that's true, we had a bigger problem than Ferguson. One that I didn't even know about. Lack of communication."

"Hence you not knowing about it," Tori snarked, miming a rim shot on an imaginary snare drum.

"Very funny."

"Can't blame a girl for trying. You're doing that whole fatalistic thing, by the way."

"What fatalistic thing?"

"The one where you act like you're never going to see Chase again," she said, "which is, like, next to impossible. There's no rule that you guys can't still talk. In fact, the rest of us would be thrilled if you did."

"What's that supposed to mean?" I asked, sounding guilty in spite of myself.

"It means those of us who love you don't like watching you come down every day with red eyes from crying half the night or having to tiptoe around every time you and Chase are in the same room."

Her words sent a flush of embarrassed heat spreading over my cheeks, but I still refused to budge. "If Chase McGregor wants to talk to me, he knows where I am. And it's not just him. I miss Myrtle."

"Myrtle would be the first one to tell you to talk to him."

That's all it took for tears to fill my eyes.

Tori plucked a tissue out of the box and handed it to me. "Okay," she said in a softer tone, "I'll back off. Please don't cry anymore. At least not until I buy stock in Kimberly-Clark."

That wisecrack finally made me laugh, but the sound came out as a sort of damp gurgle. Tori put a consoling hand on my arm. "Let's change the subject."

Excellent idea.

"What time are the moms getting here?" she asked.

I cleared my throat and said, "They'll be here for supper. Mom and Darby were on FaceTime working out the meal plan down in the lair this morning."

"Of course, they were. Apple needs to start paying us a commission the way we've been handing out iPads around here."

After we had outfitted Glory's dollhouse with an iPod Touch to serve as a big screen TV, she informed us that her biggest joy in life was attending old-fashioned drive-in movies. Couldn't we find a way to make that work for her, too?

I'd like to say "we" answered the call, but the DIY fix was all Tori. First, she bought a pink Malibu Barbie convertible on eBay, then she picked up yet another iPad and mounted it on the wall to the left of the dollhouse.

Add two squares of artificial grass and a couple of tiny Bluetooth speakers, as well as a swoopy vintage sign reading "MoonGlo," and Glory had her drive-in.

When Tori asked me for my opinion of the project, I came

downstairs to survey the miniature parking lot. Rodney rode along on my shoulder. I had one question. "How's Glory going to get the movie going?"

"Rat remote control," Tori replied. "Show her Rodney."

Giving Tori the thumbs up, Rodney ran down my arm, jumped the space to the shelf, and approached the iPad. Standing on his hind legs, he used his paw to swipe the on-screen lock. Next, he tapped the Amazon Video icon, selected a movie from the WatchList, and hit "play." On cue, the opening titles of *Blue Hawaii* filled the screen.

"Why not Netflix?" I asked.

"No Elvis on Netflix," Tori answered. "I bought the whole Elvis catalog for Glory, and now she's hitting me up to get all the Annette Funicello stuff, too."

"And the Fifties are alive and well," I declared, "right here in our basement."

Before she was done, Tori even added mini popcorn to the drive-in set up. Trust me; I never heard of the stuff either, but it's apparently one of Oprah's favorite things—and now Rodney's, too.

It would be impossible not to love Rodney anyway, but imagine a black-and-white rat kicked back in the passenger seat of a pink convertible eating popcorn out of a red-and-white striped bag.

There was, however, one unexpected complication to the arrangement—Darby's hurt feelings. We didn't expect him to look up at us with wounded eyes and ask when he would "earn" one of the "flat boxes that make pictures."

The word "earn" crushed us both so much that Tori instantly headed out to the mall and came back with a brand new gold iPad.

When she handed the tablet to the elated brownie, she said, "We had to find a really special one for you, Darby. It's already loaded up with all the Harry Potter movies."

That last announcement set him to bouncing up and down with excitement. To our considerable amusement, Darby is not only obsessed with Harry Potter; he's convinced J.K. Rowling based one of the characters on him.

Now, granted, I could see the similarity, but we only started calling our friend "Darby" because we can't pronounce his real name. Try to imagine a sound mix involving Festus tossing a hairball against the backdrop of a spoon caught in the garbage disposal—with a lot of consonants.

Tori suggested the name "Darby" from an old movie our Hollywood-obsessed moms love, *Darby O'Gill and the Little People*. We weren't even thinking about Dobby the house elf from Harry Potter.

Darby, however, steadfastly insists J.K. Rowling based that character on him. Never mind that when she wrote the book, Darby was still trapped guarding Knasgowa's grave or that at two feet tall with a shy, smiling face bears zero resemblance to a house elf.

It didn't take Darby long to figure out all the other things he could do with an iPad, including FaceTime with my mother to trade recipes.

Other than the committee meeting that morning, it had been a quiet Friday. I was locking the front door when Mom came bouncing in the back holding a huge platter encased in aluminum foil. My nose instantly told me the silver wrapping concealed a mountain of her famous fried chicken.

Tori held the door to the basement for her, and the three of us went down together. Darby already had the table set, and Beau was lighting two tall candles in massive brass holders.

"Good evening, ladies," he said gallantly. "Isn't Miss Gemma joining us?"

Beau didn't know about the situation with Tori's father. It was bad enough that the Cotterville town gossips were already wagging their tongues because Scrap's pickup hadn't left the lumberyard parking lot for days. Gemma asked us to keep the situation "just between us girls for now," and we had agreed.

"She'll be here in a few minutes," Mom said brightly, setting the platter down between two equally huge bowls of potato salad and beans. "She wanted to give Scrap his supper before he and Jeff go fishing."

Tori and I exchanged a queasy look at the fabricated story.

"So," Tori said weakly, "tonight is the night, huh?"

Mom finished folding the foil into a neat, reusable square and put her arm around Tori's waist. "It's okay, sugar. Jeff won't let Scrap fall in the river or anything."

That was Mom code for, "He'll bring him back home where he belongs."

Still looking worried, Tori leaned into Mom. "Is Jeff gonna send us a text or something to let us know . . . uh . . . if the fish are biting?"

From the stairs above us, her mother answered the question as she came down balancing a pecan pie in each hand. "If the fish aren't biting," she said, making a supreme effort to sound normal, "I gave them permission to go honky tonkin'."

"You did not," Tori said, laughing in spite of herself and standing on tiptoe to kiss her tall mother's cheek.

"I did, too," Gemma answered, handing me the pies and giving me a quick peck before hugging my mother. "Hi, Kells, Everything good?"

The moms are fiercely protective of one another. Gemma knew what a strain the Connor situation put on mom, and mom understood Gemma's pain over the estrangement with Scrap. The two of them can say an awful lot to each other without really saying anything at all.

Mom returned the embrace, nodding her answer, and holding on a few seconds longer than usual. I couldn't tell if she was drawing off a bit of Gemma's no-nonsense strength for herself or sharing some of her resolve with her friend.

If Beau found anything odd about the exchange, he didn't comment. Instead, he held out Mom's chair and then did the same for Gemma. Tori and I sat across from them, and Beau took his place at the head of the table.

That position seemed to make him happy. I think it reminded him of the days when he presided over his own family meals enjoying the company of his wife, daughter, and the two sons he lost at Gettysburg.

At the opposite end of the table, Darby had thoughtfully set out diminutive doll's plates for Glory and Rodney as well as fixing a place for himself.

To an outsider, we might have looked like an unconventional entourage, but I felt a surge of love for all the people sharing that meal. We kept the conversation light and relished the excellent food. No one watching us that night would have suspected all the hidden undercurrents flowing around the table.

When we were done eating, Darby handled the clean-up while Glory and Rodney settled into the pink convertible. They were still stuck on *Blue Hawaii*, and I thought I'd scream if I had to listen to "Can't Help Falling In Love" one more time, but I managed to hold my tongue.

Beau worked at the rolltop desk taking notes from an ancient text bound in soft calfskin while Tori and Gemma played in mounds of flour. Mom and I were drilling on the target range when Festus limped into the lair.

"Evening all," he said, stopping beside Mom and watching as I threaded a slender energy bolt perfectly through the eye of a large needle.

Mom clapped her hands in delight when I wrapped the energy back onto itself and a pulsating knot. "Honey! That's wonderful!"

"She's as good as her grandmother," Festus observed appreciatively. "Remember how Kathleen used to make those glowing yellow chains on the tree at Christmas?"

"Oh!" Mom said, breaking into a smile. "I had forgotten about those. And remember the peppermint sticks that danced to *Winter Wonderland*?"

Festus chuckled. "Those were fun to bat off the tree. Kathleen loved all the holidays. This close to Halloween, she'd have had the whole house smelling of pumpkin pies and baked apples."

As I listened to them talk, I felt a pang of jealousy. I remembered my grandmother primarily as a church lady who cranked up the volume on the TV to hear her "programs." By the time I was old enough to spend the day with Aunt Fiona in the store, Grandma Kathleen didn't come in very often. It seemed she always had some "club" meeting to attend. We saw each other at major holidays, but there was always something slightly off in her relationship with mom.

When Chase and I broke up, I didn't know how our estrangement would affect the group dynamic, but at least in Festus' case, nothing changed. He regularly joined us in the evenings, usually curling up on the hearth or playing chess with Tori on a low table by the fire. If anyone else felt the awkwardness of Chase's absence, they had the good grace not to mention it.

The aleuromancy experiment resulted in the only hiccup that evening, one big enough it almost stopped my heart in my chest. While mom and I were still practicing, we heard a frustrated exclamation from the direction of the work tables. I looked up to find both Tori and Gemma engulfed in a cloud of flour.

"Hey!" Festus cried indignantly. "Watch it, you two! You're getting that crap all over my fur."

"So groom already," Gemma barked. Turning to Tori, she said, "Young lady, I told you to *pour* the flour, not drop it."

"I didn't drop it," Tori shot back. "I think the bowl is mad at us. We've asked it the same question so many times that it wants to talk about something else."

Mom and I exchanged a bemused look. "What's going on over there?" she called out.

"We're doing something wrong," Gemma groused. "This damned bowl keeps saying someone down here is going to make a secret journey tonight."

Just as she said those words, I was directing an energy bolt toward a lantern sitting 15 feet away. I jerked my hand, sending the stream of power ricocheting off a steel file cabinet. As it shot past my head, I ducked and yelled, "Fire in the hole!"

Festus dove under one of the leather chairs by the hearth as the blue flame flew between Gemma and Tori heading straight for Glory's dollhouse. At the last second, Beau snatched up the wastebasket by his desk and fielded the energy, which immediately ignited the papers in the trash can.

Thankfully, Gemma appeared beside him and sprinkled some powder over the flames accompanied by the magical command, "*Extinctus!*"

Festus poked his head out and looked around. "Is it safe?"

"Yes," Gemma said, turning toward me. "What the heck was that?"

"Sorry," I said. "Guess I'm tired."

"Then quit before you burn the place down," she ordered. "Give us a few minutes to clean up this flour and we'll start the movie."

My heart hammered in my chest as I watched them gathering up the scattered flour, which was, as I predicted, turned over to Darby to make the biggest batch of chocolate chip cookie dough I've ever seen.

Fortunately, however, my accidental pyrotechnics distracted everyone from the "secret journey" prediction, which wasn't mentioned again.

Festus grumbled through a long grooming session before

settling down to nap by the fire. Beau excused himself and carried his books and papers off to his bachelor pad, no doubt having had quite enough metaphysical artillery barrages for one night.

Glory and Rodney were snoring in the front seat of the Barbie convertible. Darby disappeared after setting out heaping plates of gooey cookie goodness hot out of the oven.

Embracing the whole slumber party vibe, the four of us piled onto the two sofas Tori and I recently added to the lair's furnishings. Since our numbers seemed to be growing, the lack of comfortable group seating had started to be a problem.

We both agreed we should have gotten the urge to redecorate before Myrtle left, since she could have put the sofas in place with a snap of her fingers. That thought only came to us however, as we maneuvered down the stairs with the first bulky piece of furniture. The ludicrous situation triggered a fit of nearly hysterical giggling. Tori later told me that was the first time she heard me laugh since Myrtle went away.

That Friday night the moms voted to watch *Titanic* on our other new addition, a flat screen TV that drops down from the ceiling at the touch of a button. Chase installed it, since we could hardly explain to the guy from Best Buy why we would have wanted such a thing in what would have appeared to him to be a dirty, cluttered basement.

Earlier I'd used fatigue as an excuse to cover my botched energy bolt, but now everyone else truly was exhausted either from work or worry. About half an hour into the movie, I started catching the first signs—nodding heads that jerked awake only to start bobbing again in five minutes. My Mom lost the battle first, then Gemma, and finally Tori.

I waited an extra 15 minutes, set the movie to repeat so no one would wake up, left my fake note, and silently rolled one of the bikes out of the circle of light cast by the lamps.

As I pedaled into the stacks toward the portal to Shevington, I checked the time. It should take me three hours to get to the Valley, visit the stables, and get back—provided I didn't run into Chase.

The thrill of excitement that ran through me pushed that risk to the back of my thoughts. I was about to see my brother for the first time. Nothing was going to stop me.

Chapter Eight

Chase was used to hearing his father make outrageous statements, but the suggestion that Chase go to the Valley to discuss gnats with a fairy took things to a new level. At least until Festus explained that GNATS stood for "Group Network Aerial Transmission System."

Chase listened in fascination as Festus described the Brown Mountain Guard's latest tool to expand the scope of their patrols—micro drones. A single grain of fairy dust powered each of the machines that mimicked both the size and appearance of the common gnat.

If Festus had understood Ironweed correctly, the GNATS also replicated the energy signature of their namesake insect, which would make them perfect to surveil the Ionescu compound.

The walk to the Valley improved Chase's spirits. When he stepped through the portal, the verdant greens of the lower meadow worked like a balm on his aching heart, and he found himself struck anew by the incredible beauty of Shevington.

When he was a boy, his grandmother once warned him that all magic carries risks, but if used wisely, it also conveys great rewards. To experience life on a richer level appeared to mean accepting that as a werecat, he could not be with the witch he loved.

Railing against the unfairness of it all wouldn't help. Festus was right. All Chase could do was accept the situation and fulfill his obligations. Hopefully, Jinx would forgive him in time and they could be friends. If she didn't? He had to do his job anyway.

Once through the city's main gate, Chase merged with the pleasant, early morning bustle on the High Street. He exchanged greetings with townsfolk and stopped for coffee at Madame Kahveh's before making his way to the fairy guard base.

The command center sat at one end of the drill field. From the outside, the building appeared to be marginally larger than an old-fashioned phone booth. Inside, however, the structure housed a high-rise warren of fairy-sized offices, with a ceiling clearance around 8-10 inches for the command higher ups.

The offices were arranged around a central, human-sized atrium. Visitors could carefully step into the space and locate the office they needed, but most preferred to speak with the fairy personnel in the adjacent courtyard thoughtfully outfitted with furniture on a more normal scale.

Chase, however, loved the interior of the command center. It felt like literally stepping into a beehive, albeit one where the bees wore black commando fatigues, combat boots, and purple berets. Rather than rely on elevators, the fairies used their incandescent wings to move from floor to floor.

Major Aspid "Ironweed" Istra, the Commander of the Brown Mountain Guard, kept an office at the back of the building positioned to observe his troops during flight drills over the field.

At the entrance to the command center, Chase punched

the intercom button. A fairy guardsman barked through the speaker, "State your business, sir."

"I have an appointment with Major Istra."

"Roger that, sir," the guard said briskly. "Interior or exterior?"

"Interior."

"Step into the airlock, please."

Chase opened the door as instructed and waited patiently for the panel to the atrium to slide to the side. Opening the main door on windy days could cause an internal tornado and a lot of seriously hacked off fairies.

Careful to avoid any collisions with the miniature inhabitants, Chase approached the back wall. Reaching over the walkway railing, he tapped on the door of Ironweed's office with his index finger.

"Come!" Ironweed barked.

"Kinda hard to do," Chase answered. "I'm six feet tall."

Behind him, a group of fairy secretaries gathered by the water cooler giggled. Chase flashed them a smile. "Good morning, ladies."

"Quit flirting with the women, McGregor," Ironweed ordered sternly, leaning against the door of his office with his arms crossed. "Stick to your weight class."

"You're a fine one to talk."

"I'm a man of special attributes, ole boy," Ironweed said, settling his beret at a rakish angle on his head and fluttering his wings to rise to Chase's eye level. "Let's take this conversation outside so my people can get some work done."

Chase pivoted carefully and moved toward the door. Around them, fairies snapped mid-air salutes, which Ironweed returned with crisp, military efficiency.

The guards activated the airlock panel without asking. Chase and Ironweed stepped back into the daylight. The diminutive major, who was flying alongside Chase's head, was instantly all business.

"From what Festus tells me, this should be kept on a strictly need-to-know basis. Let's go to the viewing stand at the field."

"Good idea," Chase agreed, crossing the field and climbing to the top of the bleachers. He purposefully chose a seat a level below the top so Ironweed could perch on the edge of the bench by his head.

"Did Dad explain the situation to you?"

"Yep. Festus says you've got yourself a Strigoi problem and you're in need of intel. Preferably without Barnaby knowing what you're doing for the moment."

"Is that last part a problem?"

"Not if all you want me to do right now is look."

"That's all I want. Can you get in there with these drones of yours?"

"Can we get in there?" Ironweed laughed. "Let me show you something."

He reached into one of the front pockets of his fatigue pants and drew out a minuscule tablet. With a few tapped commands a magnified holographic image of the mountains around Briar Hollow projected from the device.

Chase let out a low whistle. "Nice. That's video from the GNATS drones?"

"Correct. Let me give you an idea what these babies can do." He extracted a walkie talkie from another pocket and keyed the mic. "Red Dragon One to GNATS Ops. Come in."

"This is GNATS Ops Command, Red Dragon One."

"Deploy GNAT Flight 32 low over sector 26."

"Roger that, Red Dragon One."

As Chase watched the hologram, the drones changed direction and came in low over Briar Hollow from the south. They dropped in altitude, skimming the rooftops and entering the courthouse square at the corner across from George and Irma's grocery store.

"GNATS Ops Command," Ironweed said. "Assume surveillance altitude over the courthouse."

The drones surged upward, settling in place around the clock tower on the building's roof. Chase could see the front of Jinx's store as well as his cobbler shop. He watched as the women from the historical association draped orange and black crepe paper around the entrance to the courthouse. The building would stay open that evening so festival goers could have access to the restrooms, thus decorations were in order.

"How do you overcome the time difference between Shevington and Briar Hollow?" Chase asked.

"Simple. The drone control center is on the slopes of Brown Mountain. The signal you're looking at is trans-dimensional."

"Wow. You can do real-time video at that resolution with a single grain of fairy dust?"

"Brother," Ironweed said, "you do not want to know what I can do with a single grain of fairy dust, and if I told you, I'd have to kill you."

Chase started to laugh and then thought better of it. Festus had a point about not underestimating fairies. It encouraged them to shoot for even greater heights of crazy, daredevil behavior.

"So," he said, "you can handle the Ionescu thing?"

"Absolutely. We already have the coordinates."

"You do? How?"

"We get security briefings from **IBIS**. We'll need more time to really put together a picture of what goes on out there, but let me have the boys do a preliminary fly over now."

Ironweed spoke into the walkie talkie again. He and Chase watched the display change as the drones headed out of town and started up into the mountains.

After several minutes, Chase said, "Good Lord, are you sure you have the right coordinates?"

"Yep. Verified them myself. These Strigoi seriously want to be left alone."

Finally a grouping of buildings appeared in the trees. A high fence surrounded the compound which was comprised of multiple neat homes and manicured lawns. "Place looks like somebody picked up a perfectly normal suburb and dropped it in the middle of nowhere," Ironweed said.

Then he squinted at the hologram and picked up the walkie talkie. "GNATS Ops Command, zero in on those small sheds behind the houses."

The display split as two individual drones broke off from the swarm and dived lower. One hovered above the backyard of a home on the edge of the compound while its partner flew into a shed sitting a few feet behind the residence. The camera instantly switched to black-and-white night vision for a sharper look at the interior.

"Holy freaking power consumption," Ironweed said, "would you look at that generator? That thing could light up a human high rise much less a three bedroom ranch."

The drone duo went on to examine six sheds, finding high-capacity generators in each one.

"Well," Chase said. "Dad did say they feed on electricity."

"If they're eating that much juice, you are about to cross swords with some seriously powerful bad guys."

"The point is to *not* cross swords with them. How long before you can give me a full report?"

"Can you tell me what we're looking for?"

"Not really, and there's an added wrinkle. The head of the Ionescu clan, Anton, spends a lot of time in Raleigh. He has a law practice there."

"Not a problem," Ironweed said. "We don't patrol that far,

but I have people I can reach out to. Give me a couple of days."

"That long?" Chase asked, trying not to sound annoyed.

Ironweed flew closer to Chase's face and gave him an appraising look. "McGregor, you look like hammered unicorn manure."

"Gee, thanks."

"No, seriously, are you getting any sleep after the thing with Jinx?"

"Not much."

"Why don't you take a mini vacation? You're already here. Go on up to the high valley and have a look at the new inland sea. Man, it is some kind of sweet. Those merfolk are going to be living the high . . . er . . . deep life. It would do you some good to get some fresh air. Barnaby set up a camp to oversee the work. You could spend the night. How long's it been since you slept under the stars?"

"You mean in human form? Too long."

"Then make up for some lost time."

"I do have a job, you know," Chase said, but he could feel his resolve weakening.

"Oh, please. You're not the only werecat in the world. I'll get a message to Festus. After the way he dealt with Malcolm Ferguson, surely you trust him to take care of Jinx for one night?"

"Well, I guess the old man can handle it."

"You want me to tell him you said that?"

"I do not."

"Come on," Ironweed said, "you know you want to stay."

Try as he might, Chase couldn't come up with a reason to say no. He remembered the sheer sense of relief he'd felt stepping through the portal into the Valley. The idea of a whole night away from Briar Hollow sounded more like heaven than he liked to admit.

"Okay, You've convinced me. I think I will check it out. You want to come with me?"

"No can do. Staff meeting in thirty. I'll call Festus before I go in."

Chase thanked Ironweed and then retraced his steps to Madame Kahveh's. He bought a loaf of fresh bread, a hunk of sharp cheese, and a carafe of his favorite blend to enjoy on the walk. His route would take him right by a rocky outlook that had been one of his favorite solitary places as a younger man.

"This no leak," Madame Kahveh said in her thick accent of indeterminate origin. "Coffee no get cold. I use strong magic to enchant. Here, take this for to carry."

Chase accepted the light daypack she held out with a grin. The flap was emblazoned with the words, "Cold coffee offers no comfort for the soul."

He stowed his food purchases and, slinging the bag over his shoulder, turned his steps toward the high valley. Having "camped" with Barnaby before, Chase knew he'd have access to anything he might need once he arrived at the inland sea.

As he started across the big meadow between the fairy guard drill field and the stables, Chase turned his face toward the warmth of the sun. There were plenty of problems waiting for him back in Briar Hollow, but at least for a few hours he could afford to put them on hold.

Chapter Nine

The instant I stepped through the portal to the Valley, six dragonlets landed in a perfect line in front of me, bowing their bird-like beaks low toward the earth and spreading their wings.

Then Minreinth, the flock leader, looked up. He cocked his head to the side to regard me with one glittering, jewel-like eye, and let out with a series of coos and chirps.

From the moment I met the creatures, I've been able to understand their language, but in this instance, there was no translation required. Minreinth wanted to know what I was doing in the Valley.

Sighing, I said, "You guys are worse than a bunch of parents waiting up for their kid to get home from a date."

The dragonlets' heads swiveled back and forth. I swear two of them shrugged their incomprehension.

Minreinth asked the question for the group, which I answered. "A 'date,'" I explained, "is when two people who are interested in each other go somewhere together."

Minreinth's blank expression told me he needed more detail. I tried again.

"Parents usually give their kids a specific time to come home, and if they're late, the parents wait up for them."

Now puzzlement filled the dragonlet's features. Okay, third time's the charm, right?

"The parents do that because they're afraid the kids might do something they're not supposed to do during the date."

At that, Minreinth cocked his head again and chirped mischievously. He'd been playing me the whole time.

"You are so bad!" I said. "And, no, 'make baby dragons' is not exactly the correct answer, but you're on the right track."

The dragonlet leader cackled mirthfully and reiterated his original inquiry.

"Yeah, yeah," I said. "I know I didn't tell you why I'm here."

More stares. Dragonlets have the patience of Job.

"Fine," I sighed. "I'm here to do something a lot of people wouldn't want me to do, so I'm trying to keep a low profile. Do you know what that means?"

Minreinth nodded, and to my surprise instantly began to give me useful information on getting into the city undetected. I was arriving just before the supper hour in the Valley. I didn't expect to go completely unnoticed, but it would be nice to avoid the hustle and bustle at the city's main entrance until I finished my errand.

The dragonlet explained that Bill Ruff, who guards the lower bridge, eats early and then falls asleep for at least an hour. To play it safe, however, Minreinth suggested I use the rock crossing above the bridge. The dragonlet was turning out to be an excellent co-conspirator.

"Any suggestions about avoiding the main gate?"

For an instant, Minreinth looked vaguely uncomfortable, and then he said that I *might* find a service door open on the east side of the city wall.

Narrowing my eyes suspiciously, I said, "How do you know that door *might* be open?"

The dragonlet ducked his head and dragged his talons guiltily in the dirt. He began a mournful recitation that I cut short.

"You're going into the city at night and *stealing* things?" I gasped. "Minreinth, what on earth are you *thinking*? What kinds of things are you taking?"

More chirping followed, all with a tone of reasonable self-justification.

"What do you mean 'shiny stuff?'" I interrupted.

His answer ran the gamut from purloined wind chimes to pilfered silverware. None of the thefts qualified as felonies, but since the dragonlets weren't even technically allowed to fly *over* the city, there was no way Barnaby would look kindly on these nighttime raids.

"Why on earth are you taking such a risk?" I asked Minreinth.

His vehement answer surprised me. *"The big dragons get to have treasure."*

"You mean the dragons in Europe?"

Minreinth nodded.

"Yeah, well, the 'big dragons' also get killed by people who want to take their treasure," I countered. "So count your blessings. Regardless, trying to keep up with the big dragons is not an excuse to steal. I expect you to return everything. Do you hear me?"

Reluctantly the dragonlets agreed, but now I had them over a barrel. They had to help me.

"Okay," I said, "now we're going to make a deal. You put the stuff back, don't tell anyone you saw me today, and I don't tell Barnaby what you've been up to. Deal?"

That won me nods all around.

So that, ladies and gents, is how I managed to sneak into a

walled city with the help of a gang of juvenile delinquent magical creatures. Sometimes I amaze myself.

Any miscreant behavior aside, Minreinth knew what he was talking about. The streets on the east side of town were mostly deserted. I still tried to be as inconspicuous as possible, but that mainly involved walking close to the buildings and looking over my shoulder a lot.

Things were going so well, I decided that stopping at the apothecary's for an alibi purchase should I need one, was totally doable. All I cared about was not getting caught *before* I managed to see my brother. After that, I felt confident in my ability to cook up a believable story.

When I reached the end of the sloping street, I stood partially behind a large tree and stared at the stables. Two of the pens were reserved for the descendants of Hengroen, King Arthur's stallion, and Gringolet, Sir Gawain's charger. A small herd of unicorns occupied the corral next to the invisible dome of magic that contained the winged horses, Pegasus and Tulpar, in their paddock.

Everything looked normal and deserted. Then, a single figure emerged from the barn with a wheelbarrow full of soiled straw, which he dumped in a pile. Tomorrow, the town's gardeners would obligingly haul the unicorn manure away. It's the most sought after fertilizer in Shevington.

The sun was beginning to set. I knew the worker had to be my brother, but I couldn't get a good look at his face as he moved in and out of the lengthening shadows. I waited until he went inside for another load to sprint across the open space and crouch behind a wagon filled with hay. When I heard the wheelbarrow rolling over the gravel, I cautiously raised my head.

A tall young man with my father's strong jaw and my mother's eyes came across the yard. The sleeves of his blue work shirt, rolled up to the elbow, revealed powerful muscles under skin tanned dark by long hours in the sun. The wind played through his short, sandy hair, picking up and carrying toward me the tune he whistled. *Greensleeves*. One of my . . . our . . . mother's favorites. A knot rose in my throat as I watched him work. I could see our parents in his movement and manners. I could see myself in him.

Even though I couldn't get a picture of Connor head on, I took out my phone to snap a quick image in profile. At the instant I clicked the shutter, My brother started to turn toward me. Thankfully, I have excellent reflexes. I ducked behind the wagon but banged my shin against the wheel rim. It hurt enough that before I could stop myself, I let out with a small cry of pain.

On the other side of the wagon, the sound of the wheelbarrow stopped. "Is someone there?"

I had wanted to hear his voice, but not as a prelude to getting caught. His tone was deep, like our father's but gentle, with a note of calm assurance. I knew instantly why he had such an excellent reputation for working with animals.

When I didn't answer, I heard footsteps start toward the wagon. I glanced around desperately, but there was nowhere to hide. Connor couldn't have been more than two feet from where I was standing when a raccoon hurtled past me.

The sound of skidding gravel told me the animal came to an abrupt halt on the other side of the wagon. "Whoa! Con man! Scare the fur off a guy why don't you?"

"Rube," Connor said, "what are you doing here?"

"Sorry, bro. It's an undercover thing. Top secret. You never saw me."

"Fine, but don't you go scaring my horses, and stay out of the feed shed."

"Wouldn't dream of it, man. I'm totally reformed and totally out of here. Places to go. People to see. Hasta la vista, dude."

I heard Connor walk away and then the wheelbarrow sounded on the gravel again. The raccoon waddled back behind the wagon and looked me up and down with a critical expression. "Sister," he said, "don't give up your day job. Stealth Ops ain't your thing."

"That's an understatement," a male voice agreed from behind me. "May I suggest we adjourn this conversation to a safer distance before we all get caught?"

Under normal circumstances, I might have argued, but as much as I hate to admit it, one look at the guy rendered me speechless. Don't get me wrong. The tall, lean man standing behind me was definitely good looking, but he also appeared to have stepped right out of an Indiana Jones movie.

From the bemused blue eyes to the battered fedora pushed high on his forehead, he had a look that frankly just did it for me. The collar of his white shirt was open at the throat, and he was wearing a long leather coat. If he'd pushed it back to reveal a pistol and a coiled whip hanging from his belt, I wouldn't have been one bit surprised.

Instead, he waved his hand in front of my eyes to snap me back to reality. When I blinked, he said, "Well, good, you are still in there. You've got about two minutes to decide what you're going to do. Either come with us or dive back behind that wagon before Connor returns."

My brain heard "two-minute warning" and finally reacted, sending a signal to my legs and feet to move. I followed the stranger and the raccoon across the street and into the cover of an alley. We barely made it before Connor came out into the barnyard with the wheelbarrow again.

"Now," the man said, "you want to tell me what you're doing skulking around the stables?"

Somewhat recovered, and thoroughly outdone with myself for my initial reaction, I decided I categorically did not like his tone. "I was not skulking," I replied sharply. "I don't even know how to 'skulk.'"

From the vicinity of my ankles, the raccoon said brightly, "Don't sell yourself short, doll. You're a natural at it."

Glaring down at him, I said, "And who might you be?"

"My friends call me Rube."

Something clicked in my brain. "Don't you run a cleanup crew?"

"Best in the biz."

"You did the Pike house for Festus McGregor?"

"That was us," Rube grinned, revealing a mouth full of sharp white teeth. "Some of our best work."

Turning toward the man in the duster, I said, "And who are you? The raccoon whisperer?"

"Lucas Grayson," he said, flashing me a grin of his own. "Rube is a business associate of mine."

"And your business would be what?"

"I'm an agent with the DGI,"

Oh, great. Here we go with the acronyms.

I just looked at him until he explained. "It stands for 'Division for Grid Integrity.'"

Even though I had no idea what he was talking about, one thing was clear; I'd managed to get myself busted by some kind of cop.

Before I could say anything, Grayson went on. "I know who you are, Miss Hamilton, and I know you know who Connor is, so maybe we could save each other some time by not concocting any stories."

The only thing worse than being accused of lying is being accused of lying before you even do it. Especially when that's exactly what you had in mind.

"Jinx," I said. "My name is Jinx. How do you know who I am?"

Grayson looked down at Rube. "Is she kidding?"

The raccoon shook his head. "Festus told us she don't believe her own press. Gotta admit it's kind of refreshing."

"Do you two mind?" I interrupted. "*'She'* is standing right here."

"Look Miss . . . er, Jinx," Grayson said, "you might want to start getting used to the idea that you're a pretty important person in the Fae world. Your actions have consequences."

"Meaning?"

"Meaning," Grayson said, "you can't just get it in your head that you're going to go talk to your brother when you know the potential fallout."

I started to bark back, "Who the heck do you think you are," but Grayson cut me off mid-sentence.

"The Mother Tree sent me."

Ever been called to the principal's office? Then you know exactly how I felt in that moment.

Chapter Ten

Chase lounged among the high boulders on a lonely point overlooking the Valley. To his left, he could see the walled city of Shevington, and to his right, the sparkling waters of the new inland sea. Another half hour of walking would take him to the staging area for the merfolk population transfer, but he wanted some time to himself before wading into the hive of activity visible on the shore.

After the dwarven engineers built dams in the approaches to the deep meadow, Myrtle collapsed the floor of the newly contained space to create greater depth for the merfolk. Then, in an impressive display of magical control, Moira and Myrtle held open the Atlantic Ocean portal allowing millions of gallons of saltwater to pour through. When they were done, the inland sea rivaled the size and depth of Lake Superior.

Next, the aos si and the Alchemist worked on underwater terraforming to create the rock elements and plant growth common to the merfolk's native habitat. Myrtle completed the final reef formations the day before she transitioned into the Mother Tree. Now, after several weeks of observation to verify the stability of the environment, Moira had begun to introduce designated lots of ocean species on a daily basis.

Beneath the surface, merfolk architects and builders labored to erect a submerged city for their people. If all continued to go as planned, small groups would begin to migrate to their new home over the next month.

Considering the logistical and diplomatic implications of the project, Barnaby and his staff set up camp to be on hand to help Moira and to settle the inevitable snarls and disagreements. With other species, the merfolk were by nature reclusive and shy. Their answer to any argument or conflict was generally to dive deep and remain hidden. Requesting sanctuary represented an enormous effort on their part. The Lord High Mayor wanted to avoid unnecessary stress during their relocation.

When Ironweed described the inland sea project to Chase, he hadn't done justice to the sheer scope of the undertaking. Barnaby stood by his word when he offered sanctuary to a unique species, but even by his standards, the merfolk migration constituted an epic effort.

Watching the activity from his vantage point, Chase envied Barnaby the focus and purpose of his position as Lord High Mayor. After years of friendship, the older man had confided many things to Chase, including the tragic tale of his wife's murder at the hands of a Creavit wizard who was never apprehended.

Barnaby told Chase the story over a late night game of chess during a blizzard that plunged the Valley into a whirling wall of blowing snow. Unlike Briar Hollow, where snow fell sparsely and stayed briefly, the Shevington time stream experienced winters worthy of northern New England.

Whenever Chase recalled that conversation, Barnaby's words always came back to him against the backdrop of a howling north wind. The icy punctuation more than suited the Lord High Mayor's tale of unthinkable loss and inconsolable grief. Adeline Shevington's death, in part, propelled Barnaby to leave England amidst the turmoil of the Fae Reformation, bound for the New World to found a Fae colony.

As he told Chase of those long ago days, Barnaby gazed into the flames of the fireplace in his private study, the wavering light highlighting his patrician profile. When he fell silent at last, Chase said, "How did you survive it all?"

Without looking away from the flames, Barnaby smiled. "Adeline was not the only remarkable woman in my life."

"Moira?"

Barnaby nodded. "She saved me from myself and has been my confidante and companion lo these many decades since."

Chase hadn't asked for clarification of the word "companion." No one in Shevington knew the true nature of the relationship between Barnaby and the alchemist, but their reliance on and trust in one another's abilities made accomplishments like the inland sea possible.

Now, looking down over the work site, Chase felt a twinge of guilt. Did he really have any business feeling sorry for himself about Jinx when his elders had suffered so much worse and made so much more of their loss? His own mother died rather than reveal her nature and expose the inhabitants of their hidden worlds to human fear and superstition.

Chase experienced an easy life by comparison. While he took his job as protector of the Daughters of Knasgowa seriously, everything in his world was remarkably ordinary until Jinx moved next door.

Before that, guarding Aunt Fiona presented no greater challenge than drinking coffee and eating chocolate chip cookies in her purple kitchen and listening to her endless stories. Over the years, death claimed all the members of the Briar Hollow coven except Fiona and Amity Prescott. The story of Knasgowa; her husband, Alexander Skea; and the sorceress, Brenna Sinclair became more legend than reality.

But then Fiona got it in her head to live in Shevington full time. While her staged death created an easy, humanly legal transfer of the store, it also set in motion complex developments Chase could never have anticipated.

No one realized how much the events of the past few months plunged Chase full tilt back into the magical world. He had allowed himself to become complacent about the state of Fae politics. His tiny corner of the Otherworld was peaceful, but that halcyon state didn't necessarily extend into the other realms.

When he saw Jinx get out of her car that first day in front of the store, Chase didn't immediately shut down the surge of emotion that washed over him because he didn't recognize the danger in his feelings. Certainly, he'd met Jinx before, but he hadn't seen her in years. He remembered a slightly gawky young girl, not the beautiful woman juggling multiple cat carriers who unlocked the front door of the shop and instantly became not only a part of his world but his personal charge.

Chase told himself that the speed with which he set about getting to know Jinx was just business, but, as Festus had put it so succinctly at the time, "Sell it to somebody who's buying, Romeo." Festus had known; he'd seen all the signs because he'd lived his own version of forbidden love with Jinx's mother. Chase fell for Jinx on first sight and grew to love her more every day as she gained control of her new abilities.

But from the beginning, he'd made mistakes—serious ones that culminated in their current uneasy estrangement. As soon as Jinx's powers awakened, Chase should have confessed his identity and worked to help her understand the world of which she was now a part. Myrtle, Amity, and Festus had all advised him to be truthful, but to Chase's mind, none of them understood how hard it was to say, "Oh, by the way, I can turn into a cat. In two sizes."

In fairness, Chase faced hurdles with Jinx his forebears hadn't experienced. Jinx was the only one of the Daughters of Knasgowa who was not raised with a full understanding of her powers. She never received the proper training and knew nothing about Shevington and the Otherworld. Blurting out the truth seemed to be too much too soon.

Looking back, Chase realized he waited because he liked the illusion of normalcy in the beginning of their relationship. When Jinx learned the truth, she jumped to the conclusion that Chase spent time with her because it was his job. Of course, she might not have done that if he hadn't actually used the word "job" in his ham-handed attempt to explain Clan McGregor's mission.

Now, looking out over the verdant reaches of the Valley, Chase rested his head in his hands. He couldn't even count his well-intentioned blunders. He let out a disgusted chuckle. Good intentions only paved one roadway, the one headed to the hell in which he now found himself.

Chase tried to follow every other rule, but he willfully ignored the taboo about werecat relationships because he wanted something he couldn't have. In doing that, Chase was convinced he invited Malcolm Ferguson's attacks.

When he confessed that fear to his father, Festus said, "You don't know that, boy. You can't say for certain that lunatic was after you, not until we find out who hired him."

"Are you telling me it's okay to ignore the taboo?"

Festus shook his head. "You know I won't do that, Chase. Not when I've played with fire myself. I'm telling you to stop taking on all this guilt until we sort out what's actually going on."

Part of him knew his father was right, but Chase couldn't shake the belief that his recklessness put Jinx in harm's way.

Breaking up with her was the only thing he could do to ensure she was never endangered again because of him. Couldn't she see that?

He scrubbed at his face with this hand, blinking back tears. No, of course, she couldn't. He caught her unawares and broke her heart on the same day she lost Myrtle's guiding warmth and presence.

A part of Chase suspected that the vehemence of Jinx's anger toward him was displaced grief over the aos si, but he couldn't say that to Jinx. All he could really do was put his head down and take whatever she dished out until their interactions began to improve. She had every right to grieve the aos si and to be furious with him.

The night before Festus told Chase "do your job." That's what Chase saw on the inland sea work site. Visible proof of a man who went on living by doing his job. If Barnaby could recover from the murder of his wife, a deed so foul the wizard almost lost his soul seeking revenge, Chase could settle down and find out if Anton Ionescu hired Malcolm Ferguson, and if so, why.

Chase considered talking over the Ionescu problem with Barnaby and then dismissed the idea as quickly as it came into his head. Technically, Chase answered only to Festus as his father and clan chief. The McGregors worked *with* Barnaby Shevington, not *for* him. But Chase's decision wasn't a matter of protocol. The choice was as self-serving as his decision to throw caution to the wind and fall in love with Jinx. The only hope Chase McGregor had to save himself from the pain he now felt, was to get to work.

If Ironweed came up with hard evidence to suggest that Ionescu posed a threat to the Valley, Chase would talk to Barnaby. Until then, protecting Jinx was his responsibility alone.

Chapter Eleven

The Mother Oak was one of twelve Great Trees, the daughters of the primordial World Tree, Yggdrasil. Together, they formed the Coven of the Woods. Planted at vortices of power on a vast Grid encircling the earth, the Trees were the keepers of time, the wardens of magic, and the guardians of order.

Though she had long stood in the center of Shevington, the Mother Oak traced her origin to the ancient land of the Celts. The Tuatha Dé Danann once sheltered in her roots. It was there the aos si was born and whimsically christened "Myrtle" by the Tree herself after the flowering, evergreen sacred to the Greek goddess Aphrodite.

In the days of the Fae Reformation, when the rising power of illegitimate magic threatened the laws of nature held in place by the Trees, the Mother Oak requested a most remarkable thing of Yggdrasil. She asked to be allowed to relocate with the Fae settlers who followed Barnaby Shevington, to sink into the depths of the earth and move through the channels of power running among the vortices, to rise again to her full height from the fresh earth in the place that would come to be known simply as "the Valley."

In the chronological reckoning, the Movement of the Mother Oak took place in 1584, but the Trees lived a life beyond the boundaries of time and space. Their present awareness encompassed both the history and fate of all the realms, holding intact the framework of the Otherworld, the In Between, and the World of the humans.

The 431 years that had passed since the day of her migration, and this day were nothing to the Great Oak, a mere period of waiting for what she had known all along. The agents of chaos would find and exploit a weakness in the Grid. To mend that break and restore the balance meant to underlie all creation, the magic of the New World must flow into the veins of the Old.

Even Barnaby Shevington did not realize this aspect of his journey, for he came to the Americas a man tortured by grief. The news of the murder of his wife, Adeline, sent ripples of shock through the Fae world, but none beyond the alchemist, Moira, and through her, the Mother Oak, knew Adeline Shevington carried a baby in her womb.

The journey to Shevington and the creation of a sanctuary for all who sought it gave Barnaby a renewed reason to live. As the Mother Oak foresaw, 188 years later, Shevington fathered a second child with a Cherokee witch named Adoette.

They named their daughter Knasgowa, and from her line would descend the one destined to both cause and heal the breach in the Grid.

Like the great serpent Ouroboros, who appears to swallow his tail, the chosen Daughter of Knasgowa, would close the circle and bring wholeness to that which had been broken. In so doing, the long journey to reclaim natural magic would begin. Like every hero, this Daughter of Knasgowa, would falter in her steps and even suffer comic misfortunes, but in the moment of testing, the authenticity of her heart would lead her to heal the realm.

"The Druids wove stories of myth and legend portending this great struggle," said the voice of the aos si, arising through the consciousness of the Tree.

The Mother Oak, who could drink in the warm sunlight and guard the robins in her branches, all while attending to the information coursing through the Grid, drew the aos si closer in her thoughts.

"I had great love for our brothers the Druids," the Oak said, "but I regret to say I still find myself slightly annoyed they insisted on referring to me as the 'king' of the trees."

A ripple of laughter passed along the Tree's veins. "They attempted to educate tribal humans in the mysteries of the metaphysical," Myrtle said. "The emphasis on the masculine in such societies forced the Druids to use language that would be heard."

"Language meant to veil the truth for that which might be more easily tolerated does not educate," the Oak replied. "What knows the child of the true meaning of the Grail?"

"Moira has spoken to her of the journey between the light and the dark," Myrtle said, "but I fear Jinx was too preoccupied with my state to have fully appreciated the significance of the spiritual quest that faces every living being."

The Great Tree sighed. "That is the fault of the life she led outside the circles of magic. But even that has occurred as it was meant to be. Now she must hear the great stories to understand what is required of her."

"You will tell her of the Fisher King?"

"In time she will know of the Guardian of the Grail languishing in the Wasteland that was his kingdom. For now, she must understand that she has begun her own quest, and she cannot give in to foolish temptations."

"You must be fair to the child," Myrtle said. "All who begin great tasks make mistakes. Remember you not The Fool in the cards of the Tarot? A callow youth about to plunge over a cliff saved only by the action of his faithful dog?"

"And remember you not the faithful dog represents the wisdom of nature exercising a restraining hand on a feckless human?" the Tree asked.

"Do not use such a word when you speak of Jinx. She lacks neither character nor initiative. Her only weakness is that she has not been schooled in our world. That was a matter of her destiny, not a fault of her character."

The Oak sighed again, the wind rippling the leaves on her mighty branches. "Do you recall in the tale of the Fisher King how the knight healed the land?"

"He asked an authentic question from the purity of his heart," Myrtle replied. "On seeing the wounded king, the knight innocently asked, 'What ails thee?' thus revealing the Grail that was the object of his long search. Jinx has that innocence."

"Yes, but forget you not that on their first encounter, the knight failed to ask the question that rose in his heart. All around him disappeared, and he wandered 20 years to find the kingdom again and rectify his mistake."

"Chesterfield can do great harm in 20 human years," the aos si said. "But if Jinx's dealings with him are to be from the authenticity of her heart, we cannot instruct her in the source of his black illness. She must traverse the vale on her own and ask the question in a time of her making."

Inside the consciousness of the Great Tree, an image of a child wandering into a dark wood rose before them. "He was but a boy," the Mother Oak said sadly. "He sold his soul to become Creavit, thinking unassailable power would ease his great pain. Now, that hunger has grown into the all-consuming passion of severing the realms and bringing chaos to the World of the humans. Chesterfield would make of himself a king. His wounded soul has rotted into avaricious cancer."

"If Jinx learns the truth," Myrtle said, "she will see that. She is the one for whom we have been waiting. First Rebecca died before her time. Then Kelly withdrew from our world. You foretold all that would stand between Jinx and her heritage. All the Daughters of Knasgowa, save her, have been your guardians."

"Rebecca and Kelly walked the path they were meant to walk," the Mother Oak answered. In her sister's absence, Fiona Ryan has served us well. She may not be the strongest of her line, but with your help, she has fulfilled the obligation."

The space within the consciousness of the Tree that held the aos si darkened. "You are kind in the face of my failure. I did not detect the Orb of Thoth in time. My poisoning has altered the course of our plans."

"Branches break when they cannot bend with the wind. Until you are strong enough to return, Jinx must face Chesterfield and his agents on her own. Now that she has approached her brother, we must tell her as much as we can. It is not yet time for Connor to return to Briar Hollow."

"Knowing of him and being denied his company grates on them," Myrtle cautioned. "Both mother and daughter are at risk for foolish behavior."

"They need only be patient a while longer. All must occur in the appointed time. That is what we must explain to her."

"That is what *you* must explain to her. She cannot hear my voice or she will fear to act without my counsel. Jinx must confront the coming events on her own so that when I do return, it will be as her companion and ally, not her teacher."

"You speak the correct words, aos si," the Mother Oak, "but you are troubled."

"Yes, I am. I love the child dearly. I fear for her safety."

"Jinx is surrounded by love, and for those who struggle and doubt, there is no stronger shield against harm."

Chapter Twelve

It's not like I had never spoken with the Mother Tree before, but this was the first time she actually summoned me into her presence—by sending a truant officer and his raccoon sidekick after me.

As we walked back toward the center of Shevington, I kept cutting glances at Lucas Grayson out of the corner of my eye. I thought I was being stealthy until he said, "Something you want to ask me?"

Crap. Busted.

To hide the fact that I had been totally checking him out, I said, "Yeah. What exactly is the Division for Grid Integrity?"

"We work for the Mother Trees," he said, as if that explained everything.

My next smart-aleck crack stuck in my throat as my brain kicked in. Mother *Trees*? Plural?

"You mean there's more than one?" I blurted out, before realizing how idiotic the question made me sound.

Grayson stopped and looked at me curiously. "You really don't know, do you?"

If I had been going for the cool option to hide my ignorance, I would have pretended his question insulted me. Unfortunately, curiosity won out. "No. I don't know."

We were standing on a street corner about a block from the square, right beside one of the staircases that led to the top of the city's surrounding wall. Grayson waited until a small knot of people passed us.

"Look," he said, lowering his voice, "I can't tell you anything I haven't been authorized to share, but the Mother Oak wouldn't have sent me to find you if she didn't have something important to say. The basics are common knowledge in the Fae world, so here's the lay of the land. There are twelve Mother Trees organized under the World Tree. Together they form the Coven of the Woods."

After weeks of meeting with Barnaby on a regular basis, I was more than a little put out that I was only hearing this information now, and from a total stranger.

"Uh, okay. What exactly do the Trees do?"

"Hold it all together," Rube said.

I looked down into the raccoon's black masked face. "Hold all of what together?"

"Everything, sister," he said, waving one front paw around him in a circle. "The whole shebang."

When I looked at Grayson for confirmation, he nodded. "Rube is right. The Trees are the organizing principle of all that exists. But as you can well imagine, the whole story isn't that simple. Nothing is around here."

In spite of myself, I laughed. "That's an understatement,"

Grayson smiled at me. Really smiled for the first time. Not the bad-boy smirk he'd given me at the stables or the world-weary bemusement that seemed to be his stock in trade. This smile reached all the way to his gray eyes, which in the softening light showed flecks of green.

"Maybe not simple," he said, "but certainly not ordinary and never boring. Trust me. It's all for the good. The whole system. Listen to the Mother Tree, even if you don't like what she has to say, and believe that the Grid knows what it's doing."

I frowned. "So the Mother Trees are the Grid?"

"Do you understand anything about computer systems in your world?"

"Some," I said, "but my friend Tori is the tech head in the family."

"Okay, work with me on this one. Think of the Grid as a network. The Mother Trees are its backbone. They're like core routers dispersing information across the whole system."

Under normal circumstances, I would have let loose with a flood of questions, but his description drew my mind back to an evening when I laid my hands on the trunk of a massive, aged hickory seeking information about a series of unsolved murders. When my consciousness joined with that of the tree, I knew I heard not just the hickory's voice, but the voice of all the trees everywhere. Had I been jacked into the Grid without even realizing it?

I had zero reason to trust Lucas Grayson. He ambled out of nowhere talking about some "Grid" agency and telling me about tree covens. But somehow I knew intuitively he wasn't lying. In an odd way, Grayson seemed more "normal" than anyone I had yet encountered in the Fae world. He would have been as much at home on the Main Street of Briar Hollow as he was standing in front of me in Shevington.

That thought led to an abrupt change of subject. "What are you, Grayson?"

"I told you. I'm a DGI agent."

"Are you a wizard?"

"Nope."

"Alchemist?"

"No."

"Werecat?"

"And that would be 'no' again," he grinned. "Are you going to run through the list of all the Fae races?"

"If I had the list, I would. How about you just tell me what you are?"

"I'm a guy who knows how to get stuff done," Grayson shrugged, "and what needs to get done right this minute is for you to walk over there and face the music with the Mother Tree."

At some point in the conversation, we must have started up the street again. My mind had been working so intently, I hadn't even realized we were now standing in the town square. I didn't buy the whole "just a guy" line, but I could tell I wouldn't be getting any more information from Grayson for the time being.

"So that's it?" I said. "You give me a bunch of half answers, deliver me to the Mother Tree, and go on about your business?"

Grayson's teeth flashed impossibly white in the failing light. In a few minutes, the old lamplighter would begin to make his rounds. The street lamps didn't run on gas and likely could all have been ignited with one simple spell, but the practice of an aged wizard walking under each light and snapping his fingers to make it blaze to life was a quaint and cherished local tradition.

"I don't know," Grayson said. "That depends on how things go between you and the Mother Tree. She'll let me know if I need to follow you around anymore."

Bad-boy handsome or not, this guy could seriously get on my nerves if I let him—or I could totally fall for him. Six of one, half a dozen of the other—and *not* what I should have been thinking about when I was still getting over the break-up with Chase.

As I watched, Grayson crossed the street with easy, loping strides, Rube waddling alongside. The pair disappeared into

O'Hanson's Pub on the corner without ever looking back at me.

Their departure left me with no choice. Drawing in a deep breath, I turned my attention toward the Mother Tree. Even though I was nervous, hope danced in my heart. Somewhere in the massive, gnarled trunk and spreading limbs, Myrtle's spirit resided. Would she be present for this conversation?

For as much as I dreaded what I suspected would be the Mother Tree's disapproval over my approaching Connor, I thrilled at the prospect of hearing my friend's voice again.

At the base of the Great Tree, I sat down on a stone bench and opened my mind. Since I didn't know what else to say, I went with, "Hi. I'm here."

"So you are," a voice answered, echoing slightly in my thoughts.

"Is Myrtle with you?" I blurted out.

So much for patience.

Around me, the night sounds of Shevington receded into silence as the Mother Tree surrounded us with a cloud of privacy. "The aos si dwells herein, but she will not join us this evening."

A swell of disappointment surged through me, bringing hurt tears to my eyes. The Mother Tree felt it.

"I am sorry you cannot speak with your friend. The aos si continues to recover well from her contact with the foreign orb. You, child, are an ever present thought for her. Fear not that you will be forgotten."

Swallowing hard, I accepted that was the best I was going to get. Might as well stand up and face the music. "So, I guess you're angry with me because I tried to see my brother."

"Not angry, but remonstrative. You took a great risk this evening, Jinx, both for yourself, and for he who does not even know you exist."

"What risk?" I demanded. "That curse was cast more than

30 years ago. Why hasn't someone tried to do something to clean this whole mess up and get Connor home? Do you have any idea what being separated from him has done to my mother?"

With infinite patience, the Oak said, "I have every idea. The loss of Connor led Kelly to abandon her magic for good. She retreated into a world of nervous caution and lived in constant fear something would happen to you. Her apprehensions made her smothering and overprotective. Your father ameliorated his pain by spending mindless hours alone with the rivers, ostensibly for the purpose of catching fish, but more for the solace the water afforded his aching soul."

Had she been watching my family all these years? Just watching? The Mother Tree might not be angry, but I was getting that way.

"If you knew all of that, then why didn't you *do* something? Aren't you and the other Mother Trees supposed to control everything?"

"We control the coherence of time, and we are the wardens of magic, but there is to the progression of events a natural order we cannot supersede. There was nothing we could do until all that was foretold had come to pass."

Again with the whole "foretold" thing?

"I didn't understand a single word you just said."

That's when the Mother Tree gave me a gentle slap. "Do not pretend ignorance with me, witch. You understood the words; you simply do not care for their meaning. Petulance will contribute nothing to this conversation."

So much for being taken to the woodshed with a switch. I had a whole tree coming after my backside.

Blowing out a long, frustrated breath, I said, "Okay, you're right. I'm sorry. But if you want me to understand why you, Moira, Barnaby, and Myrtle let my mother and father suffer for 32 years—and made me grow up without a brother

—then could you give me an explanation that makes some sense?"

The Tree said something next that I totally did not see coming.

"Barnaby Shevington is your seventh great grandfather."

I gazed up into the canopy of leaves over my head with a shocked expression. The Mother Oak kept talking, seeming to realize I couldn't have said a word to save my life.

Some of what she told me I already knew. Chase related the story of Adeline Shevington's murder to me, but he didn't tell me the poor woman was pregnant when she died, probably because he didn't know.

The Oak spoke to me of her personal story as well, describing her migration through the earth following the channels of power that comprise the Grid.

No. I can't explain to you how a tree could do that. Maybe it was just the essence of the tree that followed the path to rise again in the Valley. If you could hear the Oak's voice, and feel the weight of her presence in your mind as I can, you wouldn't question anything she says.

All I know is that she rose again in physical form in the spot where I now communed with her, rooted at the heart of Shevington, and tied to the community's purpose in a deeply intimate way.

You see, Adeline's death changed everything. So much so, that if she had not died, I would never have been born.

"Adeline was a Druid priestess," the Oak explained, "a rare thing in an order dominated by men. But moreover, she was the Keeper of the Oak—the keeper of me. Just as there are thirteen Trees in the Coven of the Woods, so are there thirteen keepers in their service. The child Adeline carried would have, in time, succeeded her mother as my companion and guardian. On that foul night of murder, the innocent child died first. Sensing that the life in her womb was no more, Adeline used her final breath to transfer her magic into a crystal amulet, which she entrusted to her husband for safekeeping."

Finally managing to find my voice, I said, "Did that make Barnaby your keeper?"

"No. A wizard cannot fulfill that position. Adeline's charge to Barnaby was to sire a daughter and transfer her magic into the child, thus reforging the line of the Keepers of the Oak."

But without Moira's aid, Barnaby, driven half mad by grief, might never have honored his promise to Adeline. He searched throughout Europe for his wife's killer, almost giving himself over to black magic in his relentless mission to discover the felon's identity. Moira called Barnaby back from the brink, reminding him that should he surrender to the darkness, all that was left of his beloved Adeline would be truly lost.

"He came to me and wept at my feet," the Mother Tree said, "and begged to know what he was to do. I counseled him to find a place where the Creavit heresy had not touched the face of pure magic. He quit Europe and came to this New World, waiting 188 years before the magic of another spoke to him, kindling a connection both with his heart and with the essence of Adeline he guarded."

"Who was she?"

"A Cherokee witch named Adoette. You already know the name of their daughter, my first keeper in this new land."

"Knasgowa."

"Correct," the Oak replied, "but what you do not know is that Knasgowa had a vision that one day a link would be broken in her line and thus allow the forces of chaos to seek ingress to harm the Coven of the Woods. You are the culmination of that break."

"Me?" I said. "What did I do?"

"The series of events began before you were born. Their consequences grew as you were denied the knowledge of your true nature. These factors weakened the world of the Fae. The wizard, Chesterfield, would make use of that opening to damage the integrity of the realms."

"What do you mean by sever?"

"He is Creavit, a creature of unnatural magic. Should he break our connection with the World of the humans and use the artifacts he has laboriously gathered, he will be successful in subverting the power of natural magic in that reality forever."

I won't lie to you. I didn't follow as much of that as I probably should have, but one thing came through loud and clear: we were talking about something on par with the zombie apocalypse.

"How do we stop him?" I asked.

See how I sounded all big, brave, and purposeful there? Great big ole act. I was getting more scared by the minute.

"The answer is not within my knowledge," the Mother Tree said, "but you must not create an even larger breach to be exploited by incurring more wrath from the Strigoi, or worse yet, allowing your brother to fall into their hands. You must repair the damage caused by the Ionescu thirst for revenge."

"How am I supposed to do that?"

"By finding out the truth of what happened on that long ago day when two lives were lost, setting in motion your mother's defection from the world of magic."

Oh, sure thing. I'll jump right in my time machine and get on that.

Note to self. Don't have snarky thoughts when there's an ancient tree hanging out in your head.

"Time is not so fixed and absolute as you now believe, Jinx Hamilton," the Mother Tree said. "Until you have solved the puzzle I have put before you, do not seek to contact your brother again."

Chapter Thirteen

Of all of the things I might have expected to find when I tip-toed back into the lair wheeling my bike, a disapproving rat wasn't one of them. Rodney waited for me on the corner of the work table where he'd obviously been sitting for some time staring down the corridor through the stacks.

He sat up on his haunches as I neared, revealing his snowy chest and ebony belly fur. The shirt-and-pants effect made him look like a disapproving father. Even though I think it's impossible in terms of rodent anatomy, I swear to you he had his arms crossed, and he might have even been tapping one foot.

Light snoring from the vicinity of the sofas told me my plan to sneak out and get back undetected had worked so far. On the television screen, Kathy Bates outfitted Leonardo diCaprio in a tuxedo. I had no idea how many times the *Titanic* might have gone down in my absence.

When Rodney opened his mouth to say something, I put my finger to my lips and shook my head, which did nothing but make his squeaky interrogation louder. Keeping my voice as low as possible, I said, "Stop that. Nobody likes a snitch."

Fixing me with a glare, Rodney pointed to the bike and then toward the vicinity of the sleepers. The intended message came through loud and clear. "Nobody likes a sneak either."

"Okay. Fine," I said. "I'll tell you everything, but let's go upstairs, so we don't wake them all up."

"Why don't you want to wake us up?" Tori's bleary voice asked from the shadows beyond the table. The TV screen backlighted her form, which included a serious case of bedhead.

"Thanks a lot," I hissed at Rodney. "You've clarified the meaning of the phrase 'ratted out' for me."

"What's going on with you two?" Tori asked. I could tell she was waking up.

"Shhhh!" I ordered, pointing up emphatically.

She was conscious enough to get my meaning. Whatever I had to tell her, I did not want the moms to hear.

As I watched, she carefully disentangled herself from the mountain of afghans on the couch and headed for the stairs. Then she paused, retraced her steps, and grabbed one of the platters of chocolate chip cookies. Tori is never so out of it that she forgets to think about her next meal.

I held out my hand and let Rodney run up my arm and settle around my neck. When I felt his whiskers tickle my cheek, I said, "Traitor."

From his position against my ear, I heard a very rodential "harumph."

With the basement door safely closed behind us, Tori said, "What gives, Jinksy? Why are you skulking around in the middle of the night?"

"It's more like the middle of dawn," I said. "And why is everybody suddenly accusing me of skulking?"

"Who is 'everybody?'" she asked suspiciously. "Have you been to the Valley?"

"Yes," I said. "And since Rodney the Rat Fink gave me away, I'll tell you everything, but I seriously need coffee. Let's go in the storeroom."

As she followed me around the corner and behind the counter, Tori said, "So if Rodney hadn't caught you, you weren't going to tell me everything?"

"Oh, for heaven's sake," I said. "When have I ever been able to keep anything from you? Of course, I was going to tell you. I just intended to be a little more selective about the timing of the conversation."

While I made the coffee, Tori plopped down on the sagging sofa and watched. Think of our storeroom as the "mini" lair. We still use the space for coffee breaks and lunches. It also houses Rodney's apartment, which sits tucked away behind two huge liniment cans on the back wall.

Originally, Rodney lived in what would technically be termed a "cage," but none of us liked that word or its implications. Rodney is family. Now he lives in a two-story custom-built bachelor pad.

We found a guy online who did everything to spec, including the big picture window in the "living room" and a staircase leading up to the sleeping loft. The exercise wheel sits on the roof-top terrace adjacent to a hammock strung between two fake palm trees.

The front wall snaps off so we can assist Rodney with his house cleaning. His water bottle attaches to the back out of sight and emerges in the living room as the spout of a wall-mounted fountain.

It didn't seem fair to give Glory an iPod Touch big screen and not supply one for Rodney as well. Since Glory visits sometimes, we added a miniature sectional with recliners on either end.

Because most of our group activities have moved downstairs, we offered to put Rodney's quarters on a shelf adjacent to Glory's place. He's considering the move, but I think he likes his privacy.

We did cut a special door for him in the baseboard right beside the basement entrance. It's hidden behind a shelf of second-hand books so he can come and go undetected—and so the customers in the espresso bar won't freak out if they see him.

After I handed Tori a mug of steaming coffee, I made one for myself. Normally, Rodney would have retired to his room or curled himself around one of our necks for a nap. This time, however, he sat on the back of the sofa just over Tori's shoulder. His body language screamed, "I'm waiting, and it better be good."

My narrative took the long way around getting to the point. When I finished the story of the dragonlets stealing things in Shevington, Tori said, "So that's why you went to the Valley?"

"Uh, no. I had some business at the stables."

She frowned. "You went to see if the unicorn had foaled? You don't even like unicorns that much."

"I don't *not* like the unicorns. Who can not like unicorns?"

"So that's why you went up there in the middle of the night?"

"Not exactly," I hedged again.

"Then how about you tell me *exactly* why you did go sneaking out of the lair after you made sure we were all sound asleep and . . . "

Tori was biting into a chocolate chip cookie as she talked. She froze in mid-sentence, and her eyes grew round and shocked. "Oh my God. It wasn't a dream. The aleuromancy worked through the cookies."

"What on earth are you talking about?"

"These are the cookies Darby made from the flour Mom and I were experimenting with," she said.

"Yeah, so what?"

"After I ate them and fell asleep, I had a dream you went to Shevington to meet your brother. That's it, isn't it?"

There wasn't much I could do but nod numbly. While I'm the first to say I think cookies are a religious experience, I never expected chocolate chip clairvoyance.

"So tell me everything," Tori said, making a point of biting into another cookie. "If you leave anything out, I'll know."

Since I don't know a thing about vision-inducing flour, I took her at her word and came clean about sneaking up on Connor. Then I described the arrival of Lucas Grayson and Rube.

"A DGI agent?" Tori said skeptically. "Did he show you a badge or some ID or something?"

"No, but Rube is friends with Festus."

"Like that's some recommendation. I can't believe you didn't think to get a picture of this guy."

A light went off in my head. "I didn't get a picture of him," I said, digging in my pocket for my phone, "but I think I did get one of Connor."

Sure enough, there he was, in perfect profile against the backdrop of the mountains. When I handed the phone to Tori, she let out a low whistle, turning the screen so Rodney could get a look as well.

"Big Brother is a hunk," she said appreciatively, pinching the screen with two fingers to enlarge the image. Her eyes went wide again. "Let me revise my opinion. Big brother is a *major* hunk."

"He is?" I asked, taking the phone back and staring at the screen, trying to get my head wrapped around the idea I could be related to a drool-worthy guy.

"Uh, yeah," Tori said. "So when do I meet him?"

That touched off a recitation of the events of the second part of the evening, that ended with, "And I don't know how the Mother Tree thinks we're going to find out what really happened to those girls."

"Well, for starters," Tori said, "we go up to the scene of the wreck. Then we see if we can find the car."

"After all these years? There is no way that car still exists."

"Don't be so sure, Jinksy. You know how people around here can be about legendary crashes. Sometimes those cars sit in junkyards for decades with people still gawking at them."

As macabre as it sounds, she was right. I knew one family who kept their deceased son's mangled Mustang behind their barn. His mother told my mother they couldn't bear to part with anything that belonged to him, including the machine that killed him.

"Okay," I said, "let's get this paranormal festival over with, and then we'll get started on the mystery of the wreck. I hate to do it, but we'll have to ask the moms to take us to the exact spot."

"No, we won't. I've already done that. Mom showed me the crash site a couple of weeks after they told us about it the first time."

It was my turn at minorly hurt feelings. "Why didn't you tell me?"

"Mom asked me not to. She didn't want to risk it coming up around Kelly and upsetting her."

That I understood completely. Anytime we're forced to talk about the accident, all the color drains out of mom's face and her hands tremble. Even if she has embraced her true nature again, she still blames herself for the death of those two girls. Finding out the truth wouldn't only set Connor free; it would free our mother as well.

"Okay," I said. "Then we're set."

Tori looked doubtful. "Are you sure we can pull this off?"

"Yes. It's not like the Strigoi are going to come into town and cause us any trouble in the next few days.

Yeah.

File that one under. "Famous Last Words."

Chapter Fourteen

"Anton, I fear your personal desire for vengeance is clouding your judgment."

Ionescu shifted uncomfortably. He reached for the cigar smoldering in the ashtray and drew deeply until the tip of the hand-rolled tobacco glowed cherry red. Exhaling the fragrant smoke, he said, "You are mistaken, Irenaeus."

"I am rarely mistaken," Chesterfield said, eyeing his attorney over the rim of a crystal brandy glass. "You have told your people that Kelly Hamilton broke the agreement and visited the Valley *before* you hired Malcolm Ferguson to kill her. That is not true."

"My people will believe what I tell them to believe," Ionescu said. "If I say the truce has been broken, it has been broken."

Reaching for his own cigar, Chesterfield said, "You forget that I am conversant in the ways of the Strigoi. If your clan discovers your deception, the curse becomes null. They will no longer be honor bound to seek revenge on your behalf for the deaths of your daughter and your niece."

"Seraphina and Ioana," Ionescu said tightly. "Their names are Seraphina and Ioana."

"Which I believe they Americanized as Sally Beth and Jo Anne in their desire to distance themselves from their heritage. Am I not correct?"

Ionescu flushed. "They were young. They hadn't accepted the strictures of our lives. It was a mistake to allow them to attend the human school."

"Where they crossed paths with a fledgling witch and an immature alchemist," Chesterfield said, cradling the brandy snifter in his hand. "Quite the stuff of drama."

At the taunting words, Ionescu turned purple with rage. "How dare you make light of the deaths of my children." As he spoke, every light bulb in the room shattered, plunging the two men into semi-darkness relieved only by the wavering glow of the fire.

Chesterfield casually raised his hand and snapped his fingers, lighting the tall candles housed in sconces on the walls. "That display of temper rather proves my point, does it not, dear Anton?" He reached for the cigar again. "You have difficulty controlling your temper. There is a larger purpose to our dealings. Your only job is to lure the boy, Connor, from the safe confines of the Valley. When I ransom him for a living branch of the Mother Tree, be free to do as you please with the Hamilton woman, but you are not to kill her daughter. Do you understand?"

Laboring to bring his anger under control, Ionescu said, "Yes, Irenaeus. I understand."

"SCRAP, YOU HAVE TO UNDERSTAND," Jeff said. "Gemma didn't want to drop this thing on you for good reasons."

Scrap Andrews used his fork to push the food around on

his plate. He didn't look up when he asked, "How am I supposed to live with a witch?"

"Gemma isn't a witch. She's an alchemist."

"Isn't that the same thing?"

Jeff shoved his cap back and let his hand drop to rest on the head of his best fishing dog, Bobber. "No, you moron, it's not the same thing. Gemma's more like a magical scientist. I'm the one living with the witch."

The attempt at levity failed. Unable to force himself to eat, Scrap offered his plate to Bobber, who happily ambled over and started to lick the tin clean.

"Quit spoiling my dogs," Jeff said.

"I will, when you quit buying them sausage biscuits over at Sonic."

"You forgot to mention the ice cream cones."

Both men laughed. "A man's got a right to spoil his dogs and his children," Jeff said. "Have you stopped to think what this nonsense is doing to your girl? Have you talked to her yet?"

Scrap picked up a stick and poked at the fire. "No. She quit trying to get ahold of me."

"How does that make you feel?"

Jabbing at the coals with more vehemence, Scrap said, "You know damn good and well how it makes me feel, so back off already."

"I can't do that, Scrap," Jeff said, taking a fifth of bourbon out of his backpack. "The women sent me out here to talk some sense into you."

"Figured it was something like that. Save your breath and your whiskey. Neither one are gonna work."

"Well, how about we have a drink anyway and you let me tell you a story," Jeff replied, pouring a healthy stream of amber liquid into a battered cup.

"Fine," Scrap said, accepting the drink, "but you won't

change my mind. Gemma lied to me. I can't ever believe another word she says."

Jeff leaned back in his camp chair. "I was pretty much that hard headed when Kelly and I met. We were both enrolled over at the community college. She had ideas of working as a secretary. I was learning to drive a truck. Took me asking three times to get her to go out with me."

Scrap snorted. "Pickings must have been lean that year for a pretty woman like Kelly to take up with you."

"Not just lean, bone dry. I found out about her powers after we'd been dating six months or so."

"What happened?" Scrap asked, interested in spite of himself.

"The carnival was in town. I was cutting up, showing off. I tripped and fell backward toward the Ferris wheel. Man, I thought I was a goner. I saw that next bucket coming right at me and then the whole thing just stopped an inch from my face. Nobody needed to tell me to scramble the hell out of there. I looked over at Kelly and she had her fist out in front of her like she was holding something. The minute she saw I was okay, she let go, and that Ferris wheel started turning again."

Scrap stared at him. "A little thing like Kelly held a Ferris wheel still?"

"She did, and then she burst into tears and ran as far away from me as she could get. When I caught up with her and got her to calm down, she told me everything, including how she thought she and Gemma accidentally killed two cheerleaders in high school."

At that, Scrap interrupted forcefully. "See?! I told you this stuff is dangerous."

"Hold your horses. I talked to the Sheriff about that wreck. Kelly has been blaming herself for years, but the front axle on that car was bad. If it hadn't been raining, the kid doing the driving might have been able to get the car stopped safely, but on that wet road, she lost control."

"How do you know magic didn't wear the metal in two?" Scrap argued. "You just told me Kelly held a Ferris wheel in place."

Jeff shook his head. "You sound like Kelly. Bound and determined to find the worst possible explanation. Can I get on with my story?"

The other man waved his hand. "Go on. I'm listening."

"I was so head over heels in love with Kelly I couldn't have cared less if she was a witch. She took me to where her people are from. I liked everyone I met. Even went fishing up there. Dang trout had attitude."

Scrap frowned. "Isn't Kelly from Briar Hollow?"

"Uh, yeah," Jeff said, "these were some of her folks who lived way up in the mountains. Kind of backcountry. Anyway, you remember when we got married? You were in the wedding."

"Yeah, and I can't tell you how much I didn't love that baby blue tux."

"So anyway, everything was good with us, just like it was with you and Gemma. Then Kelly got pregnant."

Scrap looked uneasy. "You don't have to talk about Connor if you don't want to. What happened with him dying of crib death like that was awful."

"My son didn't die of crib death. He didn't die at all. The father of one of those girls is another kind of magical being. He put a curse on Kelly. The only way we could save the boy's life was to send him to live with Kelly's people in that place I was telling you about. He's still there. All grown up. Thirty-two years old."

Both men sat quietly drinking their whiskey and watching the fire until Scrap broke the silence. "She made you give up your baby, and you stayed with her?"

"Scrap," Jeff whispered hoarsely, "you really can be a hard-headed idiot sometimes. Kelly didn't make me give up my son. Their world runs on a different set of rules. This was the only way he'd be safe and alive, the only way he'd have a life. They tell me he's a good man, works with animals."

"And you've never met him because of magic." Scrap said hotly.

"Most likely, magic will be the very thing that brings him back to me someday," Jeff said. "Our girls are like their mothers. Neither one of our babies would harm a living soul. Are you going to sit there and tell me you're prepared to lose your wife and daughter because you're too scared to open your eyes and see there's more to this world than we thought?"

Scrap tossed the stick he'd been fiddling with into the fire, sending up a cloud of sparks. "It's not that I'm not willing to think there's more to Creation. How am I supposed to go on living with a woman who lied to me?"

"I don't know, Scrap," Jeff said. "How are you supposed to live *without* her?"

"FESTUS IS RIGHT," Barnaby said, looking at Chase over the chessboard. "Living without the woman you love is worse. He and I both have buried our wives. I don't say that to diminish your pain over what has happened with Jinx, but only to encourage you to make the best of the reality of your situation."

Chase studied the pieces and moved his knight. "Is that what they're doing?" he said, gesturing toward the moonlit surface of the inland sea. "Making the best of their situation?"

"The merfolk?" Barnaby asked. "Yes, they are rather amazing in their approach to life. While they mourn the pollution of the seas that have been their home, they are determined to preserve their race and culture."

On the other side of the fire, Moira looked up from her book. "For a people so reclusive in their habits, they have cultivated an exceptionally synthetic world view. They lament the destruction the humans are visiting upon the earth, but they are not willing to sacrifice themselves to it."

"Are they abandoning the oceans?" Chase asked, shifting to look at her.

"No," Moira said. "They will still patrol their home waters and assist the animal friends they leave behind. The portal will be available to them at all times."

"Are they sad?" Chase asked, watching as Barnaby slid his bishop forward.

"Extremely," the wizard said, "as are you. I would be very worried about them and you if that were not the case."

As Chase reached for his rook, Moira sat up abruptly in her chair. The movement caused Barnaby to turn toward her. "What is it?"

"Jinx is in the Valley," she said. "The Mother Oak believes she means to approach Connor."

"She must be stopped," Barnaby said.

"The Oak will handle the situation," Moira said, still listening. "She will speak with Jinx."

Chase stood up. "I think I should get back to Shevington."

"Why?" Barnaby asked, looking up at him. "Do you doubt the ability of the Mother Tree to deal with our errant witch?"

"No, of course not, but I should be keeping a closer eye on Jinx's movements in case anything happens."

Barnaby was silent for a moment. "Of course," he said at last, "we would never stand in the way of your responsibilities. Fare you well, Chase McGregor."

"And you, Lord High Mayor," Chase said formally, "and you, alchemist."

As they watched him stride rapidly away into the darkening night, Moira said, "He's keeping something from us."

"Indeed, and I suspect it involves Anton Ionescu."

Moira set her book aside and moved to join him, studying the side of the chessboard Chase abandoned before making a move. "The Oak will have to tell Jinx of her true origins."

"I know," Barnaby replied, answering Moira's move. "Your queen is in danger."

"My queen can take care of herself. I fear for my opponent, good king that he is."

Smiling, Barnaby reached over and took her hand. "I am not a ruler, dear one."

"Perhaps not, but I do not want Jinx to think anything of her grandfather but that you are a good man."

"*Great*-grandfather many times over," he laughed. "Tonight the Mother Tree will instruct her in the order of our world, and when Jinx is ready, I will explain why this has all been kept from her."

"Very well," Moira said, "and checkmate."

CHASE REACHED the square in Shevington as Jinx took her leave of the Mother Tree. From the expression on her face, the Oak must have shared a great deal of information. On instinct, Chase made a move to go to Jinx, then stopped abruptly and moved into the shadows.

Lucas Grayson, with Rube in tow, met Jinx halfway across the street. They spoke for a few minutes, and as Chase watched, Lucas reached out and put a comforting hand on Jinx's arm. A surge of jealousy rolled through Chase with such intensity he looked down at his hands and was shocked to see they had partially transformed to paws with claws extended.

He hadn't shifted against his will since he was a gangly teenager.

Breathing deeply, Chase found the mountain lion in his mind and spoke soothingly until the big cat lay down and slept. This time, when Chase looked at his hands, they were normal.

Across the square, Jinx and Grayson walked off toward the main gate, while Rube dove into the nearest sewer and disappeared. Chase headed toward the gate after them, taking pains not to be seen. He needn't have worried. Jinx and Grayson were lost in animated conversation.

At the entrance to the city, they stopped, and Chase managed to get within earshot.

"You don't need to walk me to the portal, Mr. Grayson," Jinx said. "I'll be fine from here."

"My friends call me Lucas," he said, taking her hand in a way that made Chase's blood boil.

"Fair enough, Lucas. Since we're going to be seeing more of each other, friends it is."

Seeing more of each other?

That could only mean one thing. Jinx knew about the Grid, and Lucas Grayson was getting ready to become a major pain in Chase's backside.

Chapter Fifteen

Anyone looking to buy orange or black crepe paper in the state of North Carolina that Saturday would have been out of luck. Supplies of fake spider webs, foam board tombstones, plastic skeletons, hanging moss, and pumpkins dipped statewide as well.

The visual blitz Irma and the committee pulled off with their meager budget will go down as one of the great decorating mysteries of all time.

Vendors spent the morning erecting booths on the courthouse lawn. The fire department obligingly drove over to fill the dunking booth with the hose from the big pumper trunk, while local churches emptied their fellowship halls of folding chairs and tables to provide curbside seating for the street dance.

The barricades went up by noon, and Skeeter Morgan backed his semi and flatbed trailer across the far end of the street to serve as a stage for the musicians. Knots of festival goers began to stake out prime spots on the lawn by mid-afternoon, leading some of the kids' games to open early.

As soon as the women from the historical association

unloaded massive foil platters of barbecue interest picked up. Trust me, if you want to gather a crowd in these parts, set out meat. There is nothing we southerners love better than clogging our arteries during a good party.

The store did a brisk business all day. We catered to the Starbucks refugees who had bravely ventured into what they thought would be the Sahara Desert of espresso for the weekend. Our place must have looked like a caffeinated oasis given the number of shots Tori pulled before noon.

Both moms proved to be adept saleswomen, sending visitors out the door with newly acquired T-shirts, visors, caps, and mugs. I hadn't paid a lot of attention to what Tori ordered in advance of the festivities. Several weeks earlier we discussed festival-specific promotional items, but I left it to her to sort out the specifics.

That may or may not have been one of my better ideas. I was ringing up a purchase for a couple of young men who enthusiastically informed me they were representatives of some organization dedicated to hunting Bigfoot when I discovered Tori's creative genius at work.

"Mind if we put the t-shirts on?" one of the guys asked.

"No problem," I said. "Go right ahead."

As I watched, he peeled off his green polo emblazoned with a giant footprint over the left breast and shrugged into his purchase. That's when I saw the artwork.

The guy must have thought I was checking out his nonexistent abs from the wolfish grin he shot my way. I was actually staring at the ghostly profile of a Confederate soldier over a drawing of the courthouse. The accompanying caption started over the roof and ended on the front lawn.

"Visit Briar Hollow, North Carolina . . . *if you dare.*" Red stenciled letters dripping blood looked as if they'd been stamped over the center of the image declaring "SpookCon1 - 2015."

When the customer left, giving me a hopeful "call me" wave from the front door, I caught Tori's eye and gestured for her to come over to the register *now*. Leaving Mom in charge at the espresso bar, Tori bobbed over, declaring happily as she landed beside me, "Hey Jinksy, what did I tell you? We're raking in the dough."

"Let's talk T-shirts."

A guarded look came into her eyes. "You told me I could get whatever I wanted."

"'Visit Briar Hollow, North Carolina *if you dare*?'" I quoted. "'SpookCon1?' Irma is going to have a conniption."

"Please," Tori scoffed dismissively. "When isn't Irma having a conniption? As long as she sells out of her haunted Twinkie stash, she's not going to be upset about my T-shirts."

"Does all the stuff you ordered say the same thing?" I asked, already afraid to know the answer.

"Like I would be that boring? Wait until you see our cups. I think we're going to sell out."

With that, she plucked a black mug off a display table and held it out to me. The cup was emblazoned with a picture of Glory on her broom, Rodney perched behind her giving the viewer a thumbs up. The typography made it look like they were flying through the words "The Witch's Brew Espresso Bar."

I hadn't been paying *nearly* enough attention to what was going on right under my nose, and my bill was coming due.

"We have a name?"

"And a sign. Come see."

We stepped out the front door and I looked up to see the same image of Glory and Rodney atop a sign designed to mimic cracked, weathered boards complete with rusty nails. Massive iron hinges fit for a dungeon affixed the placard to the front of the building.

The Witch's Brew Espresso Bar
J. Hamilton and T. Andrews
Practitioners in Residence

My face must have gone as green as Glory's because Tori, looked crestfallen. "Uh-oh. You don't like it."

Lowering my voice to a hoarse whisper, I said, "Didn't you just out us to the whole world?"

"But that's the beauty, Jinksy. It's all about hiding in plain sight. If we go with the witchy vibe and embrace the metaphysical, we don't have to worry about customers seeing any weird stuff going on in the shop. They'll figure it's special effects. You know, coffee with a side of mojo. You're not mad at me, are you?"

After mulling it over for a minute, I shook my head. "No. I've been saying all along the store needed a theme. It never occurred to me to go with the obvious."

Tori broke out in a happy grin. "Stick with me, kid," she said, waggling her eyebrows comically, "I'll learn ya."

That's my girl. She can always make me laugh.

"Okay," I said, as we went back inside, "to prevent any spontaneous heart attacks, are there any other inventory surprises I need to know about?"

"Not really. I ordered extra on the essential oils and soaps and threw in a few crystals to up the flavor of the place. Mom helped me make the labels more interesting."

Uh-oh.

"Can I see an example, please?"

"Sure." Tori plucked an amethyst necklace off a table and handed it to me.

I squinted at the tag, which was printed with a tiny logo version of Glory and Rodney. Under that, in red, the description read, "SpookCon1 Special Price. Blessed amethyst amulet. Balance chakras / cure nightmares / access healing energy."

"You wouldn't know a chakra from Count Chocula," I said accusingly.

"Of course, I would. One is chocolate and the other isn't."

Well, that was true enough, and when in doubt, go for the chocolate.

"How much did you spend on all of this?"

"Not a dime."

"Not a . . . ." I started to say, and then my brain kicked in. "Darby?"

Tori nodded. "Who the heck needs a 3D printer when you've got a brownie in residence? He'll be updating our Instagram account all during the festival."

"We have an Instagram account?"

"We do," Tori said, "and Darby is taking the pictures." Then, seeing the look of horror on my face, she added, "He's doing it incognito. Invisible photographers get the best shots."

No doubt.

Between Tori's retail insanity and the growing numbers of people on the square, I managed to forget about the complicated things in our lives for a few hours and enjoy the day. We planned to keep the store open through the evening, rotating shifts so everyone could have a chance to walk over, eat some barbecue, and enjoy the carnival and dance.

I was so preoccupied, that when I saw Mom slip out the back door around 6 o'clock, I didn't even have time to wonder where she was going. Unfortunately, we would all find out soon enough, and the news wasn't good.

KELLY FELT an insistent buzzing in her pocket. She finished ringing up the sale of a pumpkin spice latte and pulled the phone out to look at the screen. It was a text from Jeff. "Meet me in the alley. Don't tell Gemma."

The message touched off alarms in her head. Things didn't go well with Scrap.

Gemma came in from wiping down tables and said, "Hey, you mind if I go over and see if the ladies will sell me some brisket? I skipped lunch, and I'm starving."

"That's a great idea," Kelly said, trying to sound natural. "Why don't you get enough for me, too, and some sauce. We'll make sandwiches when you get back. Darby baked bread this morning when he did all the pastries."

"Perfect. I'll be right back."

As soon as she was out the door, Kelly motioned Tori over.

"Hey, hon," Kelly said, "I need to get something out of my car. Can you watch the counter for a sec?"

"Sure thing. Take your time."

Kelly stepped into the alley and glanced around. Jeff stood at the corner of the building farthest away from Tori's add-on apartment.

After they had exchanged a kiss, Kelly said, "It's not good news, is it?"

"I'm sorry, honey. We talked all night, but I couldn't get Scrap to come with me."

"What in the world is his *problem*! Can't the fool see Gemma was protecting us all?"

Jeff shook his head sadly. "That's the worst part. I think Scrap can see just that, but he can't get past the lying. He says he can't trust Gemma anymore."

Kelly let out with an uncharacteristic burst of profanity that sent her husband's eyebrows arching up. "Kelly! That's not like you."

"Well, hell," she said hotly. "I'm mad. There's not a more honest person on the face of this planet than Gemma. If she hadn't handled things the way she did and kept up with her magic, we'd both be dead. Scrap is being an idiot."

"You won't get any argument from me, but . . . "

When he stopped talking abruptly, Kelly turned around to find Tori standing behind them with tears streaming down her face.

"Oh, honey," Kelly said, drawing her into a tight hug. "We didn't mean for you to hear about your Daddy like this."

"It's okay," Tori snuffled against her shoulder. "I knew he was gonna be like that. Daddy doesn't like to admit when he's wrong, and he *is* wrong. Mama had to do what she did and well . . . I think . . . I think . . . she's . . . *awesome*."

At those last words, Tori dissolved into broken sobs. Jeff stepped forward and put his hand on her back, rubbing comforting circles. "She is awesome, sugar. We'll figure out a way to talk some sense into your daddy, I promise. But until then, you've got us." He looked at his wife. "Should I go get Jinx?"

"Yes," Kelly said, "and then we're going to have to tell Gemma."

Tori pulled away from Kelly, wiping at her face. "She's gonna be so hurt," she hiccuped. "I could wring Daddy's neck."

Kelly set her mouth in a firm line. "You'll have to get behind me, sugar. I've got first dibs on strangling that man."

Chapter Sixteen

When Gemma came back with the barbecue, she took one look at my father and at Tori's red-rimmed eyes and knew the fishing trip/intervention failed. She looked at Mom and said, "Well, I guess that's it then."

"Mom!" Tori whispered hoarsely, trying to keep her voice low since there were customers in the store. "What do you mean 'that's it?!'"

Tori had been alternating between vows to rip into her father and bouts of flowing, silent tears ever since I put my arms around her in the alley and she fell completely apart. I looked over at my parents and signaled them with a nod of my head to go inside.

Once we were alone in the alley, I let Tori cry for a minute or two before standing back and putting my hands on either side of her face. With my thumbs, I wiped the tears away and then smiled. "Your nose is running and you look worse than you did the night you broke up with that guy who drove the red truck."

"Possum," Tori sniffed.

"You cannot possibly have dated a grown man who wanted to be called Possum."

"Grown is a relative term," Tori answered, using the flap of the apron she wore in the espresso bar to do a better job of drying her face. "And I didn't love him. I love my daddy."

I tightened my hands that were now resting on her arms. "I know you do. Scrap needs time. *You* need to get over to that lumberyard and get up in his face."

Tori nodded. "I will. Tomorrow."

"Go now if you want to. We can handle things here."

She shook her head. "No, I need to stay with you all and with Mom. If I went over there now, I'd either yell at him or I wouldn't be able to talk at all for crying."

"Fair enough. You ready to go inside?"

Tori nodded numbly and followed me into the store, temporarily disappearing into her micro apartment to wash her face and put on fresh makeup. When she emerged again, she looked better and offered a weak thumbs up in response to my silent question, *"Are you okay?"*

That's the thing with Tori and me. We can carry out whole conversations across a crowded room just by looking at each other.

Sometimes in life, you're lucky enough to find your people. Tori heads my tribe. She knows me better than anyone, and I know her just as well. Cold water and mascara might hide the obvious evidence of her distress, but I understood completely what the estrangement between her parents was doing to her.

So I also understood when my mom looked at her best friend, Gemma, and said, "Let's me and you go talk, sweetie."

At the same time that Gemma Andrews is a pillar of strength, she's also a proud woman. Falling apart in front of witnesses? Not something she would allow herself to do.

Gemma hesitated, and I saw mom's eyebrows go up. That's Kelly code for "don't you dare argue with me."

"Jinx, honey," Gemma said, handing me the covered container in her hands. "Would you and Tori fix us all some sandwiches? I got enough brisket for everyone."

"Yes, ma'am," I replied, taking the container.

We watched as the two women went into Tori's apartment and closed the door.

"Are they going to be okay in there?" Tori asked.

Dad nodded. "They'll be fine. Kelly knows how to talk to her."

He must have been right, because half an hour later, when the moms came back out, Gemma's eyes were red, too, but she was completely composed—composed enough to go behind the espresso bar, slip her arm around Tori's waist and kiss her daughter on the cheek.

I heard her say, "Temporary setback, kiddo. We'll get him to come home."

Tori leaned against her mother for a long minute and then Gemma said, in her normal voice, "Where's my barbecue?"

Thanks to a minor enchantment, the meat in our sandwiches was still warm when we sat down in the storeroom to eat. Dad volunteered to deal with any customers until we were finished.

No sooner had I taken my first bite than I heard the bell on the front door. As I was getting up to see if my father needed a retail rescue, Beau stepped into the storeroom.

"Good evening, ladies. May I join you, or is this gathering exclusive to the female contingent of our merry band?"

You gotta love the way Beau talks.

"Not exclusive," I said. "You're in a good mood."

Pulling the wooden chair away from the small work table where we prepared bundles of fresh herbs, Beau sat down and crossed his legs. He must have worked for hours to get a shine that fine on his boots. The black leather gleamed. Which made me think how much Chase would appreciate that polish job.

No, no, no, no, no, no, *no*.

I was not going to start mooning about Chase McGregor. For all I knew he was still in the Valley. What's that saying? Not my circus. Not my monkeys.

Beau's next words snapped me back. "Have you ladies ever eaten a rather remarkable fried pastry referred to as a funnel cake?"

When we all laughed, he added, "Did I say something amusing?"

That only made us giggle more.

"Colonel Longworth," Gemma said, wiping her eyes with her napkin, "you have no idea how much I needed that laugh."

Although he was thoroughly perplexed, Beau is ever the gentleman. "I am pleased to have been of service, dear lady, but while I am apparently the author of a witticism, I confess I do not understand its content."

Going to his rescue, I said, "You can't be at a carnival and not eat a funnel cake. We were laughing because it's so cute the way you discovered them for the first time."

Beau thought about that for a minute and then said, "Ah, I understand. The appeal of a modern pastry to an individual late of the 18th century proves the confection's addictive properties transcend time."

That touched off another round of laughter.

"And now you are amused by the complexity of my analysis," Beau said. "Am I not on what you refer to as a 'roll,' Miss Tori?"

"You are indeed, Beau," Tori said. "And your timing is perfect."

"As I said," he replied, chivalrously inclining his head, "I am most pleased to be of service."

We all went back to eating and listened as Beau described the scene on the courthouse lawn, ending with, "I would say the crowds portend a most successful week of festival going.

May I tend to the establishment so you may all partake of the revelry?"

Tori and I exchanged looks. "Uh, Beau," she said, "do you know how to make a latte?"

The colonel looked offended. "I am not without my resources, Miss Tori."

"You mean you'll get Darby to do it for you," she said. "Cheater."

"I do not believe that relying on a versatile member of our staff to operate a piece of modern machinery may be referred to as cheating," Beau said, with a twinkle in his eye. "It is more a matter of creatively solving a problem in advance."

From the doorway, Dad said, "For once would you hens trust the roosters to mind the barnyard? Go already."

"Jeff," Mom said, "you don't know anymore about making fancy coffee drinks than the Colonel does."

"Like he said," Dad replied, "we'll get Shorty to do it."

The night my father met Darby he'd given him the nickname, and now the two of them were thick as thieves. So it didn't surprise me that Darby instantly materialized when Dad called him.

"Good evening, Master Jeff," the brownie said, looking up at my dad with open admiration. "Are we going to make trouble?"

Dad was trying to get Darby to lighten up in the vocabulary department, which so far was leading to nothing but hysterical examples of vernacular twisting.

"That's 'get into trouble,'" Dad corrected him.

"Which means to do something most interesting and potentially adventuresome," Beau said. "I believe the appropriate phrase for which I am searching is, 'Sign me up.'"

Can you see why we were nervous leaving the store in their care?

It took some wheedling, but we finally gave in and headed

across the street. Beau's description hadn't done justice to the scene. The festival committee had a definite hit on their hands.

When I look back now on the scene that played out on that lawn full of laughing, talking people, I see it as a clip from a movie. A little girl walked past us with a Jack O'Lantern balloon. She was dressed as one of the Disney princesses. I can never keep them straight.

The band played that old song *Monster Mash*, while a bunch of guys did the Frankenstein walk in the middle of the street. Then someone called Mom's name.

We all turned around at the same time, and suddenly, I couldn't hear the music anymore. The scene around us blurred out until the four of us stood alone in a bubble of clarity. Two black figures moved toward us. I remember thinking, "They are taking the Goth look *way* too far."

Neither one of them could have been more than 16 years old. Bright red lipstick stood out starkly against their pale skin, and both sported masses of Seventies hair worthy of Farrah herself.

As usual, Tori's smart mouth came to the rescue. "Whoa! How many cans of Aqua Net died for that hair, ladies?"

The girl on the left opened her mouth and let out with an honest-to-God hiss, which was when we saw the fangs.

Yeah. Fangs. As in vampire. Which I had been told did not exist. Had to be fake, right? Keep reading.

Beside me, Mom gasped. Out of the corner of my eye, I saw her reach for Gemma's hand. The taller of the two girls laughed when she saw the movement. "Little mouse Kelly still hiding behind big, bad Gemma," she said in a nasty singsong voice that made me hate her instantly.

Gemma waded in next armed with a razor sharp tongue. "You are supposed to be dead, and frankly, I liked you better that way."

"You can't keep a good girl down," the shorter one purred.

"I'm sorry, Sally Beth," Gemma said, "exactly when were you ever a good girl?"

That won her another hiss accompanied by the snarled, "I go by Seraphina now."

"Finally decided to embrace your roots, huh?" Gemma said. "And speaking of roots, yours are showing."

For a fraction of a second, I thought the Goth chick was going to whip out a mirror and check her hair. Then she reclaimed her evil self, curled her lips, and flashed the pearly, pointy whites.

Gemma turned to the taller girl, "So, Jo Anne, I guess that makes you Ioana, now. News flash, honey, the Seventies are over."

"News flash, *honey*, so are you," Ioana said, raising her hand.

On instinct, we all answered with the same gesture, and suddenly there was a wall of power in front of us six inches thick.

"Let's stay on our respective sides of the fence, ladies," Gemma said. "One of you want to explain what you're doing back from the dead rocking the whole Elvira, Queen of Darkness look?"

"We are Strigoi," Seraphina said.

"Yeah, we got the memo," Tori said. "You're supposed to be *dead* Strigoi."

"Then you know nothing of the ways of our people," Seraphina answered. "We came to this pathetic gathering tonight to make ourselves known to you. When you least expect it, we will be back."

With that, the world righted itself. Seraphina and Ioana were nowhere to be seen. The music swelled, and we all hastily turned off the power we were putting out in time to see a group of people walk onto the lawn.

Nothing seemed unusual about that, until all the lightbulbs on the square dimmed and one of the band's amps blew up.

I know it didn't really happen this way, but in my mind, I saw the strangers coming at us in slow motion with some theme from a bad spaghetti western playing in the background. They looked normal, but my Spidey sense told me they weren't.

"Oh, great," I said. "Anybody want to tell me who they are?"

Beside me, Mom whispered, "They're the Ionescus."

Chapter Seventeen

The dramatic, slow motion movie effect existed only in my mind. No one else on the lawn noticed a thing. All around us people went on eating barbecue, playing games, and having a good time. Even the brief electrical show didn't interrupt the activities.

The band dragged out a replacement amp, asked the crowd how they liked the pyrotechnics and broke into a decent cover of *Witchy Woman* by the Eagles.

If I hadn't felt quite so much like I'd been run over by two freight trains with bad mascara, I might have laughed.

Gemma's brain kicked in first. "We need to get back to the store. We're too exposed out here."

Her suggestion triggered an old caution in my mind—something dad used to say when Tori and I would head into the woods for day hikes. "You two come up on something that wants to eat you, don't run. Don't ever look like prey."

"Hold on," I said, plastering a fake smile on my face and answering the wave Irma shot my way from the vicinity of the dunking booth. "We can't let the Ionescus think they're scaring us."

Beside me, Tori croaked, "Even if they *are* scaring us?"

"*Especially* because they're scaring us. We're going to turn around and walk back across the street like nothing is wrong. Can you guys handle that?"

Tori and Gemma agreed immediately, but my mother stood rooted in place. "You can do that, right, Mom?" I prodded.

At first, I didn't think she heard me. Then she blinked as if she were coming out of a trance and gave me a jerky nod. Her reaction worried me, but this wasn't the place to have a mother/daughter talk.

As a group, we moved, and instantly that slow motion effect took over again. In my perception, agonizing hours passed before my hand turned the knob and I held the front door of the store open, so the others could go in first.

For once, we caught a break; no customers in sight, just Dad and Beau playing cards in the espresso bar.

"What's going on?" Dad asked. "You all haven't been gone 20 minutes."

No one answered him. Instead, Gemma turned back toward the now closed door, raised her hands and commanded, "*Et immundum ne admittito.*"

Admit not the unclean.

The spell attached itself to the top of the door frame and flowed down over the wood and glass until it reached the floor. The barrier briefly shimmered and coalesced into a solid, transparent rectangle before dissolving into invisibility.

Gemma instantly turned on her heel, went to the back door, and repeated the incantation.

During all of this, Mom stood alone in the center of the store with her arms wrapped defensively around her body. Dad got up from his chair and went to her.

"What's wrong, honey?"

All she could do was look at him and shake her head, so he

tried with me. "Jinx, *what* is going on?" he demanded. "Somebody talk to me."

What was I going to say? *"Oh, you know those girls Mom thought she killed back in high school? Yeah, they're alive."*

Mom held out one trembling hand, which was all the signal Dad needed to fold her in a tight embrace. Finally, in the safety of his arms, she found her voice.

Pulling back enough to look up at him, she whispered, "They're not dead. It was all for nothing, Jeff. We gave him up for nothing."

He looked down at her in complete confusion. "What on earth are you talking about, Kelly?"

Gemma came up beside them and laid her hand on Mom's back. "Jeff, we just ran into Sally Beth and Jo Anne Ionescu and they definitely weren't dead."

Before dad even had time to digest the words, the basement door opened, and Festus limped through.

"Sorry to eavesdrop," he said, "but I can save you all some time getting up to speed on this one. Those chicks may not be dead, but trust me, they're not alive either."

Behind him, Chase appeared in the doorway holding an iPad in his hand. "We need to talk," he said. "Can you all come down to the lair?"

Any plans we might have had for keeping the store open through the evening were out of the question now. Our current concerns were far bigger than selling coffee and t-shirts.

Without hesitation, I locked the front door, turned the "Closed" sign over, and flipped off the lights.

"The lair is the best place we could possibly be," I said. "Somebody get Rodney. I don't want him up here alone. Gemma, are you sure that spell will work against Strigoi?"

"Technically," Festus said, "those two dames aren't Strigoi. They're vampires."

You want to know how casually he threw that one into the

mix? Substitute the phrase "Sunday school teachers" for "vampires."

I don't know how anyone could be blasé about the bloodsucking undead, but Festus pulled it off.

Everyone froze, except Beau. He was coming out of the storeroom with Rodney on his shoulder when Festus dropped the "V" word. Instead of being creeped out or registering shock, Beau said, in a fairly clinical tone, "If they are indeed vampires, we now enjoy double protection."

Every head in the room, including Rodney's, swiveled in his direction.

"How do you figure that?" Gemma asked.

"I promised Myrtle I would be of assistance to Jinx," Beau said. "To fulfill that promise, I am laboring to correct my ignorance of the Fae world. For some weeks now, I have been researching the Strigoi."

That explained the mountains of old books Darby pulled from the deepest stacks in the basement and piled on Beau's desk daily.

"It is my personal belief," Beau continued, "that the Ionescus hired the assassin, Ferguson. At any rate, I have consumed a rather vast body of literature regarding vampires. Bram Stoker and other novelists drew on the Strigoi legends for inspiration. In endeavoring to separate fact from fiction, I have determined that the creatures cannot enter a home into which they have not been invited. Since the store is also our home, the Strigoi are naturally barred from entrance."

"Good to know," Gemma said, "but I'm not taking down that spell."

Dang straight she wasn't.

Beau inclined his head in acknowledgment. "I am ever the advocate of the secondary plan, dear lady."

Dad calls that being a belt *and* suspenders man.

Tori hadn't said a word since we left the courthouse lawn,

so I didn't realize how scared she was until she started to babble.

"Are you sure? Because maybe we should find some garlic. Which isn't going to be easy since coffee shops don't really need garlic. But vampires and garlic, bad mix, right? Which is good for us . . . "

I put my hand on her arm to halt the flood of words. "Unless you're craving lasagna, we can pass on the garlic."

Under my fingers, I felt her shaking, but I knew what I was doing. Tori has a superpower. She rises to every occasion. Sometimes you just have to activate the ability by throwing her a straight line.

The shaking began to subside. She took a deep breath before asking in a stronger voice, "So, are you saying lasagna is an option here?"

"Lasagna is always an option."

Her eyes locked on mine, and I saw she was back. "Then I'm in."

Everyone took that as a signal to follow Chase and Festus down to the lair where we all more or less collapsed into the nearest available seat. Bless Darby's ever-attentive heart. He showed up immediately with trays of steaming coffee mugs, and when Mom shivered, he was instantly by her side with a heavy cardigan.

"Thank you, Darby," she said, accepting the sweater.

"Please tell me if there is anything I can do to help, Mistress Kelly," Darby said earnestly. "I do not like to see my friends so upset."

Mom smiled at him and scooted over a bit on the sofa where she and Dad were sitting. "Come sit by me. I'd like that."

Darby happily accepted the invitation, snuggling into the space between Mom and Gemma. Dad, who was on the other side of Mom, said, "Okay, now, will one of you please tell me exactly what happened out there?"

I gave him the short version of our encounter with Seraphina and Ioana and watched as he realized what Mom meant when she said "it was all for nothing."

When I finished, Dad slipped his arm around Mom. She leaned into him, resting her head on his shoulder, while he kissed the top of her head. Neither of them spoke. They were too shocked. The death of those two girls completely changed the course of my parents' lives. Had it all been a hoax?

Festus said he could save us some time on the learning curve, so I tossed the ball in his court. "Festus, you seem to have some idea what's going on here, so talk."

While I had run down the encounter on the courthouse lawn for dad, Festus assumed his usual position on the hearth. Now, he sat up and shook his head. "I don't know *everything*, but I'll tell you what I do know. I was watching from the front window of the cobbler's shop when the Strigoi pulled that mesmerizing stunt. That stuff doesn't work with cats. We don't see light and color the way other humans do."

"I thought cats could see color," I said.

"We can, but we can also tune in frequencies you can't."

"Okay, so what did you see, and what do you mean by 'mesmerizing?'"

Chase answered before his father could. "All the old stories say Strigoi can make themselves invisible, but that's not really how it works. They cloud the minds of the people around them. The creatures you encountered this evening seem to be able to do that to the power of ten."

The interruption annoyed me, and I let it show. "Suddenly you're an expert on the Strigoi, too?" I asked, shooting him the arched eyebrow.

For people who know me, the arched eyebrow is a *bad* sign.

I'll give Chase credit for not looking away, but a cautious veil fell over his eyes. "I've been doing some research, too."

A wise voice in my head reminded me that it didn't matter who had been doing the research so long as the information helped us. I took a deep breath and made an effort to sound more cordial. "Then by all means, enlighten us."

Chase told us he'd only returned from the Valley a few minutes before our encounter with the two girls Tori promptly christened "The Strigoi Sisters."

"That makes them sound like bad back-up singers," I said.

"They *look* like bad back-up singers," Tori replied, "and it's easier to say than Seraphina and Ioana."

"At any rate," Chase said, grinning at Tori, "while you all were dealing with The Strigoi Sisters, I was in the shower. Dad was keeping an eye on the festival from the front window."

Festus took up the story at that point. "I saw them throw that energy field around you, and knew we had a situation on our paws."

"What did the energy field look like?" I asked curiously.

"A bubble," Festus answered, "right down to the shimmering, oily colors on the surface. Thing is, no one else saw it. People who walked in your direction would get within a foot or two and then veer right or left and go around."

Which was a good thing.

"Okay," I said, "so how did you jump from 'chicks in black blowing a big soap bubble' to 'the vampires are coming, the vampires are coming?'"

That's an inside joke. Ever since we saw *Abraham Lincoln Vampire Hunter*, Tori and I have been imagining the same treatment for *Gone with the Wind*. Come on. Tell me you can't see Scarlett driving a stake through a Yankee's chest on the staircase?

Before Festus could answer, Beau let out with an "Ah, ha!" He wheeled his desk chair around and regarded Festus with the air of an over-excited academic who had discovered some hidden scroll. "I've got it! They were not buried properly, were they?"

"Well, well, well," Festus said. "Chalk one up for the warmed-over dead guy."

"Would one of you please speak English?" I said.

"Beau has landed on the same theory we've come up with," Chase said. "We think the girls are here because some necessary death rituals weren't performed. We need to get to the Valley and talk to Moira about this as soon as possible to confirm that."

Uh, no, Mister Man, we don't.

"The only thing you need to do," I said, in a low, even voice, "is talk to *me*."

An uneasy silence fell over the room. I had just pulled rank on Chase McGregor for the first time.

Now, to be truthful, I wasn't really sure what my "rank" was supposed to be, but from everything I knew so far, Chase was my bodyguard, not my boss—and I had seriously had enough of his "this is what *we* need to do" attitude.

Amidst the anxiety radiating off the group, Festus caught my attention. I saw a gleam of admiration in his amber eyes. That was all the confirmation I needed. I was doing the right thing.

Festus may be a mouthy old scoundrel, but he's not to be underestimated. He didn't retire because he has a lame hip; he retired because he didn't have my mother to protect anymore.

Well, Mom is back—and so is he. In a big way.

While Festus gave me encouragement, Chase shot me annoyed impatience, which is what I always get from him when he's trying to tell me what to do and I balk.

Whether he knew it or not, that dance was officially over.

The muscles in Chase's jaw worked back and forth as he

started to argue with me. Festus saw it, too, and decided to pull some rank of his own.

"Answer her, boy."

Chase blinked at his father in shock. "Dad . . . "

The protest died on his lips when Festus snapped, "Remember your place, Chase McGregor. She is a Daughter of Knasgowa, and I am your chieftain. Answer her."

Imagine the scene if you will. A scruffy yellow tomcat sitting beside a fireplace staring down a grown man. The image should teach you an important lesson. Power and authority have nothing to do with size.

In the end, Chase opened his iPad and started to speak, occasionally referring to what I guessed were notes on the screen. He did as he was told and answered me, but he didn't like it.

We learned that all the Ionescus descend from a single human cursed to be *Strigoi Viu*, which Chase translated for us as the "undead living." Technically, that makes them the "good" kind of Strigoi, especially since a kindly Romanian priest working with Benjamin Franklin, of all people, figured out how to feed them with electricity so they wouldn't have to harm people.

Both Tori and Beau had begun to take notes of their own. Tori held up her hand to interrupt Chase. "So Father Damian and Ben Franklin figured out how to domesticate the good vampires and dumped them around Briar Hollow? What's up with that?"

Instead of answering her directly, Chase looked at me. "I saw you in the Valley. You were talking to the Mother Oak, so I assume you know about the Grid now."

The words "I saw you" carried the unmistakable tone of an accusation, which I did not like.

"Yes. I know about the Grid."

"*You do?*" Mom gasped.

Without taking my eyes off Chase, I said, "I'll tell you about it later, Mom. What about the Grid, Chase?"

He couldn't help himself. He had to go there.

"Did you talk to anyone else in the Valley?"

And we have a winner, folks! Suspicions confirmed. Chase saw me with Lucas Grayson, thus the attitude.

My reaction to that?

Oh, *hell* no.

Thankfully, Festus followed the whole silent exchange and stepped in again before the sparks ignited into an open argument.

"I think I'll take it from here, boy," he said smoothly. "Finding out about the Grid and understanding it are two different things, Jinx."

Festus rarely uses my name. At that moment he did it to get me to ignore his son, who was acting like a jealous idiot, and focus on what I was being told. It worked.

"Good point," I said. Help me understand."

"The Grid is like a net of power overlaying the globe. The points at which the Mother Trees are placed are called vortices."

When he paused to make sure I was following, I nodded and said, "Go on."

"The vortices form centers of power in the Fae world. At the time Damian and Franklin figured out how to feed the Strigoi, electricity was a novelty. Their earliest feeding system relied on proximity to the local vortex to generate enough power to be effective."

"That makes sense," I said. "The Strigoi were placed in a location that would maximize their ability to stick to their feeding program and stay away from human prey."

"Exactly, and that's the part of all of this that doesn't make any sense. The Ionescus have been here since the American Revolution. In all that time, there hasn't been a single report of one of them hurting a human. I think the problem here is Anton and not his people."

Dad had been listening intently to the whole conversation. "Wait a minute," he interrupted. "We've always known this was a personal revenge thing with Anton. What do the rest of his people have to do with this?"

"That," Festus said, "is an added complication. Anton might have cast the curse on Kelly originally, but because he's the head of their clan, all of his people have to honor the curse. If he has decided that the truce is broken, all of the Ionescus are in on the hunt now."

Great. I can't get one vampire. I have to get packs of them.

"If I may?" Beau said. "Am I to infer that you believe it possible the majority of the Ionescus are not in favor of pursuing this revenge?"

My ears perked up at that.

"That's exactly what I'm inferring," Festus said. "The Ionescus have a good thing going here. Why risk losing all that?"

Yeah, good argument, but I saw some major problems with the theory.

"If that's the case, what was with that group appearance tonight and what's the deal with the Sisters not being buried the right way?"

"I think the Ionescus showed up *en masse* to reel in those two teenage vamps for being out of bounds," Festus said. "If I'm right, those girls are as big a problem for their family as they are for us."

"What makes you think that?"

Festus inclined his head toward Chase. "Because unlike my boy here, I read the footnotes."

In rare cases, it seems that a third kind of Strigoi can crop up. When a *Strigoi Viu* dies, no matter what the cause, they have to be . . . well, disposed of . . . and I'm not talking embalming.

If you don't want a dead *Strigoi Viu* to rise as a supercharged *Strigoi mort*, the body has to be staked with silver and beheaded. Otherwise, they really do rise from the dead as the creatures most people call vampires. Once that happens, the only energy that can satisfy their hunger comes from warm, living blood.

Which explained everything except the source of the information Festus shared with us.

"Exactly what footnotes have you been reading?"

Festus looked me in the eye and told me the truth. "At my request, Earl, Merle, and Furl worked up a dossier on the Strigoi."

"And why would you have them do that?"

There's one thing you need to know about Festus McGregor. He doesn't flinch from the consequences of his actions.

"I lied to you about what happened the night Ferguson died."

"What did you leave out?"

"Ferguson was able to say one word to me before he died," Festus answered. "He said, 'Ionescu.'"

Chapter Eighteen

Festus was rocking the one-word bombshells. First I get vampires, and then I find out he—and by extension Chase—knew Ferguson and Ionescu were linked all along.

So. Not. Cool.

Trying to control my temper, I said, "If this secrecy thing is a McGregor family trait, I don't like it, Festus. When were you going to tell me about Ferguson's dying words?".

Still looking me straight in the eyes, Festus said, "I owe you an apology. I seriously underestimated your ability to deal with all of this. I should have told you what Ferguson said the night it happened."

"Yes, you should have."

"On my honor, I had no idea those two girls were alive in any form until I saw them walk up to you this evening. I would never have put any of you in that position had I known."

From the sofa, Mom spoke up in his defense. "Listen to him, honey. Festus wouldn't hurt us." She paused and glanced at Dad, and then added, "He would never hurt *me*."

There wasn't much I could say to that with my father

sitting right there. Or at least that's what I thought until Dad voiced his support. "Festus would give his life for Kelly in a heartbeat. There's no way he knew Sally Beth and Jo Anne were alive."

Truth be told, I didn't need them to convince me. I didn't think Festus would put us in danger either—and neither would Chase, at least not intentionally, but his pig-headed streak was starting to be a problem.

"I believe you, Festus." Then I looked at Chase. "But *you* should have told me regardless of what was going on between us personally. If I'm going to trust you to do your job around here, nothing like this can ever happen again. Understood?"

"Understood," he said tightly.

"Good. Now, let's figure out . . . "

Chase interrupted me. "I'm sorry, but in the spirit of transparency, there are still a couple of things you don't know."

The spirit of transparency? Nasty *nice* was not going to cut it with me, but I was trying to keep the conversation on track.

"I'm listening."

"Anton Ionescu is Irenaeus Chesterfield's lawyer."

Un-freaking-*believable*.

"And?"

"I went to the Valley to ask Ironweed to start surveillance on the Ionescu compound."

And that, ladies and gents, officially qualified as *enough*.

"Tell me that you at least discussed that with Barnaby first."

"No. I didn't talk to Barnaby."

Festus tried to step in and defend his son. "Jinx, in all fairness, that was my . . . "

Too little. Too late.

I was already on my feet and pointing a finger at Chase. He must have expected me to hurl a bolt of energy in his direction because he flinched.

Silly man. I didn't need magic to take him down a peg or two.

"You and I need to have a private conversation. Come with me."

With that, I turned on my heel and marched off into the stacks. I wasn't about to look back. If Chase McGregor knew what was good for him, he'd follow me.

After a few seconds, I heard footsteps behind me. I kept walking until I knew there was no chance anyone in the lair could hear us and then I turned to face him.

We were standing in an open area where four sections of the archives converge. I hadn't meant for the setting to look quite so much like a fight ring, but considering the tension between us, maybe that was apropos.

"With everything else that is going on in our world, Chase, I do not need a lone wolf werecat on my hands."

Yeah, I know. Mixed species metaphors. It was a heat of the moment thing.

"Jinx, I just wanted to . . . "

I held up my hand. "Stop right there. Festus is right. You work for *me*. I've let all this paternalistic, protective, misogynistic *crap* go on for too long. I might have been in over my head at the start of the summer, and I appreciate everything you did to help me adjust, but those days are long gone. You either start treating me as an equal in all this *stuff* we get into or get out of my way. Your pick."

The red flush creeping up from the neck of his shirt could have been anger or embarrassment. "It doesn't work that way. You can't fire me."

"Watch me. I'm a grown woman and a perfectly capable witch. If you can't deal with that, stop coming around. I saw what Festus could do when he took down Ferguson. Lame or not, there is at least one werecat who is actually fulfilling his responsibilities, and I'm not looking at him."

"Fine," Chase said, giving in to his anger. "Whatever you say."

Since we were both already mad, I went for broke. "Is there anything you haven't told me? Because we're not going back to the lair until everything is on the table."

"No."

"Then come on. They're waiting for us."

"I thought you said you wanted everything out on the table," Chase shot back, his eyes blazing.

Unbelievable. I gave him the chance to drop it and he barrelled ahead anyway.

"Something you want to ask me, Chase?"

"Why were you talking to Lucas Grayson on the square in Shevington?" he demanded—in entirely the wrong tone of voice to get a good response from me.

I took a step forward until I was right up in his face.

"Listen to me carefully, because I'm only going to say this once. You gave up the right to ask me a question like that when you decided to implode our relationship. If there's anything you need to know because we have a job to do, I'll tell you. Otherwise, what goes on in my personal life is none of your business."

Since I didn't need an answer, I didn't wait for one.

I turned around and went back to the lair. This time, there were no footsteps behind me.

The group stayed busy while Chase and I had our . . . discussion. To my surprise, Glory appeared to have joined the effort. She was standing on a book lying open on Beau's desk, reading the text. In relation to her size, the print was enormous.

"Hey, Glory," I said. "I guess you heard everything we were talking about?"

"Oh, yes," she said, craning her neck to look at me. "I didn't mean to listen in without permission."

"You don't need permission," I said, sitting down. It didn't put me at eye level with the Barbie-sized witch, but at least I was no longer towering over her. "I apologize for not asking you to be a part of the meeting."

Her green face colored with what I think was a blush of pleasure. It's hard to tell. Normally she's sort of spring green, and now she was more forest, or maybe pine. You get the idea.

"That is so nice of you," Glory said. "When I heard about everything that's going on, I came down here to the desk to ask Colonel Longworth if I could please help. Those creatures you all were talking about sound awful. Even worse than the *Creature from the Black Lagoon*."

She looked so earnest I managed not to laugh, even as my mind flashed on the phony rubber-suited "monster" of movie fame.

"Thank you. I know I speak for everyone when I say your help is much appreciated."

"You are so welcome," she gushed. "Could I ask you for a favor?"

"Sure. What do you need?"

"I left my megaphone up at Graceland East. Would you mind getting it for me? It's in the living room."

Glory is right at 11.5 inches tall. When you're up close to her, hearing what she has to say isn't that hard, but across the room or when we're all in the lair, she can have a hard time making herself heard.

As it turns out, Glory and Barbie are the same size, which has made facilitating Glory's life a lot easier. We ordered the Barbie cheerleading outfit complete with pink megaphone, and Glory had instant voice amplification.

I carefully reached through the door of Graceland East, snagged the megaphone, and sat it down beside Glory on the desk.

She thanked me, and then said, "I might have something

important to say. You know, I worked in the state archives when I was a normal-sized person. I'm very good at research, even if I don't have a clue what any of this stuff means."

While that statement didn't necessarily bolster my confidence in our tiniest team member, I didn't say that to her. Instead, I turned toward Beau who was standing in front of the bookcase to the right of the fireplace consulting a text he held open in his hand. I could make out Rodney's slumbering form tucked inside the collar of Beau's shirt.

"Hey," I said, "So what's the scoop?"

Beau was so absorbed in what he was reading; he must not have heard me come in. "Ah, there you are. I trust you resolved matters of . . . protocol to your satisfaction?"

Getting up from the chair and joining him, I said in a low tone, "To my satisfaction, yes. I don't know about his."

In an equally soft voice, Beau said, "I believe you took young Mr. McGregor by surprise with your uncharacteristic assertiveness, which he did not appear to appreciate. I, on the other hand, am quite proud of you. I do not like to see your talents downplayed."

"That makes two of us. And thank you. So, what's everyone doing?"

"We are going through the various elements of vampiric lore in an attempt to determine the potential physical and magical capabilities of the two creatures you encountered. Since they have already appeared to you in daylight, for instance, we can rightfully assume their movements will not be limited to darkness."

"Is that supposed to make me feel better or worse?"

Beau ignored the sarcasm and gave the question serious consideration. "Rather worse, I should think," he said finally, with a twinkle in his eye.

"Gee, thanks," I said, smiling in spite of myself. "What else are you looking at?"

"The standards. Holy water, mirrors, and crosses."

I frowned. "Aren't all of those things just movie props?"

From across the room, Gemma spoke up. "Not necessarily. Now that you're starting to learn about the Grid, you may be realizing different woods have varying levels of associated power. I'm not ready to rule out crosses because of that, but we need more research."

Just then Chase walked into the lair. We all paused for maybe the space of a heartbeat, and then went right on with our business. He'd apparently taken the extra time to get his temper in check, so I opted for the high ground and treated him with the level of professionalism I expected to receive.

"Has Ironweed found anything?" I asked.

Although his tone was subdued, the earlier note of arrogance was gone. "I don't know. He's using some new micro drones called GNATS."

"As in small annoying insects that stick to your sweaty skin in hot weather?" Tori asked. "'Cause *ewwwww*."

Everyone laughed, easing the undercurrent of tension. When Chase spoke again, his voice sounded normal.

"Yes, except these GNATS are powered by fairy dust and outfitted with high definition cameras."

"Sweet!" Tori said. "You have to get me in to see one of those things."

"Down, Geek Girl," I said. "Have the drones found anything?"

"When I was with Ironweed, he did a preliminary fly over of the Ionescu compound. Every one of the houses has a super-sized generator in a shed behind the residence. I imagine that's their food source. I wasn't able to give Ironweed any specifics about what he might be looking for, so that's all I know right now."

"Actually," Tori said, "I have some ideas in that department. Let me throw some stuff up against the wall and see what sticks."

Beside me, Beau frowned. "Why do you need to throw things against the wall to share your thoughts with us?"

"It means she's going to think out loud," I said. "Come on, let's sit down for this."

Everyone settled in their previously claimed spots, and I nodded at Tori, "Go ahead."

"Okay, so go with me on this. We know the Strigoi Sisters died in the wreck even if it was only temporary dead. Since they're here now, somebody didn't do the old stake/beheading two-step, which should mean those chicks have been running around as vampires for what, 35 years?"

"Closer to 40," Mom said. "Gemma and I were 15 the year the wreck happened."

"Right," Tori said. "So where are the reports of strange deaths? They have to feed on blood, so there should be unexplained bodies piling up. I did a search online. Nothing. The only unsolved murders in this area for the past 30 years were the girls on the hiking paths, and we took care of that one. So what, exactly, have the Strigoi Sisters been eating?"

No one had an answer, but Glory piped up with an idea. "Maybe whoever was taking care of those girls put a stake in their heart."

"You know about real vampires?" I asked in surprise.

"Of course," Glory said, "I know them all. Bela Lugosi, Peter Cushing, Christopher Lee . . ."

Right on cue, my movie trivia-obsessed mother chimed in with, "Peter Cushing didn't play *Dracula*."

"He did *so*," Glory said.

"He did *not*," Mom countered. "Cushing played Van Helsing . . . "

Oh, for Heaven's sake. Not. Productive.

"Ladies," I said, "a little focus here. Glory, what is your point?"

"Well," she huffed, "in those movies, if someone staked a vampire he turned into a skeleton, but if the stake was pulled back out, the vampire got all flesh and blood again."

Festus, who had been staring into the fire, turned his head. "Dang, the cocktail pickle may be onto something there."

"Hey!" Glory cried. "Who are you calling a pickle, you, you, you . . . yellow tomcat."

Turning impassive eyes toward the desk, he said, "I'm sorry, but is that supposed to be an insult? I *am* a yellow tomcat."

"Enough, you two," I said. "Festus, is there something to what Glory said?"

"Maybe. What if staking the girls put them in a state of limbo? Ionescu could have kept them stashed for years."

"But why would he do a gruesome thing like that?" Mom asked. "He doted on those girls."

"Think about it," Festus said. "The only reason the Strigoi are here in Briar Hollow is because someone thought they could be cured. Maybe Ionescu got it in his head that he could do something like that for the girls; control their transformation into *Strigoi mort* or even reverse it.

I turned to Beau. "What do you think?"

"It would seem reasonable that such an attempted cure would be a natural line of thinking for a man with Mr. Ionescu's family history. Especially since your mother tells us that he was inordinately fond of both young women. Perhaps he was incapable of letting them go."

Gemma reached for Mom's hand. "You remember the funeral?"

Mom nodded. "Mr. Ionescu was completely shattered. He sobbed through the entire service."

"You went to the funerals?" I asked, shocked.

"It was a memorial service," Gemma said. "There was just one for both of them. The actual funeral with the caskets was private. Sally Beth was Ionescu's daughter. Her mother died when we were in grade school. Then Anton's brother and sister-in-law were killed a couple of years later. That's when the niece, Jo Anne, went to live with them."

"What's up with the name switching thing?" Tori asked.

"I think as they got older the girls wanted to fit in more," Mom said. "The Ionescus have always been extremely reclusive people; homeschooling their children, never coming into town. I'm not sure why Ionescu let them go to public school with the rest of us. When we were in the 8th grade, they changed their names from Seraphina and Ioana to Sally Beth and Jo Anne."

"Okay," I said, "I like this theory. But if Ionescu did manage to put them in suspended animation, why would he wake them up?"

"Perhaps he believed that he had the means of curing or controlling them, and he woke the girls up to test it," Beau suggested.

"Yeah," Festus said. "Or maybe someone conned him into *believing* there was a cure."

"Chesterfield," I said.

"Chesterfield," Festus nodded.

I turned my attention back to Chase. "When will Ironweed have more information?"

"Late Monday afternoon or early Tuesday morning."

"Okay," I said, "so here's what I think we should do. Tori and I should try to find the car so I can see if I can get a reading off the wreckage psychometrically."

Mom paled. "Oh, honey, is that really necessary?"

"It's the closest thing we have to a time machine, Mom. No one else was there when the accident happened. The car is the only 'witness,' but finding it is a long shot."

She looked at Dad, then at me again, blinking back tears. "I can tell you exactly where the car is. They towed it to Murph Lawson's junkyard. It's sitting in the far back corner by the fence."

Dad turned on the sofa to look at her. "How do you know that, honey?"

"Through the years I've . . . I've gone there to . . . see it."

For as much as I hated to think of my mother visiting what she had always believed to be the scene of her "crime," she was saving us a lot of time.

"Thank you, Mom. That's a big help."

From the stricken look on Dad's face, I could tell he wasn't dealing well with Mom's admission that she had been torturing herself with those junkyard visits.

"Hey, Dad," I said. "I need you to do something for me. You up for a little errand?"

I had to ask twice before he answered. "Hmm, what? Oh. An errand. Sure. What do you want me to do?"

"Get Chesterfield's chessboard the hell out of my store."

"Not that I'm objecting," Tori said, "but is that a good idea?"

"If Ionescu and Chesterfield are working together," I said, "there is no way that Chesterfield doesn't know we've figured out the truth about the chessboard. We can't take even the slightest chance that he has a way to use it to get information."

Behind me, a pen hit the floor. When I looked over my shoulder, I saw Glory standing on the edge of the desk looking for all the world like she might be thinking about jumping.

"I didn't do anything bad," she said in a choked voice. "I haven't told him one thing since you all made me bigger and gave me a place to live and music and movies. I haven't. I really haven't."

I got up and went to the desk. At least if she did do some dramatic dive over the side, I'd be in position to catch her.

"We know that Glory. No one is accusing you of being in touch with Chesterfield, but there could be a chance that chessboard can work without you. Wouldn't you feel better if it was gone?"

She nodded so vigorously she looked like one of those dashboard dogs. "Oh, I would. I truly would. But I'm afraid if you do anything with it, Mr. Chesterfield will find me and do something even worse than . . . worse than . . . turning me into a cocktail pickle."

At that, she burst into tears. I shot Festus a murderous look. "See what you've done? Get over here and apologize."

Festus rolled his eyes, but he limped over to the desk and sprang up to the surface with surprising ease. When he put his paw out, I was half afraid he might be about to try to smack some sense into the wailing witch. Instead, he gently patted her on the back.

"I'm sorry, Glory. I shouldn't have called you a cocktail pickle."

"That's alright," Glory sniffed magnanimously. "I shouldn't have called you a yellow tomcat."

Festus started to say, "But I am . . . " and then opted for, "No problem."

Sometimes trying to sift through Glory Logic is just not worth it.

Chapter Nineteen

With the Glory drama resolved, everyone got down to business. Beau volunteered to help Dad move the chessboard. I wanted the thing gone, but I didn't know where to put it. Beau suggested a long-abandoned crypt at the back of the cemetery.

"The inhabitants died shortly after the Revolutionary War," he said. "They have not put in an appearance among the spirits in at least a hundred years. The crypt, however, is well built. With a chain and lock on the door, I do not think the chess set will be disturbed."

"Won't somebody notice a brand new lock and chain?" Tori asked.

At that, Darby jumped on his yellow bicycle and went tearing off into the archives, only to return in under five minutes with an old wooden box balanced precariously in the bike's basket.

Dad grabbed the box before it fell and knocked Darby over in the process. "Whoa there, Shorty. What have you got here?"

"I thought these would be of help, Master Jeff," Darby said excitedly. "They are not new."

"Not new" didn't do justice to the mass of rusty chains and ancient, massive locks in the box. I've always thought it was a rule that no lock ever gets stored with either its keys or the combination. You know, the way the dryer eats socks and Tupperware lids never match the containers?

In this instance, however, every single lock sported an equally rusty skeleton key.

"Perfect, Shorty," Dad grinned. "You want to come with us to the cemetery?"

That set Darby fairly jumping up and down with excitement. "Road trip!" he crowed. Then, remembering himself, he turned to me and said, "May I go, Mistress Jinx?"

"Oh, for heaven's sake, would you guys get out of here already!" I laughed.

As they went up the stairs, I called out to my father, "Take Darby to Dairy Queen while you're out, Dad. He likes their ice cream with hot fudge."

Darby came rocketing back down the stairs and jumped into my arms to give me a big hug before he went trotting happily after Dad and Beau.

That's how things are in my world. Dark and complicated one minute; light and endearingly simple the next.

After that, Chase excused himself, and for once, Festus didn't linger behind on the hearth. I suspected father and son would have a long talk when they got home. So far, the evening could not have been pleasant for Chase.

That left me, Mom, Gemma, and Tori alone for the time being. We walked upstairs into the dark store to have a look out on the square. By then it was after 11 o'clock. The band had been hired to play until midnight, and there were still plenty of people dancing in the street.

"Irma must be ecstatic," Tori said. "The festival is a huge hit."

"Yes," I said, "but we have to make sure that none of the

attendees turn into juicy Strigoi snacks before the week is over. I think we should all stay here at the store until this business with the Sisters is resolved."

Gemma would bunk with Tori in the micro apartment, and Mom and Dad could stay with me. The cats would be thrilled to death to have me on the couch. There was one nagging question however. Was Tori's dad safe at the lumberyard with the Strigoi Sisters on the loose?

By the time that problem came up for discussion, we'd migrated to the espresso bar and were talking over a pot of tea. Tori confessed that she had been planning to drive to Cotterville the next morning and see her father.

"I think I better come with you, honey," Gemma said. "He might listen to me and agree to come back here for a few days until all this blows over."

"And if he doesn't?" Mom asked.

"Then Tori can distract him long enough for me to ward his office," Gemma said. "That may be the best we can do."

TORI BROUGHT the car to a stop in front of her father's business, Andrews Lumber, which sat on the northern edge of Cotterville several streets away from the downtown business area.

After she cut the engine, Tori and her mother sat quietly, listening to the Sunday morning stillness.

"I always loved this place," Tori said finally. "When I was a kid there wasn't a square inch of it I didn't know."

Her mother's eyes roamed over the bins of wood. "It's the smell I love. The scent of new lumber always makes me think of your father."

"Guess it's a good thing he didn't go into pig farming, huh?"

Gemma chuckled and shook her head. "You get that smart mouth from me and your level-headedness from your father."

"Daddy isn't being level-headed, he's being unreasonable."

On reflex, Gemma said, "Don't criticize your father, young lady."

"Mom, this time he deserves it."

Still looking at the stacks of wood, Gemma said, "When your Dad first bought this place, and you were just a baby, we'd get hamburgers at the M&M Drive-In and come over here for family picnics. Remember?"

"I remember."

Pointing to one of the upper bins at the far end, Gemma said. "That one was our favorite because of the view of the mountains. Your Daddy kept a box of wood scraps up there for you to use for blocks."

"I remember that, too. When I told him I needed arches for the palace I was building, he cut them for me himself."

Gemma swallowed hard. "Scrap has always been a good father and a good husband, but I'm starting to wonder if I've been a good wife."

Tori took her mother's hand. "Don't even think that. You are the heart of this family."

Squeezing her daughter's hand, Gemma said, "Thank you, sugar. But your daddy is right. I lied to him all these years."

"You thought you were doing the right thing, and honestly, Mom, I think you were. If anyone had known you were still practicing magic, Brenna Sinclair could have found out after she was released. You got the drop on her because she underestimated you."

Gemma sighed. "We understand that, Tori, but I don't know if your father will ever be able to see it that way. When he gets an idea in his head, sometimes dynamite won't blast it back out."

"Well, we're not going to make any progress with him by sitting here. Let's do this thing, Mom."

They got out of the car and crossed the parking lot, moving toward the outside stairs that led up to Scrap's office, which sat above the main loading dock. About halfway up, Tori suddenly laid a hand on her mother's arm.

Gemma opened her mouth to ask what was wrong but stopped when Tori shook her head and put a finger to her lips. She pointed up and mouthed, "Listen."

The sound of voices floated down to them. Female voices.

"The Sisters?" Tori whispered.

Before Gemma could answer, a woman's voice called out. "Do join us, Gemma, and bring your spawn with you. We're having a lovely talk with your husband. He's just the most *interesting* man."

"These bitches have got to go," Tori said tightly.

"They do," Gemma said, starting back up the stairs, "but you may have noticed they're hard to kill."

When mother and daughter stepped through the door, Tori took one look at the scene in the office and started forward only to be blocked by her mother's restraining arm. "Easy," Gemma said, under her breath. "Let this play out."

Scrap sat behind his desk with a dazed expression on his face. Seraphina lounged across his lap while Ioana, who was standing behind the desk chair, ran her fingers through his hair.

"Hi, Gemmy," Seraphina purred. "Wherever did you find this one? He's fun."

"Leave. Him. Alone," Tori said through clenched teeth.

"Now why would we want to do that?" Ioana asked. "He smells so nice."

"We haven't hurt your Daddy, kitten," Seraphina said. "We're just getting to know him a little better."

"Yeah, well, pardon me for saying so," Tori said, "but it doesn't look like he's into either one of you."

Seraphina laughed, waggling her fingers in front of Scrap's eyes. "He's dazed. Men are ever so much easier to control when they're dazed. Ever so much easier to . . . drain."

She emphasized the last word by dragging a razor sharp fingernail across Scrap's cheek opening a thin, scarlet trail on the skin. Leaning closer, she ran her tongue along the blood.

"Ohhhhh," she said, "he is *tasty*. Salty *and* sweet, with a hint of fatty flavor. Like good barbecue. Maybe we'll have him with a side of coleslaw."

Later, when Tori tried to describe the next sequence of events to Jinx, she only remembered the wind. The hot torrent swept through the doors and windows all at once, wrapping them in ever-tightening tendrils of pressure. When Tori thought all the breath would be sucked from her lungs, the air stilled, leaving a tall, red-haired woman dressed in black standing in the center of the room.

The woman turned toward them, and said, in a lilting Scottish brogue, "Sorry for the dramatic entrance. In a bit of a hurry. No time to knock."

"No problem," Gemma said. "As long as you're on our side."

"Totally," the woman replied, looking toward the Strigoi. "Isn't *this* adorable? The Romanian vampires want to play."

"Mom, do you have any idea who that woman is?" Tori asked.

The red-haired woman glanced over her shoulder. Green fire now danced in the depths of her emerald eyes. "Greer MacVicar, at your service."

Seraphina gasped. "You are the baobhan sith."

"Ah," Greer said, "my reputation precedes me. How gratifying."

"You can't kill us," Ioana said. "You can't kill one of your own kind."

"Oh, no, dear. No, no. *You* are not one of my kind. You're a cheap Transylvanian vampire knock off. I may not be allowed to kill you without cause, but I can certainly make you wish you were dead. Now . . . *leave*."

Seraphina and Ioana hastily disentangled themselves from Scrap and joined hands. "This isn't over," Seraphina said. "Gemma and Kelly ruined our lives. We will have our revenge."

With that, they raised their clasped hands high in the air and disappeared in a cloud of acrid, gray smoke.

Greer wrinkled her nose in disgust. "Repugnant creatures, and smelly. Are either of you harmed?"

"We're okay," Gemma said, "but what about my husband?"

"He'll be perfectly fine when the mesmerization wears off," Greer said. "Give the poor man ten or fifteen minutes and he should be coherent."

"Are you really the baobhan sith?" Gemma asked curiously.

Tori interrupted. "Okay, could I at least get the Cliffs Notes' explanation here? What is a *baa-van shee*?"

"A Scottish vampire," Greer said. "The only sort that counts."

"Uh, okay," Tori said. "So, Romanian vamps bad, Scottish vamps good?"

"Precisely," Greer said. "You can, in general, assume that any product of Scotland is superior."

"Oh," Tori said, "Festus is going to *love* you."

Chapter Twenty

As for the rest of Tori and Gemma's visit to the lumberyard, things didn't get better. Waking up out of the mesmerized state scared Scrap half out of his mind. Then he looked in the mirror, saw the bloody scratch on his cheek, and lost the other half.

He chose to cope with his fear by getting mad as hell at everyone and everything in sight, but most especially his wife. The longer he ranted, the madder Gemma got, with Tori not far behind.

She didn't hear everything her parents said to each other because Gemma asked her to wait in the car, but on the way down the stairs to the parking lot, Tori heard the word "divorce" used for the first time.

Whether Scrap was serious or overreacting under the circumstances remained to be seen, but it was safe to say the Andrews' spat was rapidly escalating toward an actual separation.

Mom and I listened as Gemma described what happened after Tori left the office. Scrap not only wouldn't come back to the shop, he refused to let Gemma ward the office.

"That's when Greer stepped in," Gemma said.

The red-haired woman fixed Scrap with an almost feral smile, and said, "Mr. Andrews, what goes on between you and your wife is none of my business, but I'll venture to say you don't want Seraphina and Ioana coming back, now, do you?"

The suggestion of dealing with the Strigoi Sisters again made Scrap turn as pale as one of the cemetery ghosts. "I most certainly do not, and if those women show up again, I'll call the law."

Gemma paused and took a sip from the glass of Scotch in her hand. "Greer laughed in his face." "Then she told him 'the local constabulary cannot protect you from the Strigoi.' He demanded to know what the hell a Strigoi was, so I told him."

Mom was sitting beside Gemma on one of the sofas in the lair. She had her own glass of single malt, a request that shocked me—especially since it was 10 o'clock on Sunday morning. My mother drinking whisky neat almost rocked my world more than the whole vampire thing.

"What exactly did you tell him, Gem?" Mom asked.

"The truth. That the Strigoi are vampires. And do you know what that man had the nerve to say to me?"

None of us had to ask because she was fired up and ready to tell us.

"Scrap said, I wasn't just a liar, I was a crazy liar. There I was trying to protect his sorry butt, and he has to go and say something like that."

We all knew what was going on. Anger was the only thing holding Gemma together at the moment, so we let her be mad.

"So that's when Greer offered him this amulet you told us about?" I asked.

"Right," Gemma said. "It was in a linen bag. Scrap laughed at her and said he wasn't going to wear some sack on a string when he didn't even know what was in it."

Now we were getting somewhere. Gemma related Greer's

explanation of the amulet; a bag holding nine pieces of elder twig cut before the full moon to be worn over the heart.

When Scrap responded with a less than polite answer, Greer suggested he get a civil tongue in his head when he addressed his wife.

Way to go, Scrap. Piss off your wife *and* a Scottish vampire.

Never a man to back down, Scrap tried to get up in Greer's face, and she handily turned the tables on him. At that point in her story, Gemma couldn't help herself. She laughed.

"It was a thing of beauty. Greer let that green fire come back into her eyes and said, 'If you don't start treating this woman with some respect, the Strigoi may be the least of your worries.'"

Good answer.

"What did Scrap do?" Mom asked.

Gemma snorted. "What do you think he did? He took the amulet. Would you argue with that woman?"

As she spoke, Gemma gestured with her glass toward the hearth where Festus and Greer were trading stories by the fire about great bars they had known and loved.

Tori was right when she predicted Festus and Greer would hit it off, but she got the timeline wrong. They already knew each other. Correction. Make that "knew each other well" judging from what little of their conversation I overheard.

"Did Greer tell you why she's here?" I asked Gemma quietly.

I shouldn't have bothered whispering. It didn't work.

"*She* did not," Greer answered cheerfully.

At my startled expression, she said, "You know what they say about vampires. We all have bat ears."

Festus cracked up and laughed himself to the point of a hairball toss. "Bat ears," he wheezed. "That one never gets old."

Actually, the line was so old it was mummified, but I let it slide.

"Come on over, ladies," Greer said. "Join us by the fire."

Chase hadn't come around since the evening before, and Beau and Dad were up in the espresso bar, so it really was just us girls plus Festus.

"Do I need to get everyone together to hear this?" I asked.

"Oh, heavens no," Greer said. "We're going to have a professional girl talk."

That got a grumbled, "Seriously, Greer?" from Festus.

"You can stay, you old rascal," Greer replied, reaching over and ruffling his ears. "You'd just go slinking off in the shadows and listen anyway."

"Dang," Tori said, "you *do* know him."

"Better than he knows himself, sometimes," Greer laughed. "But we're not here to talk about Master McGregor's misadventures. You want to know why I've shown up on your doorstep."

"Not only that," Gemma said, "But how did you know to come to the lumberyard this morning?"

Greer smiled, "Now, if I had a mind to self-aggrandize like some yellow tomcats I know, I'd tell you my timely arrival was due to a vampiric superpower. Truthfully, luck was on our side. Ironweed Istra called me and told me his GNATS drone picked up the Strigoi girls going into the office."

Now that was an interesting development.

"Ironweed is watching Scrap's movements?" I asked.

"Yes," Greer said. "Chase asked him to put a GNATS unit on Mr. Andrews when he learned there was some . . . dissension in the family."

For once, I blessed Chase for doing something without talking to me.

"Are the drones going to keep watching him?" Tori asked anxiously.

Greer patted Tori's knee. The woman had beautiful hands with slender, elegant fingers. She wore a single gold signet ring set with a ruby the size of a dime on her left ring finger.

"Don't worry about your father," Greer told Tori. "The fairies will keep a close eye on him, and he'll be none the wiser."

Tori thanked her, visibly relaxing at the news that Scrap had more protection than a cloth bag around his neck. There had been no time yet for me to get Tori alone and find out how she was really doing, but if I had to guess, the answer would be, not good.

"Why did Ironweed call you?" I asked.

"He knew I was on the way to you with a package," Greer said. "Lucas would have delivered it to you himself, but he's on an errand in Istanbul."

An *errand* in Istanbul?

"What's the package?"

"Elder amulets," Greer said. "One for each of you, and wee ones for your rat and the little witch. The werecats don't need any extra protection beyond their own magic."

She reached into a leather pouch hanging at her waist and drew out the amulets, each one bound in the same kind of linen bag on a heavy thread cord that Gemma had described to us.

After Tori's description of the way Greer literally blew into the lumberyard office, I wasn't going to inquire into her magical credentials. I slipped the amulet over my neck. When the material touched my skin, a cool blanket of power wrapped around me.

"Why elder twigs?" I asked, putting my hand over the bag, which now rested above my heart.

"In Scotland," Greer said, "elder and rowan are used to ward off witchcraft and evil spells directed at you. Don't worry. It won't affect your powers. Either wood could be used under these circumstances. I happened to have a bit of elder on hand, and the amulets have to be made before the full moon, which will be Tuesday night. I saw no reason to waste them."

"How do the amulets work?" Mom asked, tucking the linen pouch in her blouse.

"The amulet will protect you outside of the ward guarding the shop," Greer said. "The Strigoi cannot mesmerize you so long as you're wearing the elder, or cloud your mind in any way. The amulet won't stop them coming after you claw and fang, but it will keep them from being stealthy about it."

I would have preferred a magic Easy button that would make Seraphina and Ioana go "poof," but beggars can't be choosers.

"Uh, Greer," Tori said, "not to be indelicate about this, but aren't you a vampire, too?"

The woman's green eyes sparkled with mirth. "Only if you believe that Bram Stoker nonsense. Not that Bram wasn't a most interesting man, but I am Fae, not some demon risen from the dead."

"But the girls said you aren't allowed to kill them." Tori said. "That you were their own kind."

Greer made a dismissive noise. "They should be so lucky as to be baobhan sith. Bram's novel and all the vampire myths it created have caused quite a lot of trouble among those of us who require the taking of energy to survive. Around 1900 there was a conclave of the various creatures—the Strigoi, the baobhan sith, the Incubi, and such. The meeting led to a peace accord. After all, if the humans were all trying to kill us, the least we could do was not help them."

Seemed reasonable.

Tori looked uncertain, so Greer helped her out. "You want to know if I drink blood to survive."

"Uh, yeah," Tori nodded, adding hastily, "no offense intended."

"None was taken. My ancestors used rather unrefined methods to gain the life force they needed. Traditionally we feed on the throats of young, male travelers. The hunger need not be addressed daily. Periodically I attend corporate conventions and spend a pleasant evening with an attendee. The next day, my companion remembers only the best parts of the evening."

"And the marks?" I asked.

"Are not on the neck."

From the hearth, Festus chuckled, which told me my interpretation of the remark was accurate—which also meant we were going to let that topic go.

"*Sooooo*," I said, "do you and Lucas work together at the DGI?"

Mom and Gemma exchanged glances. "Uh, honey, I think we're out of the loop here. How did you find out about the Grid and the DGI?"

First, the Mother Tree busted me, and now the moms were going to get their turn at bat.

I shared a somewhat abbreviated version of my excursion to Shevington to spy on Connor, which did win me a lecture from both moms, but then my mother said, in a small voice, "May I see the picture you took of my son?"

When I held my phone out to her, she took it and cradled the device in her hands like a priceless, fragile object. As she gazed at the screen, her face filled with light. "Oh, Gemma, look at him. He's so handsome."

Gemma put her arm around Mom's shoulder, and they leaned their heads together, staring in unison at the photo. "I never thought I'd see him again," Mom whispered. "My baby. He's a grown man now."

"And a fine man," Greer said. "I know Connor Endicott. Strong as the Mother Oak herself, but hands like an angel with the animals. You should be proud, Mrs. Hamilton."

Mom regarded her with shining eyes. "Kelly," she said. "Call me Kelly. And I *am* proud . . . of both of my children." She looked at me. "That was a sweet and incredibly stupid thing you did, young lady."

I shrugged, "You know me. A real multi-tasker."

Everyone cracked up at that.

"You gave Lucas a good fright," Greer said. "We were in Reykjavík when the Mother Oak told him to get to Shevington. The poor man had to jump three portals to make it in time."

"So you're a DGI agent, too?" I asked.

"In a manner of speaking," Greer said. "You wouldn't happen to watch a television program called *Scandal* would you?"

"Oh my *God*," Tori said. "Team Fitz or Team Jake?"

"Please," Greer said, "Jake might be a sociopath, but I'll take him any day over that milquetoast nitwit Fitz."

"Sister friend!" Tori declared, holding out her fist, which Greer bumped on cue.

Grinning, I said, "So you and Lucas fix things like Olivia Pope does?"

"We do," Greer said, "but Scottish vampire or not, I'm not half as scary as that woman."

Somehow, I doubted that.

Chapter Twenty-One

A little before 2 o'clock, Beau, Tori and I prepared to walk to the library for Linda's program, "The Haunting of Briar Hollow: Past and Present." Technically, we were leaving Gemma and Mom in charge. However, since my folks were huddled together looking at the picture I took of Connor, which had now been emailed to both their phones, Gemma was pretty much on her own.

"Hey, Mom," Tori said with barely disguised hope, "maybe I should stay and help you with the shop?"

"*Maybe* you should go to Linda's lecture like you said you would. There haven't been half a dozen people in here all morning. Don't worry about it."

When she asked the next question, Tori's words were more uncertain. "Are you sure you're alright? I mean . . . about . . . things."

"Honey," Gemma sighed, "I really don't have much choice right now. Your Daddy needs a few days to cool off, and so do I. It's good to know someone is keeping an eye on him."

Tori agreed, but as we stepped out the front door, I saw her cast a worried glance back at her mother.

"Hey, Beau," I said, "would you mind going ahead? We'll be right behind you."

"Of course," he said, bowing slightly. "I will reserve seats for you."

As I watched him walk away, I said to Tori, "How about we take the long way around?"

"Okay," she said, falling in beside me as we started down the sidewalk past Chase's shop to the corner.

"How are you doing, kiddo?" I asked, keeping my eyes forward.

I heard Tori swallow hard. "He won't even talk to me, Jinksy," she said, her voice breaking. "What if he really does want a divorce? I can't imagine us not being a family."

A lot of people might have offered some platitude about "you'll always be a family," but Tori and I shoot straight with each other. If her parents did divorce, nothing in her world would ever be the same again.

"I am so sorry, honey. You want to know what I think?"

"Always."

"I think Scrap is hurt and scared. Gemma cut him out of a huge part of her life for a really long time. He doesn't know anything about magic, and he's afraid to find out. You remember how I felt when I found out about my powers?"

Out of the corner of my eye, I saw her nod. "Yeah. You were seriously freaked out, but you were willing to *learn*. Dad won't even listen."

"You said yourself those girls were creepy."

"No," Tori corrected me. "I said they were creepy as *hell*. But if dad had let us, Mom and I could have explained."

"Could you really, Tori? Because I'm right in the middle of this and I don't understand how two dead girls rise from the grave and turn into those creatures. How do you know the explanation wouldn't have upset your Dad even more?"

"Yeah, you have a point."

We turned and headed down the side of the square where the Stone Hearth Pizzeria was located. As we approached Pete's door, we both fell silent, not taking up our conversation until we crossed the street.

"We have to find out what's going on with that guy," Tori said. "If I don't get a supreme with anchovies pretty soon, I'm going to expire."

Truer words were never spoken. Thinking your pizza man is in league with the dark side can put a serious crimp in a girl's food supply.

"It's on the to-do list," I said.

Before we reached the library, I stopped and caught Tori's arm. "Seriously, are you okay?"

"No," she said, with tears in her eyes, "but don't worry, my head's in the game."

"Tori," I said, "of all the things I'm worried about, your head not being in the game isn't one of them."

That had the opposite effect of what I intended. Two big tears rolled down her cheeks.

"Whoa, whoa, whoa. That was supposed to make you feel better, not turn the water works on."

Tori laughed. "I'm sorry," she said, wiping her eyes. "It does make me feel better. Lots."

Linda's talk drew a standing room only crowd. She took the attendees through the major stops on the weeks' ghost tours, giving the history of each location, complete with a PowerPoint presentation.

When I first met Linda, she was an incredibly stereotypical librarian complete with a graying bun. However, shortly after she began working with Beau on the festival, she'd turned up sporting a perky pageboy.

Now she was wearing dark jeans and a bright red sweater that made her look years younger. The transformation was remarkable, and I suspected it had something to do with trying to catch Beau's eye.

From what I could tell, he was oblivious to her interest, especially since he still considered himself to be a married man. I honestly didn't know if dating would even work for Beau given his changeable form, but at the very least, Linda was his first new friend outside our tight circle. With her extensive knowledge of the Civil War, I think talking to Linda made Beau feel less like a man out of time and place.

Even though I hadn't wanted to attend the lecture, Linda gave an interesting talk. She didn't come right out and overtly claim any of the local sites she discussed were *actually* haunted, but she spiced her comments with enough historical gossip to make a convincing argument for paranormal activity.

At the conclusion of her remarks, Linda said, "Those of you interested in touring the courthouse with us this evening can sign in at the desk. We'll be investigating the site of Mayor Howard McAlpin's alleged murder and attempting to make contact with his spirit."

A hand went up in the back.

"Yes, sir? Do you have a question?"

"Is it true that Mayor McAlpin's ghost only appears from the waist down?"

Linda deflected smoothly. "I haven't actually seen His Honor since he passed to the other side, so I'm as intrigued to discover the answer to that question as you are."

Another attendee raised her hand.

"Yes?"

"Do you think the Confederate officer will appear this evening?" the woman asked excitedly. "I want to see him as much as I want to see the levitating Twinkies."

Beside me, Beau cleared his throat in irritation. I couldn't say that I blamed him. I wouldn't like being compared to a cream-filled pastry either.

"He doesn't keep a schedule," Linda said, "but you're more

than welcome to camp out near the monument all week to try to get a glimpse of him."

"And the Twinkies?"

"That incident occurred in the corner grocery. The proprietors are hosting an investigation on the premises Thursday night. I hope we'll see you there."

"Oh, you will," the woman said earnestly, making a note on the legal pad in her lap.

Linda wrapped things up, and we went over to congratulate her on the presentation before joining Beau on the sidewalk for the walk back to the store.

As we crossed the courthouse lawn, I asked Beau, "Have you been able to coach Howie into a full manifestation yet?"

"His Honor is an amazingly slow study," Beau said crossly. "At best we have progressed slightly north of his belt buckle."

Tori snickered but didn't say anything.

"Are you going to the tour tonight?" I asked him.

"Yes, but in corporeal form. Howard was quite adamant that the courthouse interior is his exclusive territory. I assured him I would not dream of perpetrating an encroachment."

The way he said that made Tori and I both crack up. Beau made no bones about Howard being a thorn in his side.

The rest of the afternoon passed uneventfully. Greer told us she had to "keep an appointment in Edinburgh" but would return in a few hours.

"You're coming back?" I asked.

"I am. The DGI higher-ups think it's a good idea for either Lucas or myself to be on site as much as possible until this issue with the Strigoi is settled."

Lucas. On site. Meaning he and Chase would have to interact. Oh. Joy.

"So does that mean Lucas will be here later, too?" I asked, trying not to sound interested, and failing, judging from the way Greer grinned at me.

"He will, but I doubt he will arrive before morning. Do try to avoid getting into too much hot water in the next few hours."

Yeah. No guarantees on that one.

We had a trickle of customers, probably because a lot of people had jobs to get to on Monday morning. The diehard ghost hunters, on the other hand, seemed to be in town for the duration. The courthouse tour was scheduled to begin at dusk, and the building would stay open until midnight. We planned to keep the store open as well, in case any of the paranormal groupies came out of the ghost hunt with a case of the munchies.

That evening, Beau left a few minutes early to see if Linda needed any help. As he started for the door, I said, "Do you have your cell phone with you?"

"Yes," he said, patting his pocket. "Miss Tori has instructed me quite well in the use of the camera and the art of sending a text message. If anything of interest occurs during the tour, I will let you know."

As it turned out, we didn't need Beau's newly acquired text messaging skills to know something major happened. About an hour into the tour, three women ran screaming out the front door of the courthouse as the words, "ride to the sound of the guns," flashed on the screen of my phone.

"'Ride to the sound of the guns?'" Tori said. "What does that mean?"

"It's cavalry speak for 'get to the scene of the battle,'" Dad said.

Lord. Now what?

Tori and I came out the front door of the store in time to see more people streaming out of the courthouse. The tour must have drawn a bigger crowd than I realized. I spotted Beau standing off to one side and steered for him.

"Beau," I said, "what happened?"

Drawing us farther away from the milling tourists, Beau said in a low voice, "I fear I underestimated Mayor McAlpin's abilities."

"So more than half of him showed up?" Tori asked.

"Indeed. The good mayor strolled directly into his office as a full-body apparition, moved his desk chair, and actually spoke to one of the participants."

"He *what?*" I said. "How is that even possible?"

"I do not know," Beau said. "In an effort to enhance the ambiance, the lights were not on in the room at the time. Linda was delivering a somewhat embellished version of the details of Howard's murder. As she described the pool of blood that formed under his desk, Howard moved through the crowd."

I fought the urge to put my head in my hands. "What did the people do?"

"It has been my experience that living souls curious to interact with the dead, flee rather quickly when actually afforded the opportunity to do so. Three women immediately fled the vicinity, while others backed away still attempting to capture photographic evidence of the event."

"Do you think anyone got a good picture?" Tori asked.

"It is a distinct possibility."

"How did you get everyone out of there?" I asked.

Beau smiled. "I merely suggested to Linda that the festival committee is not insured against the personal injury of participants, especially by potentially dangerous paranormal entities. For the safety of those present, retreat was the better part of valor."

"*You,*" I said, "are a genius."

Inclining his head in thanks, Beau said, "Hardly, but the ruse worked. Now, we need to speak with Howard immediately and get to the bottom of this."

Before we could move, Linda threaded her way through the excited crowd and joined us. "Beau, did you see him?"

Trying to play down the incident, Beau said, "I was standing toward the back of the room, but I did see . . . something."

"Something?!" Linda exclaimed. "It was Howard McAlpin plain as day. I'd know him anywhere!"

Beau hedged diplomatically. "I'm afraid I did not have the pleasure of the gentleman's acquaintance in life."

"Oh, trust me," Linda said, "knowing Howard was no pleasure. But I'm telling you, that was him. I have to see if anyone got a picture for the website. This is fantastic!"

We watched her wade back into the crowd, calling out, "Did anyone get a photo of the manifestation? If so, we'd like to post it on the festival website immediately."

"Quick," I said, "inside while no one is looking. We need to have a talk with the *manifestation*."

I was pretty sure everyone outside was too preoccupied with checking their phones and cameras for pictures of Howard to notice when we ducked in the door, but we were careful not to run into anyone *inside* either.

We found Howard in his office looking inordinately pleased with himself and altogether too solid. As the three of us walked into the room, he said, "See there, Longworth? You're not the only professional spook in Briar Hollow."

"Can it, Howie," I said. "This is not a contest. You agreed to abide by the rules. You were supposed to make a vague and *brief* appearance, not talk to the living!"

McAlpin frowned. "All I did was ask the woman to step out of the way, and I *might* have brushed her arm."

"You *touched* her?"

"Potentially, but I'm not prepared to confirm that detail at this time."

Once a politician, always a politician.

"Show me what you did," I ordered.

Somewhat reluctantly, Howard tapped me on the arm. His fingers were cold, but the pressure was unmistakable.

"And you just *stood* here in a room full of people and let yourself be seen like this?" I asked. "Seriously?"

"I did no such thing. When I realized I was not necessarily in control of my . . . output, I slipped into the file room."

"And no one followed you?"

"The door is locked, and I can still go through walls," he said. "Give me some credit here, Miss Hamilton. I'm not an amateur."

"That's exactly what you are," I said, looking over to Beau. "Something's not right here. There is no way Howie has the energy to appear with this much coherence."

"Now see here!" McAlpin protested. "I do not appreciate the implication that I am normally incoherent."

The last thing I wanted to do was listen to a wounded politico's post-mortem ego issues. "Howie, if you know what's good for you, you'll fade your butt right on out of here."

"Fine, I have more important matters to attend to anyway."

And . . . he just stood there.

"Well?" I said. "Go, already."

Looking completely confused, Howie said, "I, uh, I'm trying. It's not working."

Chapter Twenty-Two

We couldn't leave Howie in the mayor's office. Someone might see him, and we had no idea if he'd fade to invisibility when the sun came up. A ghost walking around the courthouse in broad daylight would put Briar Hollow more on the "paranormal map" than we'd planned.

But if we wanted to get him out of the building and over to the store, we had to find a way to cover up his pale, glowing form.

"Can a ghost wear clothes?" Tori asked, eyeing Howie as he rifled through the drawers of the current mayor's desk. "I mean, other than the ones he was buried in?"

Beau suggested a different solution. "We could put the Amulet of the Phoenix on Howard. As I have greater control over my spectral form, I should be able to quite easily cross the street undetected."

There was *no way* I was going to agree to that. For one thing, I was fairly certain he'd shoot his mouth off and say something stupid before we reached our destination. There was also a real risk that we might not be able to get the amulet back.

"Besides," I said, "for all you know, you have the same problem he does. It might not even work."

"Then let us test that hypothesis," Beau said. He pulled the amulet over his head and held it out to me.

As soon as I took the artifact, Beau reverted to ghost form, but he was even more solid than Howie. For the first time since I met him, Beau stood before us in full, albeit faded, color.

"*Oh*. Not good," Tori said. "Not good at all."

"Not necessarily," Beau said. "I would still stand a far greater chance of passing casual human inspection than Howard."

That's when I put my foot down.

"No," I said. "You're not giving him the amulet, and that's final."

My stubborn stance confused Beau, but Tori realized where I was coming from immediately. If I couldn't have Myrtle in my life, I would have Beau, and I would *not* risk his corporeal existence for the likes of Howard McAlpin.

As a ghost, Howie rated somewhere on the scale between bumbling idiot and outright moron, but in the world of the living? He specialized in corrupt, small-town politics.

"Beau," Tori said softly, "put the amulet back on. Jinksy can't take you being all self-sacrificing."

When he took the amulet from me and returned to what we now considered "normal," Beau put his hand on my shoulder. I covered it with my own.

"Sorry," I said. "Your idea probably would have worked, but you're too important to me, Beau. We have to find another way."

"I understand," Beau said, "and I am deeply touched."

During this whole conversation, Howard had been ignoring us completely. He's never shown much of an attention span for any topic but himself. As we watched, he flipped through the pages of the living mayor's notebook.

"This guy is a weakling," Howie grumped. "I would never have let the city council get away with trying to tell me what to do."

"Isn't it the city council's *job* to tell the mayor what to do?" I asked.

"Not in *my* administration, it wasn't," Howie declared. "As soon as the so-called mayor gets here tomorrow, I'm having a talk with him."

"Don't get used to being like this, Howie," I warned. "We're going to find a way to put you back."

"Oh, *right*," the mayor snapped. "Mr. I-Fought-in-the-Civil-War gets to be solid, but I'm supposed to wander around like half a mannequin for the rest of my afterlife? I don't think so. And *stop* calling me 'Howie.'"

"I'll call you anything I want, *Howie*," I snapped. "If you keep giving me lip, I'll see to it that you don't *have* an afterlife."

"You can't do that," he blustered, but I heard the note of doubt in his voice and used it.

"Do you really want to find out?" I asked, raising my hands to give him the impression I was about to zap him with some kind of super witch magic.

You'd be surprised how fast a politician can issue a retraction when he's faced with potential oblivion.

"Now, now," Howie said, pushing the desk chair back until it hit the wall. "There's no need to overreact. We're merely exploring options here."

"You haven't seen me overreact," I said. "Now shut up while we figure out what to do with you."

Since I had firmly ruled out using the amulet, a disguise seemed like the best option. Tori went off scavenging and came back with a jumpsuit and cap she found in a custodian's closet.

"I am *not* putting that filthy thing on," Howard said.

"Yes, you are," I shot back, raising my hands again. "Don't make me tell you twice."

Even though I heard him mutter something about witches waking up on the wrong side of the broom, Howie took the jumpsuit and put it on. To our great relief, it stayed on.

"I don't get it," Tori said. "How can he still walk through walls, but manage to wear clothes?"

Neither Beau nor I had an answer, and we didn't have time to worry about it.

"Put the hat on," I said, "and let's get out of here."

Howie jammed the purloined cap on his head. "Do I look as ridiculous as I feel?" he groused.

"Turn your collar up," I said. "We need to hide as much of your face as possible."

Even when he did as he was told, Howie still glowed in the dark.

"Keep your hands in your pockets," I ordered. "And keep your head down."

We took the stairs at the end of the building opposite the Confederate monument. Linda and the tour participants—at least the ones we could see—were still gathered there.

Once outside the door, we stood in the shadows long enough to surveil that side of the square and then we made a break for it, sprinting across the lawn and diving behind the dumpster left over from the dance.

"Did anybody see us?" I whispered.

"I don't think so," Tori said, "but I vote for taking the alleys around to the back of the shop."

That route took longer, but we managed to get behind our building undetected. Unfortunately, when I peeked in the back door, the espresso bar was full of hyper-excited ghost hunters.

Good for business. Bad for stealth.

"Now what?" I asked.

Tori pointed up. The lights were on in Chase's apartment. Going through his place to get to the lair was the only answer.

I took out my cell phone and dialed Chase's number. He answered with a cautious, "Hi."

As briefly as I could, I outlined what we were dealing with.

"I'll be right down to let you in," he said.

In seconds the back door opened and we all filed into the cobbler shop.

Howie instantly tossed the cap to one side and peeled off the jumpsuit, making a show of brushing himself off like he'd been exposed to some deadly contagion.

"Wow," Chase said, "you weren't kidding. He's actually knocking dust off his sleeves."

"Yeah," I said. "His Honor is way too solid for my tastes. Where's Festus?"

"The Dirty Claw," Chase said. "He's meeting with Merle, Earl, and Furl."

"Red Dot?"

"No. He's trying to find out if the Registry has any information on Seraphina and Ioana . . . "

He paused, a look of panic coming into his eyes.

"It's okay," I said. "I know you asked Ironweed to put a GNATS unit on the lumberyard. Thank you. If Greer hadn't gotten there, I don't know what would have happened to Tori's father."

Still looking guarded, Chase asked, "You're not mad at me?"

"No. I'm grateful. Truly."

Chase let out the breath he'd been holding. "You're welcome. I'm glad Scrap is okay. Just as soon as Dad gets back, we'll let you know what he found out."

His cautious manner melted away the lingering traces of my anger. I'd made my point. It was time to let Chase in out of the cold.

"Why don't you just come hang out in the lair?" I suggested. "It's easier when you're in the middle of things with the rest of us."

The poor man looked so relieved, I felt genuinely sorry for what he'd been through over the last couple of days, no matter how well deserved.

"I'd like that," Chase said. "I've missed . . . being in the middle of things."

When he smiled at me, I answered him with one of my own. Behind Chase's back, Tori gave me the thumbs up. As we followed Chase down to the basement, she leaned toward me and said, "Looking better on that Miss Congeniality thing there, Jinksy."

"Zip it," I ordered, but I was grinning when I said it.

As I descended the first few steps, the familiar sense of passing into the fairy mound came over me. We found ourselves in a long corridor, which opened into the stacks in our basement a few feet away from the lair.

"Sit down, Mr. Mayor," I said as we walked into the room, "and don't get into any trouble."

Beau went immediately to the shelves and started pulling down volumes. "I will endeavor to find an explanation for Howard's new found solidity, but Barnaby and Moira may have to be consulted."

"Let's put that off until we can talk to Greer and Lucas," I said. "Barnaby and Moira have their hands full with the merfolk migration. We can keep Howie stashed down here out of sight."

That elicited more protest from the mayor. "What am I supposed to do to entertain myself while you people play with magic?"

"How do you entertain yourself at the courthouse?"

"I spend the days collecting data."

"Meaning?"

"Attending meetings, listening to private conversations, reading correspondence..."

"Snooping," I said. "We'll put a soap opera on for you to watch. Now hush."

Chase, who had been quiet the whole time, said, "I'll watch him. You play cards, Howie?"

The mayor's eyes lit up. "For money?"

Apparently, Howie never heard "shrouds have no pockets" or even "you can't take it with you."

"Sure," Chase said. "Do you have any money?"

"Uh, no, but if you'll spot me, I'm good for it."

Chase rolled his eyes. "No problem. Five card stud, penny ante."

Howie made a face. "Can't we take the stakes a little higher?"

"We cannot," Chase said, opening one of the desk drawers and taking out a deck of cards. He pitched them at Howie who caught the box in mid-air. "But I'll let you deal."

I caught Chase's eye and mouthed, "Thank you."

"No problem," he mouthed back.

Tori and I left Chase and Beau in charge of our reluctant guest and went upstairs. The moms hid their surprise when we came through the basement door. Even though it was almost midnight, the espresso bar was full of patrons engaged in lively discussion.

"How'd you get in the basement?" Mom asked when Tori and I stepped behind the bar.

"Through the cobbler shop," I answered. "We have a visitor we need to keep incognito."

"Who?" Mom asked.

"The late mayor all these people just saw over at the courthouse. He's having a little trouble controlling his manifestation."

"How much trouble?" Gemma asked.

"He's sitting downstairs dealing cards with Chase right now."

Her eyes widened. "He can touch the cards?"

"Oh," Tori said, "it's better than that. He touched one of the people on the ghost tour."

Before we could explain more, the front door of the shop burst open, and the two guys from the Bigfoot hunting group who bought the t-shirts from me charged in.

"We've got ghosts on video," one of them yelled. "They're playing baseball! We've already uploaded it to YouTube. Y'all have *got* to see this."

A dozen people whipped out iPhones while others crowded around the laptop the second guy opened and put down on one of the tables. The four of us pushed through the crowd to get a better view of the screen.

The clip was about 90 seconds in duration. It showed the baseball diamond at Briar Hollow High. Both teams from the cemetery were engaged in a game, with Hiram on the mound and one of the gingham grannies at bat.

Every single one of the spirits was fully formed and clearly visible. Hiram let loose with a fastball. The granny's bat connected. She hitched up her skirts and ran for first base. One of the infielders sent the ball sailing to the third baseman, who launched it toward Duke in hopes of tagging the hairdresser out as she trotted toward home.

As we watched, she looked up, realized they were being filmed, and let out a scream. Duke whirled, spotted the cameraman, bared his teeth and charged. The image started to wobble. One of the boys screamed, "Run, run!" Then everything went black.

The espresso bar fell completely silent, then a lone voice said, "Why'd you stop filming?"

"Wouldn't you?" the guy gasped. "That hellhound charged

right at us! He was like the freaking Hound of the Baskervilles or something."

At that, the shop erupted.

Tori leaned in and whispered in my ear, "Status revision, Jinksy."

"What do you mean?" I whispered back."

"Houston," she said, "we have a *big* problem."

Chapter Twenty-Three

Although I didn't stick around for the whole thing, Tori later described the Monday morning follow-up committee meeting as "tripping." George and Irma pounded on the front door before 7 a.m. and started babbling excitedly the instant I let them in.

"Can you *believe* how many people we had this weekend?" Irma enthused. "And what happened at the courthouse last night?! How did we get so lucky? I never thought Howard McAlpin was much of a mayor, but he certainly came through for us this time. And now the YouTube video! I swear, the deceased citizens of this town are showing exceptional civic pride. I just *know* they've come back from the other side to help us."

Before I could answer, Linda charged through the door. "We've had so many viewers, the festival website crashed," she announced enthusiastically. "Isn't that *fantastic*?!"

"Uh, Linda," Tori said, "'crashed' is a bad thing."

"Not when the ghost baseball video has had more than a million views on YouTube," she said proudly. "We're a virus."

Smothering a grin, Tori said, "I think you mean we've gone viral.'"

"Viral. Bacterial. Who cares? The point is, everyone is talking about Briar Hollow!"

So much for damage control.

"There's not a hotel room to be had in town," Linda went on. "All the ones in Cotterville are booked, too. Ghost hunters are pouring in from all over the state. Maybe the country! I think we need to revise the festival agenda and have a gathering every night on the courthouse square between now and Halloween."

"That's a wonderful idea!" Irma said, opening her bulging portfolio. "Let's see what we can pull together."

As other committee members came in and joined the planning, Tori and I quietly retreated to the back of the shop. "We have to get control of this situation," I said, "and make sure no more videos go up on YouTube."

Tori took out her iPhone and found the incriminating footage. She scrolled through the comments with her thumb. "It may not be quite as bad as we think. The skeptics are betting even money the whole thing is a fraud."

From somewhere near my knee, a quiet voice said, "Mistress, the Red Headed Woman has returned."

I almost jumped out of my skin. While I appreciated Darby using his powers of invisibility, the lack of an early warning system was going to result in me having a heart attack one of these days.

"Thank you, Darby," I whispered. "Tell her I'll be right down."

Tori looked out at the committee. "Sooner or later Irma will notice if we're both gone, especially since Chase and Beau aren't here either."

"Good point. Why don't you wade back in there? I'll go down and send Chase up while I talk to Greer."

"Oh joy," Tori sighed. "I'll try not to let them get too carried away."

"Yeah, good luck with that," I said, quietly easing the door to the basement open and slipping through.

Downstairs, I found Howard stretched out snoring on one of the sofas. Greer, Chase, Beau, and Festus were all sitting around the table, and Glory was literally jumping back and forth between two books on the desk.

"How are things upstairs?" Chase asked as I pulled out a chair for myself.

"Today is your lucky day because you get to find out for yourself. We can't all ditch the meeting. Time for you to get up there."

He groaned. "What have I missed so far?"

"They're talking about having a gathering on the courthouse every night between now and Halloween."

"You know," he said thoughtfully, "that could actually be a good thing for us. If the crowd is concentrated on the square, they'll be easier to watch."

"True, but what do we do about stragglers like those two guys who shot the video? They were supposed to be going on the courthouse tour and decided to wander off on their own."

"Actually," Festus said, "that's what we've been talking about. What would you think about asking Ironweed to put more GNATS units in town? He can pipe the video feed into our tablets so we can keep an eye on people. We should have enough manpower for that."

From the desk, Glory shouted through her megaphone. "Rodney and I can help if you put the picture on our drive-in movie screen."

"Okay," I said. "Surveillance is covered. No more excuses, Chase. Run along to the committee meeting now."

He raised his eyebrows. "*Run along?*"

I made a shooing gesture with my hand. "Have fun."

His footsteps on the stairs struck the cadence of a condemned man climbing the gallows.

After we heard the door open and close, I caught Festus looking at me as he lazily wagged his tail back and forth."

"What?"

"Glad you lightened up on the boy," he said. "I'm tired of having to listen to him. Disrupted my nap time."

"All 23.5 hours of it?"

Festus raised one paw and gave it a disdainful lick. "I'll have you know I was awake a full 22 hours yesterday."

"How grueling for you," I said with mock sympathy. "Beau, have you made any progress on figuring out why the spirits are suddenly so much stronger?"

Just then, a gurgling snore emanated from the sofa.

"No," he said, "nor have I been able to divine why Mayor McAlpin seems to be able to sleep—if you will pardon the pun—like the dead. I have spent most of my time on this earth in non-corporeal form and never experienced sleep. I believe I should pay a visit to my compatriots in the cemetery and ascertain the facts of the last 36 hours from their perspective."

That confused me. The baseball game captured on the video happened right around midnight, now roughly 7.5 hours ago.

"Why the last 36 hours? Isn't that going back too far."

Greer answered. "Before His Honor, the Mayor, decided to take a nap, he told us he was watching out one of the courthouse windows when the Ionescu family walked onto the lawn. He said he saw waves of energy emanating from the individual Strigoi that radiated across the square. Beau and I believe that surge from the massed Strigoi may have been sufficient to supercharge any spectral form present on the square."

"You make them sound almost radioactive," I said. "Does it take that much energy to keep a Strigoi up and running?"

"Not normally," Greer said, "but this clan is a bit unique.

They've been feeding themselves on pure electricity for generations. It seems plausible to me that their metabolisms could have become altered over the last couple of centuries. My own kind used to rip out throats. Now we're tidier and more efficient in our feeding habits."

Okay. Grossly detailed TMI there, but overall the explanation made sense and accounted for how Beau had picked up a dose of the extra energy as well.

"Why did Beau's ghost energy seem stronger than Howie's after they were both exposed to the Strigoi?"

"Again, we have only a theory," Greer replied, "but Colonel Longworth has been dead longer and is more skilled at manifestation thus his form better assimilated and distributed the influx of energy."

If they were right, the cemetery ghosts would have had to be present on the courthouse square last night. "So the ghosts caught on video playing baseball sneaked into town?"

"Yes," Beau said, "that is what I suspect. I think their curiosity about the event clouded their judgment. At any rate, that is the question I wish to put to them at the cemetery."

"How are you planning to get there?"

"Before your father retired for the evening," Beau said, "he volunteered to drive me. He told me when I was ready to leave to 'give him a shout.'"

"Hold on," I said. "If Mom is actually getting some rest, I don't want her to wake up. Let me send him a text."

Dad answered my message immediately. "Your Mom is sleeping. Will slip out and meet Beau out back."

"Then I am off," Beau said.

"Wait," Festus interrupted. "If you go upstairs and Irma spots you, you're sunk. Go through our place. Chase told me you came that way last night."

"Indeed we did," Beau said, "and that is an excellent plan.

I do not relish the idea of being dragooned into more festival planning."

After Beau left, Greer said, "I'll be on hand today. What may I do to help?"

"I really need you to stay here and make sure Howie over there doesn't cause any problems," I said. "Tori and I want to go to the junkyard as soon as the meeting breaks up so we can check out the car Seraphina and Ioana died in."

"*Temporarily* died," Festus said.

"Merle, Earl, and Furl didn't have any ideas about all of this?" I asked.

"They're working on it. I told them what I really want to know is how those girls wound up the way they are now."

That made two of us.

JEFF PARKED his pickup outside the cemetery wall. He and Beau silently watched small knots of tourists walking among the gravestones.

"This," Beau said, "is an unexpected development."

"Guess we should have figured people looking for ghosts would come out here, but I would have thought they'd come after dark."

"I suspect they will," Beau said, opening his door, "which is all the more reason we must still attempt to ascertain the lay of the land."

Jeff got out on his side."How do you want to play this?"

"We should wander among the gravestones as if we are conducting research. If any of my friends are visible in the daylight, they will find a way to contact me. Due to their experiences interacting with the world of the living, I believe they would know to secret themselves in some way."

Once inside the grounds, the two men strolled slowly

through the plots, occasionally pausing to gaze down at a monument. The passersby had no idea Beau was introducing Jeff to his spectral friends through their tombstones.

As they walked, Jeff said, "This must all be one wild ride for you, Beau."

The colonel smiled. "I have never been known to select tame horses. Sampson, my mount on the day of my demise, was a high stepper.'"

"What happened to him after you died?"

"I am most gratified to report that Chase's grandfather, James McGregor, took Sampson from the battlefield. I only learned of this recently, but James told me Sampson died peacefully of old age in a warm barn."

Beau's voice broke on those last words, and he looked away to hide the tears that filled his eyes.

Jeff let the colonel collect himself, and then asked casually, "Done any riding since you've been . . . back?"

"I have not had the pleasure."

"If you'd like to get back in the saddle, a friend of mine from high school runs a horse farm between here and Cotterville. We could take a drive out there soon as things calm down. That is, if you're interested."

"Most interested, and most grateful for your kindness."

During their conversation, the men worked their way to the far end of the cemetery near the woods. Beau paused in front of a tall monument, appearing to look up at the inscription when in fact, he was scanning the treeline for movement.

"There, by that big hickory fifty yards in a straight line from my nose. Do you see him?"

Jeff's eyes tracked the course Beau described. "I'll be damned. Is that a dog?"

"It is. His name is Duke. I imagine the rest of the spirits are hiding out there under deep cover."

Glancing over his shoulder, Jeff said, "You go in and talk to them. I'll keep a look out here, and if any of these people start getting too close, I'll distract them best I can. Send me a text message when you're ready to come out and I'll let you know if the coast is clear."

Beau moved swiftly through the underbrush until he was sure he could no longer be seen from the graveyard. "Duke!" he called. "Here, boy!"

The ghostly coonhound obediently trotted out of the woods and jumped up to greet Beau, resting his forepaws on the colonel's chest and licking his face enthusiastically.

"You've been waiting a long time to do that, haven't you boy?" Beau chuckled." I'm glad to see you, too. Now, get down."

Duke obediently sat in front of Beau, his tail lashing back in forth in the leaves.

"Where are the others, boy? Can you take me to them?"

The dog instantly jumped up and plunged deeper into the woods, occasionally looking over his shoulder to make sure Beau was following. After 200 yards or so, Duke drew up outside a small culvert with thick brush choking the entrance.

"Colonel Longworth?" a woman's voice called out. "Is that you?"

Straining to see through the brush, Beau spotted Susie Miller. "Yes. Stay there, I'll come to you."

With some effort, he pushed the limbs aside and stepped into the culvert, finding both baseball teams in hiding and clearly visible in the daylight. All the spirits started talking at once, but Beau held up his hand. "Can one of you please supply me with the narrative? I cannot understand your meaning when you all speak at once."

Hiram Folger stepped forward. "Afternoon, Beauregard. Reckon us getting caught like that at the ballfield stirred up a peck of trouble, didn't it?"

"I fear it did, Hiram. The young men who saw you there

recorded a brief portion of your game with a motion picture camera. It has now been seen by far more people than you might be able to conceive. Can you tell me what happened?"

Hiram explained that the cemetery ghosts felt left out of the festival even though they would be supporting the event throughout the week with their appearances.

"We didn't think it would hurt to come to the opening night so long as we stayed invisible," Hiram said. "But then that group of people showed up, and all the electrical stuff started going haywire. We all felt the energy move through us, and some of us blipped into sight for a second or two. That seemed like a pretty good cue to skedaddle. On our way out of town, we saw the baseball diamond. It was just too big a temptation to play on a real field. Couple of us came back and got our gear. We waited until almost midnight thinking nobody would be awake. We didn't count on those two fellers catching us."

"Did you realize how visible you had become?"

"We knew we were all kind of extra juiced up. but we figured it was because we were having fun and enjoying the game. Soon as we saw the fellers with the cameras, Duke chased'em off and we high-tailed it on back out here. When the sun started coming up and we weren't fading, we reckoned we ought to get out of sight."

"Most prudent of you," Beau said. "The cemetery is filled with curiosity seekers as we speak. You must stay here as long as you cannot control your level of visibility."

"If it helps any," Hiram said, "we think it's starting to wear off a little bit. We're not as solid as we were this morning, especially the younger ones."

"That is exceptionally good news. Do not return to the cemetery until you are quite restored to normal, and do not make any of your scheduled appearances unless you receive confirmation from me."

"What about the tour tonight?"

"That," Beau said, "is my concern as it is to be on the very battlefield where I lost my life. I will come up with something sufficiently intriguing to satisfy the people in attendance, but not as damning as what happening at the ballfield."

"We're awful sorry, Beauregard. We didn't mean to cause any trouble."

Around him, the other ghosts mumbled their apologies as well.

"It is alright, dear friends. You could not have anticipated what occurred on the square. We will set this to rights, but we must be more cautious as we move forward. I cannot stress this enough. No one is to attempt a manifestation without explicit instructions from me. Do you all understand?"

Everyone in the group promised. As Beau started to leave, Duke fell in beside him. "No, boy. You have to stay here."

Duke looked up at him and whined.

"None of that. Soldier on, old boy. We will have a fine game of catch as soon as this is all sorted out. I'll even give you a special treat."

Duke cocked his head to one side when he heard the word "treat."

Beau reached into his shirt and showed the dog the Amulet of the Phoenix.

"If you're a good boy, I'll let you wear this on your collar long enough to have a dish of ice cream from an establishment called the Dairy Queen."

He wasn't sure if Duke understood the words "ice cream" or "Dairy Queen," but the dog instantly laid down in the leaves and didn't try to follow as Beau walked away.

At the end of the woods, Beau took out his phone and sent Jeff a text. "All clear?"

"Yep," Jeff texted back, "come ahead."

The two men reunited at the base of the white marble obelisk marking Beau's grave.

"This is some tombstone you've got here," Jeff said, craning his neck back to examine the top of the column.

"My wife's doing. I'm afraid she possessed a rather inflated opinion of me."

"Lots worse fates a man can face in life than having a wife who thinks well of him."

"Indeed. Were things quiet here in my absence?"

"Oh," Jeff said, "I don't know about that. I spoke with a group out of Charlotte. They heard about what happened last night and packed up all their gear and drove up here today. They're doing a full-scale investigation in the graveyard tonight. All kinds of infrared cameras, some gizmo called a 'spirit box,' and a bunch of K2 meters, whatever the hell that is."

"Your daughter is not going to be amused by this information," Beau said, as they both got back in the truck.

"You know, Beau," Jeff said as he turned the key in the ignition, "Jinx told me you've got kind of a talent for understatement. She's not wrong about that."

Chapter Twenty-Four

Dad knows me pretty well. While I wasn't sure any of those spook-detecting gizmos the people in the cemetery told him about *worked*, the chance that they *might* didn't bode well for our containment efforts.

I *was*, however, relieved to learn that the cemetery ghosts believed they were slowly fading back to normal. For his part, the Honorable Howard McAlpin stoutly denied that any such thing was happening to *him*. In life, I doubt the mayor ever had a self-aware moment, but his craving for power certainly transcended death.

Admitting to a waning of his newfound energy was not on the late mayor's current agenda. Sitting on the sofa complaining that he had "important work to do" and railing against "being denied free access to his sphere of influence," however, were major line items.

Putting all of his vehement denials aside, I thought Howie was getting more transparent by the hour. Beau agreed, but to test his perception, he briefly took off his amulet and did a self-color check. In spectral form, Beau's deep maroon vest now registered pink pale. Progress.

With Greer on-site to deal with anything magically unknown that might crop up, and the moms and my dad watching the store, Tori and I felt safe enough to go in search of the wrecked car.

Murph Lawson's junkyard lay hidden from view down a dusty dirt road three or four miles outside of town. When we pulled up in front of the shack that did double duty as the office and Murph's home, the proprietor himself was sitting on the front porch in a well-worn recliner held together mostly with duct tape.

That image was picturesque enough, but he also had a double-barreled 12-gauge shotgun balanced over his lap.

"Don't care what you ladies are sellin'," he called out, "I don't want none. And me and the Lord are on good speaking terms, so if you're here to witness, don't."

"We're not selling or preaching, Murph," I yelled back. "I'm Kelly Hamilton's daughter, Jinx."

Murph stood stiffly on arthritic knees and propped his shotgun against the porch railing. Hiking up his pants, he limped down and peered into my face. "Yep. You look like her. You here to see the wreck?"

I wanted to ask how often my mother had been out there, but then decided just as quickly I really didn't want to know.

"Yes, sir."

Murph scrutinized Tori. "Who's that?"

"My best friend."

"That hair color ain't natural."

Since Tori's spiked blond locks currently featured orange and black highlights in honor of Halloween, Murph's assessment was both unnecessary and incredibly obvious.

"No, sir," Tori grinned, "it's not. Want me to do your hair the same way?"

At that, Murph cackled and slid his greasy John Deere tractor cap up and back revealing a perfectly bald scalp.

"Reckon you'd have to use spray paint, missy. Car's all the way in the back corner. Veer right when you walk through the gate there and follow the trail. Be careful not to get yourselves hurt. Ain't got no insurance and I don't aim to be getting stuck with medical bills."

We thanked him and set out in search of the wreck. Mom told us that morning that we'd be looking for a red 1975 Toyota Corolla. Without the color, we'd never have figured out the model of the mangled hunk of metal overgrown with weeds wedged against the back fence.

"Is that it?" Tori asked in a stunned tone of voice.

"It must be. Mom said it went over the shoulder and down into a ravine."

"That thing looks like a giant crushed it up and used it for a spitball. No wonder the Ionescus are bitter. So, how do you want to do this?"

"Same as usual. I touch the car and let my psychometry kick in. You pull me out if I get in trouble."

Tori and I have experienced some mild degree of telepathy on a daily basis after using blood magic against Brenna Sinclair, but when I'm using my psychometry to read an object, the ability is much stronger. I rely on being able to call out to Tori to help me break the connection during these encounters. She's my safety valve.

We both waded through the weeds around the car. I couldn't reach what was left of the driver's window, so I decided to lay my hand on the back fender, now located under the door handle. I was pretty sure the car had been a coupe, but it was hard to tell.

As I stepped forward, I tripped on something and Tori reached to steady me. Our hands hit the car at the same moment and reality melted. One minute we had been standing in the junkyard and the next we were sitting in the backseat of the Corolla listening to a pelting rain hitting the windows.

The driver of the car did a very Eighties hair toss and said, "Kelly and Gemma will never make the cheerleading squad, Jo Anne. Quit worrying. They're nobodies."

Tori looked at me with horror. "Jinksy, what the *hell*?"

"Sorry," I said. "When you touched my hand, I guess my psychometry pulled you into the vision as well."

"You *guess*?"

"Lighten up," I groused, "it's a work in progress."

"Those two can't hear us, right?" Tori asked, leaning forward to get a better look at Seraphina behind the wheel. "Dear Lord, get a load of that baby blue eyeshadow."

"No on the hearing us. And yuck on the eye shadow."

"So we just sit here and . . . what?" Tori asked. "Go over the cliff with them?"

"Pretty much."

"You do realize that if we get into trouble in here there's nobody to pull us out?"

"I didn't *plan* this, Tori. We have to wing it. Now, hush so we can hear what they're talking about."

If we expected vapid cheerleader/mean girl dialogue to be illuminating in any way, we were wrong. That morning, Seraphina and Ioana had been two girls calling themselves Sally Beth and Jo Anne to fit in. They were engaged in trading lively gossip and complimenting each other's hair when the car suddenly skidded toward the shoulder. Seraphina fought to right the vehicle, but over-corrected.

Tori and I went from sitting upright in the backseat to tumbling inside the rolling car as it plunged through the guardrail and into the ravine. Ioana screamed and I saw her reach for Seraphina, who clasped her hand a second before the vehicle hit the rocks and bounced drunkenly.

The impact knocked the breath from my lungs. Tori slammed into me and I caught hold of her, trying to minimize the beating we were both taking. Then, as quickly as the whole thing began, the car landed for the last time, rocking back and forth before coming to a stop.

We sat there in shock, listening to the wreck groan and steam. One of the hub cabs fell off and clattered against the rocks. Fragments of glass mingled with the raindrops beating a steady rhythm above our heads.

Blinking to clear my vision, I gently shook Tori, who was wedged against me. "Hey, are you okay?"

"Yeah. I think so. Just dizzy."

Then she looked in the front seat. I followed her gaze.

The two girls might have been broken dolls. Their heads lolled to the side. Seraphina's face was covered in blood, and Ioana was pinned in her seat by what was left of the passenger side dashboard. But the most heartbreaking thing of all? They were still holding hands.

"It's hard to see them like this and think of what they are like now," Tori whispered. "This makes me feel sorry for them."

"Me, too. Who would let such a horrible thing happen to them?"

"Which horrible thing? The wreck or the resurrection?"

"Both. We need to get out of . . . "

Before I could finish the thought, Tori and I were standing outside of the wreckage on a large, flat boulder. Heavy rain pounded around us, but we stayed dry as a bone.

"Whoa," Tori said, "how did you do that?"

"I have no idea," I said, looking around at the rocky, rugged terrain and up the face of the cliff. "No wonder the car was so destroyed after bouncing around on these boulders. Between that and the distance, it must have fallen . . ."

When I stopped speaking, Tori looked up as well. "Oh. Crap. Who is that?"

Above us, inside the shattered and splintered railing, a figure in a long, black raincoat stared down into the ravine.

The brim of a fedora covered his face and his hands were jammed in his pockets.

As we watched, the man turned his head towards us.

"Uh, Jinksy, he can't see us, right?"

Before I could answer, the man slowly raised his right hand and tipped the brim of his hat. With that, he turned on his heel and disappeared.

"Tell me that did *not* just happen," Tori said.

"It happened. I just don't know *when* it happened."

"What do you mean?"

"Was he there *during* the original wreck or is he here *now* in our vision?"

"Or is it both?"

There was no good answer to that question.

We stayed in the vision long enough to see everything that happened after that—the trucker who found the scene of the accident and called it in, the firefighters who climbed down to reach the girls, and the arrival of Anton Ionescu.

I don't know how Anton learned about the wreck or if he came on it by accident driving down the mountain as if that day was like any other. But no matter what else I thought of the man then, or what I think of him now, my heart broke as I watched him fight to scramble down the cliff.

"Damn you!" he cried, striking at the state trooper restraining him. "Those are *my girls* down there. I have to get to them. Let me *go!*"

It took that trooper and two others to hold Anton, until his legs buckled under him and he dropped to his knees. The wail of agony that rose from his throat in that moment echoed through the surrounding hills.

As his head fell into his hands, the scene around us dissolved, and Tori and I found ourselves back in the junkyard with our hands resting on the cold metal of the car. Far from answering any of the questions we had about the accident, our vision raised new and more frightening uncertainties.

"Do you think the man in black caused the accident?" Tori asked.

"I don't know, but one thing is for certain. Our mothers weren't responsible."

Chapter Twenty-Five

Sometimes when I tell you about our magical adventures, you may forget that Tori and I run a business. Let me pause for a capitalist identification moment here. Profit wise, that Monday was fantastic!

Tori and I walked into a store clogged with tourists when we returned from the junkyard. The retail scene seemed even more jarring than vicariously plunging over a cliff in a 1975 Corolla.

Mom waved from the cash register. We side-stepped our way through the milling crowd to get to her. "When did this start?" I asked.

"Right after you all left." She signaled my Dad to take over for her and drew us into the storeroom.

"We were running out of SpookCon1 merchandise," she said. "I hope you don't mind, but I put Darby to work creating more inventory."

"No," I said, "that's great. What did you have him make?"

"Everything's there on the table," Mom said, sticking her head out the door to check the status of the crowd. "I'm sorry, honey, but I have to get back out there. Gemma is swamped in the espresso bar. Have a look at the new stuff, and then if you two could pitch in, that would be great."

With that, she was gone.

"Did your mother just tell us to get to work right in the middle of a magical crisis involving vampires?" Tori asked.

"She did," I said, examining the items on the table.

"And did she ignore the fact that we've been out psychometrically reading the wreck that completely changed her life?"

"Mom didn't forget," I replied, "she's not ready to hear about it. Let's see what she and Darby cooked up."

As Tori stepped over to the table with me, she said, "The little guy is good with captions. Once Darby understands the theme and you toss him a few suggestions, he can run with it."

And run with it he did. The Witch's Brew t-shirt line now included three designs in addition to Tori's original "Visit if You Dare" concept, starting with the provocative question, "Do you *really* want to be in Briar Hollow when the lights go out?"

That one showed the courthouse square festooned in spider webs with jagged bolts of lightning shooting across the sky. Tori lifted the shirt up to get a better look at the graphics.

"Oh my God," she said. "They included the Strigoi Sisters."

Sure enough, the two figures dressed in black planted dead center in the middle of the scene, fangs extended, were Seraphina and Ioana.

"Well," I said, "you do have to admit that Elvira thing they're got going fits the theme."

"True, but with our luck, they'll demand a cut of the profits."

"Check this one out," I said, holding *Good Government from the Grave* over my chest. The panel featured Howie in spectral form hard at work at his desk in the mayor's office. The caption under the image read, "Confirmed sightings of the late

Howard McAlpin, Sunday, October 25, 2015," along with the festival's website address.

I didn't even have to ask Tori to get her phone out and have a look. Linda and her webmaster, a senior at Briar Hollow High, apparently spent their Monday building a new page devoted to Howie filled with pictures taken by tour attendees.

Fortunately, none of the photographers qualified as "steady-handed," probably because the majority of them were running at the time. You could definitely make out a human-shaped figure, but calling the ID "confirmed" stretched credulity to the breaking point.

"The baseball video was bad luck," Tori said, "but we dodged a bullet on Howie's appearance. The people on that tour were ordinary tourists curious about a haunted courthouse not professional paranormal investigators."

"I know, but from what Dad tells us, the pros are in town now, which is probably why we're selling this." I held up the last t-shirt, which read, *Haunted Briar Hollow - Not for Amateurs*.

Just then, Dad's head appeared around the door frame. "Hey, we really need some help out here, kids."

Tori and I had no choice. We went to work. The crowd didn't thin out until around 5 o'clock. Judging from the conversations I overheard as I wiped down tables and rang up purchases, most of the people were heading out for an early supper so they would be able to get to that night's ghost tour on time.

The scheduled destination? The battlefield where Beau died in 1864.

We went downstairs with the moms, leaving Dad in charge. The four of us collapsed on the sofas in the lair, shell-shocked from the day. Darby appeared instantly with a platter of sandwiches and a huge bowl of chips. We did pause long enough to compliment him on the new Witch's Brew merchandise before attacking the food like a pack of ravenous she-wolves.

Greer, who was sitting by the fire, closed the book in her hands and regarded us with a mixture of amusement and horror.

"What?" I asked, as I realized there was a piece of roast beef dangling from the corner of my mouth.

"Oh, nothing," she said pleasantly. "I was pondering the irony that most people think we vampires are the messy eaters."

Beside me, Tori laughed, choking on her pastrami and necessitating a back pounding from Gemma.

"Sorry," Greer grinned. "Couldn't resist. Do you suppose you might be able to intersperse chewing with an account of your afternoon's excursion to the junkyard?"

"Sure," I said, "but everyone needs to hear this. Let me send Chase and Festus a text message. Where's Beau?"

Behind me, I heard the now familiar slap of a saber scabbard on boot leather. First I glanced over my shoulder, and then I pivoted completely to behold the resplendent Confederate colonel standing behind me.

Beau wore a new tunic of soft heather broadcloth. Two rows of gold buttons gleamed brightly against the gray fabric, matching the intricate braid sewn on the shoulders and cuffs. The gun belt and scabbard were his own, but polished to a high ebony gloss. He held his white non-regulation Panama hat in his hand as he would say "in deference to the presence of ladies."

I put my food down and got up, moving to stand in front of him. "Colonel Longworth, I have never seen you looking so handsome."

Bowing deeply at the waist, Beau said, "Nor you more comely, Miss Jinx."

For the record, I had on a plain navy sweatshirt and jeans, but his gallantry flattered me all the same.

"Are you planning to appear in ghostly form tonight?" I asked, hoping the answer would be "no." We needed to tone down the perception of Briar Hollow as the go-to place for on-demand haunts.

"No. I am leading the tour of the battlefield. I plan to present myself as the descendant of the Beauregard T. Longworth who died on that ground. I wear the uniform in honor of the men who fell there so bravely under my command."

I asked Beau once if any of his soldiers were among the spirits that frequent the cemetery since many of the men are buried there. He told me that his cavalry troopers are at peace, implying that he, himself was not. Over time, I've come to understand that Beau carries a heavy burden of guilt for the ambush that claimed the lives of his entire unit.

"That's a beautiful tribute, Beau. I know your men would be honored."

"The honor is mine for having had the privilege to command such splendid soldiers."

"Come join us," I said. "Tori and I have a report from the junkyard. We're just waiting until everyone is here."

After I sent a text to Chase, I went over to Graceland East and tapped on the door with my forefinger. Glory opened it immediately. "Hi," she said, "is everything okay?"

"Yes, we're going to talk about what Tori and I found at the junkyard. I thought you might like to be included."

Her face lit up to an almost neon green. "Oh, *thank you!* Do I need to change?"

She was wearing a velour warm-up suit and white tennis shoes. I half expected a Ken doll in a white sweater to appear behind her at any second.

"No, you look great. May I offer you a lift?"

"Please," she said, stepping out the door and closing it carefully.

I held my hand out flat, and Glory sat down on the edge of my palm. We crossed to the sitting area, and I let her down on one of the end tables. "Hi everyone!" she called out happily, waving to the room.

Everyone waved back, while Glory climbed atop a stack of books to get a better view. Tori sent a message to Rodney's wall-mounted iPod and within seconds the black-and-white rat bounded down the steps.

"Okay," I said, "that should take care of everyone. . . "

For the first time, it occurred to me that the Honorable and Annoying Howard McAlpin was no longer in the basement.

"What happened to Howie?" I asked Beau.

"I am happy to report the Mayor faded to normal and returned to his usual haunts. I must add that his departure came not a moment too soon. Howard can be rather trying."

Footsteps sounded from the stacks, signaling Chase's arrival. Then I realized I was hearing two people walking. Was Festus in human form?

I got my answer soon enough. Chase and Lucas Grayson walked out of the shadows side-by-side with Festus limping along. One look told me the two men had a history—one Chase didn't like.

After being introduced all around, Lucas sat down on the hearth beside Greer's chair. I caught myself studying them carefully, trying to figure out if there was any involvement between them other than a working partnership.

As he sat, Lucas said, "Hey, Red."

Greer smiled at the nickname. "Laddie," she said, inclining her head in greeting. "Is Istanbul contained?"

"Buttoned up hard and tight, but there may have been a leak."

I had no idea what they were talking about, and was pretty

sure neither would tell me if I asked. But given their body language and level of professional cordiality, there didn't seem to be any romantic involvement there, which pleased me more than I expected.

That's when I caught Chase studying me from the other side of the room. I telegraphed a silent message with my eyes, *"We talked about this."*

To his credit, Chase understood and answered with a curt nod. He saw my interest in Lucas Grayson and didn't like it, but was abiding by the rules. Smart man. I wanted to go on working with Chase, but I wasn't going to tolerate jealous nonsense.

Festus, who had gone immediately to the fire, took in the whole exchange. There's not much that gets past that old yellow scoundrel no matter how much he plays up the boozy bad-boy persona.

"Somebody want to tell me why I had to interrupt my nap?" he asked crossly. "How's a man supposed to digest his tuna if he can't get some shut eye?"

"More to the point," Greer said, wrinkling her nose, "what is a man to do about his breath when he has consumed his tuna?"

"This from a woman who likes her Type O shaken, not stirred."

Vampire humor was going to take some getting used to.

"Mom," I said, "are you sure Dad wants to be upstairs? Shouldn't he be here for this?"

"Yes, honey. I'm sure. Your father feels better when he's doing something normal like running the store. I'll fill him in later. Tell us what happened at the junkyard."

The group let me get through the whole account, including the sighting of the man in the trench coat. When I finished, Lucas said, "Could you tell what the man's face looked like?"

I shook my head. "He was standing too far away, and we

couldn't make out details through the rain. All I can tell you is that he was dressed in a black trench coat and wore a black fedora. He didn't say anything, just tipped his hat at us and walked away."

"Do you think he caused the accident?" Greer asked.

Tori and I had discussed that topic on our way back from the junkyard. "I don't know," I said. "We didn't see him on the side of the road before we went over the cliff, but honestly, I was paying more attention to what was going on inside the car. It's certainly possible that he was there."

"And yet," Lucas said, "he was both in the past *and* apparently aware of your presence psychometrically. That's interesting."

No, it was creepy as hell. "So what's the verdict?" I asked. "Was he really at the scene of the wreck all those years ago or was he some kind of stowaway in my vision?"

"I suspect he was both," Greer said. "As you have learned from your journeys back and forth to Shevington, time is not so static as humans believe. It sounds as if you were dealing with a wizard who has the capacity to time shift."

"Do you know any wizards who can do that?" Tori asked.

"Just one," Lucas said. "Irenaeus Chesterfield."

Well, that answered that question. Ionescu and Chesterfield *were* working together.

Mom, who had been listening with a kind of frozen expression, returned her focus to the room. "If Chesterfield was there," she said, speaking slowly and cautiously, "does that mean that I . . . that we . . . didn't . . . "

Gemma caught hold of her hand. "I knew we didn't send that car off the road, Kelly, but from what I'm hearing now, I think Chesterfield wanted us to think we did."

"I would tend to agree," Greer said. "There was no reason for Chesterfield to be there unless he was targeting you, Ionescu, or—and this is much more likely—all of you."

We let that sink in. If Irenaeus Chesterfield orchestrated the car accident, he had been pulling strings and affecting our lives for more than 30 years. That meant there was something far larger and more serious going on.

When I said as much, Greer said, "Perhaps we should work with one crisis at a time, starting with the young women. From your description, they were most certainly killed in the accident. According to Strigoi burial custom, they should have been staked and beheaded prior to burial to prevent their rising as *Strigoi mort*."

"Okay," Tori said, "I'm confused. Anton and all the other Ionescus are *Strogi viu*, right?"

"Correct," Greer said. "Their ancestor was cursed by a witch."

"When Chase told us about all this the other night," Tori said, "I thought the *Strigoi mort* were sort of like demons."

"They are," Greer said.

"So what kind of *Strigoi mort* are Seraphina and Ioana?"

"Excellent question," Greer said. "They are *Strigoi mort blasfematoare*. The 'blasphemous undead.' The witch who originally cursed the Ionescus and others of their kind granted them the mercy of real death if they followed the prescribed rituals. If they did not, the creatures they would become when they arose from a false death were even more demonic than the regular *Strigoi mort*. Those creatures merely drain the energy of their victims. The *Strigoi mort blasfematoare* require living blood to survive."

"Super-charged Strigoi," I said.

"Precisely," Greer said. "They retain all the powers of their kinsmen as well as a driving hunger that only blood can satisfy. To become *Strigoi mort blasfematoare* is a fate worse than death. They are exceedingly rare, but where they exist, they are reviled and feared."

"Uh, yeah," Tori said, "after what I saw at the lumberyard, I'm good with the reviling part."

Mom spoke up. "But why would Anton do that to the girls when he loved them so much? I don't understand why he would stake them, keep them somewhere for years, and then allow them to rise from the dead."

I'll never forget the look that came over Tori's face. She gets that look when all of the pieces of a puzzle she's working on suddenly fall into place. Only this time, I could tell the answer was a shocking one.

"What? Tori? What is it?"

"Jinksy," she said breathlessly, "Anton didn't raise those girls from the dead. You did."

Chapter Twenty-Six

"Me?!" I squeaked. "I don't know anything about raising the . . ."

The words died in my throat. My mind flashed back to the night I used a spell downloaded from a voodoo wiki, to accidentally free Brenna Sinclair and raise a cemetery full of ghosts.

The only two people in the room who didn't jump on that memory train with me were Greer and Lucas—or so I thought.

"Is there something you need to tell us about?" Lucas asked.

"Laddie," Greer said, "is it so impossible for you to read your incident reports? They're correlating the present set of circumstances with the raising of Brenna Sinclair."

"Ah," he said, "I do remember that. The office pool was running 5 to 1 you wouldn't be able to put the cemetery ghosts back."

"*Seriously?*" I said. "You people knew what a mess we had on our hands and you thought running an office betting pool was a better idea than helping us out?"

"It wasn't time for us to get involved," Greer said. "From what I can tell, you handled it quite well."

Somewhat mollified, I said, "Thank you. Is there any chance I could get a copy of this mystery time table that seems to be running my life?"

Greer laughed. "Doubtful. The Grid works with us on a need-to-know basis. I can't tell you how many times the Mother Trees have uprooted my plans. No pun intended."

"Try working with the Registry," Festus groused. "Some werewolf lifts his leg on a rose bush in sight of the humans and it takes six werecats and a crew of raccoons to contain the fallout."

Lucas snickered. "Before we head down the endless rabbit trail of interdepartmental politics, would you mind running through your foray into raising the dead for me?"

As briefly as possible I laid out the details. While I was talking, Greer got up and crossed to the liquor cabinet. She took out a bottle of Oban single malt and poured herself a dram. From the brief amount of time I had spent with Greer MacVicar, I already knew the woman only drank the expensive stuff.

Rather than take her seat again, she leaned on Beau's desk, watching me with obvious interest in her liquid, emerald eyes. In fact, she was watching everyone in the room.

Let me give you some advice from the vantage point of retrospection. Don't bother trying to lie to Greer or getting anything past her. I have no idea how old she is or how powerful, but her presence fills a room. When that woman is on your side? You're loaded for bear.

When I finished my account of the graveyard incident, Lucas flashed me another grin and said teasingly, "Come on. You have to tell us. What did you Google to come up with the spell?"

Blushing to the roots of my hair, I said, "Necromancy, how to."

At that, Lucas laughed outright, and I smiled in spite of myself. "I was new to the business."

Out of the corner of my eye, I saw Chase cross and uncross his legs. My easy banter with Lucas seemed to be annoying the hell out of him, which both irritated and pleased me. Chase was the one who called it quits on our relationship, not me. If watching me talk to a good-looking, roguish man gave Mr. McGregor a hairball, he could figure out how to swallow it.

As I turned my full attention back to Lucas, my gaze crossed Greer's. She had taken in both Chase's behavior and my reaction to it. When our eyes met, she smiled, and raised her glass an imperceptible fraction as if to say, "That a girl."

Tiny though it might have been, that accolade sent a thrill of power through me.

"So what do you think?" I asked. "Did I have some effect on Seraphina and Ioana?"

"Regardless of the source of the incantation you used," Greer said, "you gathered a tremendous amount of magic that night. I think it is possible that your spell could have awakened Seraphina and Ioana."

Chase cleared his throat. "What would you say the radius of a spell like that would be?"

Greer considered the question. "That's difficult to measure. Why? Do you know where Ionescu might have been keeping them staked in their coffins?"

"No," he said, reaching for the TV remote and lowering the big screen, "but I think I know where he may have been keeping them since they woke up."

Chase tapped a few buttons and streamed the image from his tablet to the television. We all moved to get a better view of the screen, which showed a recorded sequence from a GNATS camera.

Festus hopped up on the back of Chase's chair. "Talk to us, boy. What are we watching?"

"This is a video that Ironweed's pilots shot yesterday," Chase said. "They've been observing activity in the Ionescu compound for several days, and frankly, there's nothing out of the ordinary. From what I can see, these people are trying to go about their business in peace. Now, the building that is coming up is where Anton lives."

The drone's view took us down an ordinary residential street before turning up a sloping drive to approach a large two-story home set back from the compound's main street. The front of the house was open, but a high wall protected the backyard.

We listened to the radio chatter as the GNATS pilot received directions to fly the drone over the wall. The camera showed a good-sized pool, an outdoor kitchen, and what at first glance looked like a guest house.

"Do you see it?" Chase said.

"Other than a grill that set Anton back several thousand dollars?" Tori asked.

"No. Look at the guest house as the drone circles the yard."

As he spoke, the camera panned, so we saw the small structure as a whole for the first time. There were bars on the windows.

"That," Festus said, "is one high-rent jail."

"That's not all," Chase said. "Look at the door."

When no one spoke. He froze the video and zoomed in on the entrance. The wood around the door handle was splintered and broken, with one end of an industrial strength hasp dangling at a drunken angle.

"He had someone or something locked in there," Greer said.

"Something he was feeding," Chase said, shifting the image to magnify a sliding iron panel at the bottom of the door.

Cats can't snap their paws, but Festus would have done just that if he could have pulled it off. "That's it! That explains the livestock."

"What livestock?" Tori asked.

"I met with Merle, Earl, and Furl at the Dirty Claw yesterday to see if they had heard anything that might help with the Strigoi Sisters," Festus said. "They didn't have much to say, so we wound up having nip nachos and shooting the . . . er . . . . talking over Litterbox Lagers. Earl was bitching about trying to get to the bottom of a bunch of mysterious livestock deaths in the area around Briar Hollow over the past couple of months. He was thinking there might be a werewolf passing through, except the carcasses were drained of blood and dumped miles from where the animals disappeared."

"So," Greer mused, "the girls awaken without warning and wander back to their people. Typical behavior for a newly risen *Strigoi mort*. Anton secrets them in the guest house behind bars and feeds them animal blood until he can develop a plan. The girls escape, which could explain why the Inonescus made an uncharacteristic appearance in town Saturday night to retrieve them."

"Which didn't work," Gemma said, "because Sunday morning they were going after my husband at the lumberyard."

The whole scenario made sense, with a few glaring exceptions. "That's all well and good," I said, "but why did Anton hire Malcolm Ferguson? And if Anton is working with Chesterfield, what's in it for him? From everything I've learned about Chesterfield, he always plays the long game."

From the couch, Mom said softly, "Maybe Chesterfield is offering him a way to help the girls."

Given the depth of the grief Tori and I witnessed Anton

display in our shared vision, I had no difficulty believing Ionescu would do anything to help Seraphina and Ioana, especially if he was partially responsible for turning them into *Strigoi mort blasfematoare.*

"We have suspected for some time that Irenaeus Chesterfield is not merely an antique dealer and rare book collector," Greer said. "His involvement with Brenna Sinclair made that rather obvious."

"But what does he want?" Beau asked. "We have presumed that his goal was to gain access to The Valley and Moira, as she is, to my understanding, the last person capable of performing the necessary magic to create a Creavit witch or wizard."

"*Veneficus trajectio,*" I said. "The magical transference. Moira would never do that."

"Moira would never do it *willingly,*" Greer corrected me. "Chesterfield is quite skilled at the art of leverage."

Leverage. The Mother Oak told me it wasn't time for Connor to come to Briar Hollow yet. Was she afraid he would fall into Chesterfield and Ionescu's hands?

When I put that idea on the table, Mom turned deathly pale. "We can't put Connor's life in danger."

I sat down beside her. "We won't let that happen, Mom. We just have to figure out which one of the bad guys is the biggest threat."

"I'm afraid that's not quite true," Greer said, still leaning against the desk. "The greatest threat could be what they plan to do together."

"Separate or together," Mom said in a steely voice, "makes no difference to me. I gave my son up once. I'm not losing him again."

FOR AS MUCH AS I hated to leave the store with so many things coming together at once, I couldn't send Beau out to conduct the battlefield tour alone. Everyone else thought he was dressed in uniform as an enthusiastic Civil War buff. I knew he was a commander honoring the men who died with him.

On one of our long walks through the hills, Beau had already taken me to the place where he lost his life. It's a narrow cut between two low hills where a dirt road used to run before the highway was built. There's nothing left but a two-rut country track connecting adjacent farms.

More than fifty people showed up for the ghost tour, so Beau broke them into two groups and delivered his presentation twice. He spoke in precise and moving detail about the ambush and then helpfully positioned knots of ghost hunters around the battlefield.

When they were all settled with their infrared cameras, recorders, and other paraphernalia, Beau and I walked off into the woods to talk in private. "How are you doing with all this?" I asked him.

"The sadness I carry for my men has long been with me," he said, resting one gloved hand on the hilt of his saber. "There has not been a moment of my afterlife that I have not grieved for them."

He was standing with his back to the woods, so he didn't see them at first, the spirits dressed in Confederate gray who cautiously picked their way through the trees, quietly forming into two straight lines behind him.

"Beau," I said softly, "they've been thinking about you, too. Look."

When Beau turned, a young officer with a thick drawl called the men to attention. "The troops await your inspection, Colonel Longworth, suh."

At first, I didn't think Beau could move, but then he drew

himself up to his full height. "Lieutenant Broward, I would hope death has not given us over to any laggards."

"Not our boys, Colonel," the Lieutenant grinned. "Point us at those Billy Yanks and we'll give'em hell."

"Our war is long since over, son. I thought you all to be at rest. Why have you come here tonight?"

"This was the day, suh," Broward said, "the day we all died. We've come back every year since looking for you."

I saw the muscles in Beau's jaw work back and forth. "I did not know. It was only recently I have been able to wander far from my own grave."

The Lieutenant eyed him curiously. "Have you come back from the dead, suh?"

"No," Beau said, "but I have been granted the incalculable privilege of walking among the living."

"If you have a few minutes, Colonel, would you walk with us tonight?" one of the soldiers asked.

Beau looked at me with tears in his eyes. "Will you keep the others away from this part of the woods?"

"Of course I will, Beau. Be with your men."

The Lieutenant tipped his hat, "Much obliged Miss . . ."

"Hamilton," Beau said. "Boys, I have the deep honor of presenting to you Miss Norma Jean Hamilton, my benefactress and a great lady."

As I watched, work-roughened hands reached for caps as one after another the men bowed.

I have no idea what came over me, but I think I actually curtsied. I do recall saying, "My pleasure, gentlemen."

Beau took my hand and kissed it. "I shall not be long."

"Take as much time as you like," I said, my own eyes now filled with tears. "You've earned this."

Chapter Twenty-Seven

Beau and I returned to the store well after midnight. True to their word, the festival committee managed to pull together an abbreviated version of the carnival to run each evening through the week. All the stores on the square, including ours, were staying open until 9 or 10 o'clock.

Locals who had at first been skeptical about the festival were now enthusiastically supportive, decorating their homes and yards as well as coming downtown in the evening to picnic on the courthouse lawn. Tori reported brisk business—so brisk she looked exhausted, as did the moms and my dad.

"So nothing on the Strigoi front? I asked.

"Nope," Tori said, "everybody is off working their own leads."

Since she finished the sentence with a massive yawn, I decided it was time to call it a day.

"Everybody go to bed and get some rest," I said. "Things are quiet for now."

Nobody argued.

"Aren't you coming up, honey?" Mom asked as she started to climb the stairs. "You're just as tired as we are."

She wasn't wrong, but I was also wired. With the episode at the junkyard that morning, a full afternoon of work in the shop, and then witnessing Beau's emotional reunion with his soldiers, my mind wouldn't stop churning.

When we got downstairs to the apparently deserted lair, Beau excused himself to "reflect on the remarkable events of the evening."

I planned to unwind with some magical drills on the target range until a voice from the vicinity of the fireplace stopped me.

"Won't you join me?"

Greer was sitting in one of the wingbacks by the fire with the chair turned toward the hearth. Since the lights were off in that area and she wore black from head to foot, I hadn't seen her sitting there.

I walked over and claimed the opposite chair. "Hi. Where is everyone?"

"Chase and Festus went home a while ago. Lucas is at the Registry looking into this matter of livestock disappearances."

"And Rodney and Glory?"

"They went upstairs earlier to spy on the patrons in your store. They assured me they would stay well out of sight."

I laughed. "Which probably means they're tucked in some hidden spot sound asleep."

"Undoubtedly. Theirs is a strange, but rather lovely friendship. Miss Green went on at some length explaining her predicament. She is effusively grateful that you have taken her in as a magical refugee."

"I'm assuming those are your words?"

"They are. I believe Glory's phrasing involved being 'trouble tossed on life's terrible black ocean.'"

"That sounds more like her."

"Was Colonel Longworth's tour a success?"

Greer listened as I described the arrival of Beau's soldiers and the time he spent with them.

"The afterlife is such a complicated place," she said when I finished. "The spirits who remain earthbound find themselves forever caught between a past they cannot live and future they will never realize."

"But aren't you . . . "

Ever have one of those sentences you start and don't know how to stop? No sooner had I opened my mouth than I realized how rude it would be to ask Greer if she was dead—or at least *technically* dead.

"Aren't I dead?" Greer asked.

"I'm sorry. That wasn't very nice of me."

"Don't be silly. I would expect you to be curious. I am *baobhan sith*, which makes me a fairy."

That surprised me. "Like Ironweed?"

"Well, after a fashion. Ironweed and his kind are Seelie. I am Unseelie."

"Now you've lost me."

"The Seelie inhabit the Light Court. I am of the Dark Court."

My face betrayed my next question before I could even say it, touching off a round of merry laughter from Greer.

"That does not mean I am malicious or evil, although many of the Dark Court are those things and more. I long ago allied myself with the forces of the Light. It makes me something of an outcast with my own kind, but grants me certain advantages in my work with the DGI."

"Like what you did to help Tori's father with the Strigoi Sisters," I said. "Thank you, for that, by the way."

"My pleasure."

Since this was my first chance to really get information on the DGI, and Greer was more forthcoming than Lucas

Grayson, I asked. "So are you and Grayson watching me or something?"

Greer arched her eyebrows. "Didn't Lucas tell you anything?"

"No, he just dragged me away from my brother and took me to the Mother Tree like I'd skipped school or something."

"I commiserated. I have had my share of uncomfortable conversations with the Mother Tree."

"You have?"

"Yes. When I first began to work with the Grid my appetite was, shall we say, a bit rough around the edges. There were incidents."

Since I had no earthly idea what to say about that and *really* didn't want any details on those "incidents," I said nothing. Greer didn't seem to mind; she continued talking.

"We are not watching you. We are here to work with you."

"Doing what?"

"You really are in the dark about all this, aren't you?"

"Completely. The whole thing with my mother getting cursed and me not being trained is kind of catching up with me. Half the time I'm not even sure I'm up for this."

Where did that come from? My admission was the truth, but normally I wouldn't have said such a thing to somebody I'd just met.

As I watched, the green fire Tori described to me slowly filled Greer's eyes. She looked me up and down, almost as if she was searching for something. Then, as quickly as it had risen, the fire receded. "You're 'up for it,'" Greer said. "Yours is one of the most powerful auras I have ever seen. But if I may, I'd like to give you a piece of advice."

"Go right ahead. I'll take all the help I can get."

"Hold your power close. The likes of Chase McGregor mean well, but you are no hot house flower, Jinx Hamilton. Direct your own affairs. You work for no man or woman. Not

Chase McGregor, not Barnaby Shevington, not Moira. You are at least their equal and at times their better because you are one of those chosen by the Trees."

"Chosen?"

"Aye. They have waited a long time for your coming. I cannot tell you everything because I am not allowed. The Trees will only tell you when they are ready, but trust me, *Quercus de Pythonissam*, I speak the truth."

Beau's Latin lessons were paying off. She called me "Witch of the Oak."

At the time, I had no idea what that meant, but the words sent a frisson of familiarity through my soul—and I liked it.

THAT WAS MONDAY NIGHT. Tuesday, the *Briar Hollow Banner* came out with a huge headline proclaiming, "Howard McAlpin, Hiram Folger Among Haunts Spotted."

When I read the words and groaned, Tori said, "It was too much to hope that someone wouldn't recognize Hiram. He was kind of a local legend back in the day."

Still scanning the paper, I pointed at the white blob in the center of the Mayor's office. "At least they're stretching it on the identification of Howie.

"Yeah," Tori agreed, "that was a win for our side. Now if we can get rid of the Strigoi Sisters, figure out what Ionescu is up to, break the curse, get your brother home, go after Chesterfield . . . "

"STOP!" I commanded. "One thing at a time. Right now, dealing with Seraphina and Ioana tops the list. I don't like not knowing where they are."

"Oh, I don't imagine you'll have to wait long for them to show up."

By Wednesday evening, when things were still calm, I was

starting to get antsy. If we'd been in some old Western, I'd have been the steely eyed cowboy gazing out over the Indian-infested prairie intoning, "It's quiet. Too quiet."

Of course, I should have known it wouldn't last—and it didn't.

After the sun went down, the movie fired up over on the courthouse lawn. *Poltergeist*. The carnival was going full swing and everyone seemed to be enjoying themselves. The evening was cool. We had the front door of the store open to let the breeze in. I was restocking the SpookCon1 t-shirt display when I heard it—the mournful baying of a hound, but this was no ordinary hound.

The undulating notes of his doleful cry rose up on the night air growing more shrill and piercing until the sound raised chill bumps on my arms.

Instinct propelled me toward the door.

Beau came charging past me. "I'm guessing you have some idea what's going on?" I asked as I hurried to catch up with him.

"That's Duke. He is attempting to alert me that something is wrong."

Out on the square, people who had stopped in their tracks at the first high-pitched howl were now gathering in nervous groups. I could see their eyes shifting restlessly toward the side streets like they were expecting packs of wolves to come charging into the square.

Someone cut the sound to the movie in time for a man's panicked shouts to echo off the building. It was one of the Bigfoot hunters who shot the viral video.

"Oh my God! That's him! The hellhound from the baseball field! Run for your lives."

Great. Just great.

Beau and I were now standing on the sidewalk outside the store. Duke raised his voice in another keening wail.

"Can you tell where he is?" I asked.

"There, I think," Beau said, taking off past the cobbler shop and toward the pizzeria. Instead of going down the sidewalk, however, he made for the alley, with me in hot pursuit. We didn't have to go far to find Duke and the reason for his distress.

Less than 20 yards down the alley lay the body of the second Bigfoot hunter. He was face up, his eyes open and staring. I knew he was dead even before Beau reached down and felt for a pulse in his neck—right above a set of round puncture marks.

Duke, who had stopped howling, danced nervously back and forth, whining.

"There, there, boy," Beau said. "I'm here now."

When he moved to pet the ghostly coonhound, Beau's hand passed entirely through Duke's head. At least we wouldn't have to worry about anyone seeing the "hellhound" they'd just heard.

But then I was treated to a hellish sight of my own. When Beau reached for Duke, he cleared my line of sight to the body, and I spotted the second pair of puncture marks on the other side of the boy's neck.

The Strigoi Sisters.

Chapter Twenty-Eight

For years, Tori and I have made jokes about getting a shovel and hiding a body. Now, confronted with a real body to hide, my mind worked faster than I ever could have imagined.

In that moment, I didn't stop to consider that the boy lying there in the dirt had a family and friends. I didn't think about his potential in life so needlessly wasted or wonder if he died in helpless terror.

With a calculating efficiency I didn't even know I possessed, my thoughts jumped over all of that to the simple equation, "Three dead bodies in three months in one little town equal panic."

If my studies in magic and witchcraft taught me nothing else that summer, I learned panicked humans present a serious danger to people like me.

Until that moment, I purposefully shied away from the question, "Am I human?" I'll spare you the elegant theorizing about what constitutes humanity. That night I reacted like a Fae witch. I protected myself and the people I love.

"Beau," I said urgently, "we can't let anyone find this body."

When he looked up at me, I knew Beau's mind had already jumped to the image of Fish Pike propped up outside our front door with his throat ripped out. People had accepted that Malcolm Ferguson was responsible for that murder, but how would we ever explain this one?

"I agree," he said. "We cannot risk throwing the town into a mass hysteria. The puncture marks are indelibly associated with vampiric lore."

His calm and reason made me finally understand Beau's talent for understatement. He was a soldier. One who kept a clear head when the bullets started flying. His job as a commander was to minimize the danger by example, and he was teaching me to do the same thing.

"Any chance you have a plan?" I asked.

"At least a partial one," he replied, standing up and taking off his belt. "We must first take steps to explain Duke's howling. In the presence of fear, people will accept the explanation that most immediately appeals to their sense of logic."

Accepting the leather strap more on reflex than comprehension, I said, "Okay, I'm with you so far. What am I supposed to do with this?"

"Use it as a leash," Beau said, pulling the Amulet of the Phoenix out of his shirt and affixing it to Duke's collar. "We are about to enlist the assistance of a corporeal coonhound."

The instant Beau took his hands away from the amulet, Duke's coat turned coal black, and the brown accents on his muzzle and face became visible. Beau, on the other hand, faded to ectoplasmic gray as he leaned down and spoke seriously to the faithful dog, who never took his eyes off his master's face.

"Duke, you were smart to call us. I am in need of your further assistance. Can you do as I ask?"

The steady beating of the hound's tail raised a cloud of dust beneath him, and a willing grin split his face.

"Good boy. You must go with Miss Jinx. She will speak harshly to you, but she will not mean it. People must believe that you escaped her care and are in trouble for howling and frightening everyone. She will play as if she is dragging you home. Do you understand?"

In response, Duke dropped his head and then cut his eyes up at me in mournful regret. I swear if the dog had asked, "Like this?" it wouldn't have surprised me.

"Oh," I said admiringly, "you are good, Duke. You are *really* good."

That touched off another round of enthusiastic tail wagging. At least the dog had his part in this caper down.

"What about the body?" I asked. "Should we try to drag it out of sight."

"There is no time. You must use the cloaking spell you have been practicing to temporarily disguise the corpse. I will stay here and guard the scene until you have consulted with Miss MacVicar. I should think that a problem of this nature falls within her area of expertise."

Getting Greer sounded like a fantastic idea. Me cloaking the corpse, not so much.

"I can barely hide a pencil with that spell. I can't cloak this guy."

Beau fixed me with a kind, but firm stare. "Jinx, perhaps you have heard the assertion that necessity is the mother of invention?"

The sound of voices from the street settled the matter. We couldn't keep standing in an alley over a dead man. Explaining the scene would be far harder than trying the spell.

Closing my eyes, I searched within for the spark of my power, fanning it into a bright flame in my mind. When I opened my eyes again, I brought my hands up and quietly chanted the incantation.

A gentle wave of blue light flowed from my fingers. It washed over the body at my feet, which appeared to grow thinner and fainter. Gaining in confidence, I channeled more energy toward my hands. In seconds, we were looking at bare, rocky ground, but when I cautiously extended my foot, it made contact with the corpse.

"Excellent!" Beau said. "How long will the spell hold?"

"I have no idea," I said, looping the belt under the dog's collar. "Stay put until Greer and I get back. Come on, Duke. Show time."

The instant we came out of the alley, the hound dropped his head until his ears almost dragged on the sidewalk. As we neared a group of people on the corner, I said in a loud, angry voice, "Bad dog, Duke! *Bad* dog. What were you thinking? Howling like you're trying to wake the dead! Bad, *bad*, dog."

One of the men turned at the sound of my voice and looked at me with wide eyes. "My God, lady, was that your dog making that awful sound?"

"Yes," I said crossly. "He got away from me. He's all stirred up because there's so many people in town. He's been trying to get out all day, and he finally pulled it off."

"Are you sure?" the man asked. "That guy over there on the square said a hell hound was on the loose."

At that, I delivered a disdainful laugh. "Yeah, right. Duke may be an old devil, but he's no hell hound. Duke, howl, boy. Howl."

Right on cue, Duke threw his head back and let out with a piercing, blood-curdling yodel. Every head on the square snapped in our direction.

Perfect. We had their attention.

I waved and called out. "Sorry, folks. Just my uncle's dog. Guess he's in the Halloween spirit, too!"

Waves of relieved laughter floated over the courthouse lawn. I made a show of dragging Duke back into the store. The dog executed a flawless performance, even digging his feet into the sidewalk and making me pull at the lead to get him to come.

Getting inside the store didn't put us in the clear, however, since there were customers inside. Thank God Tori catches on quick.

"Did Duke get out *again*?" she asked with exasperation.

"He did. That was him howling. Scared everybody out there half to death. Uncle Beau is going to have to do a better job of keeping this damn dog in the house."

The people in the store bought it. No one batted an eye when Duke and I headed down to the basement.

The instant we were out of sight, I took the leash off and leaned down to give Duke a big kiss between his sweet, brown eyes. "You are a very, very *good* dog and don't ever let anyone tell you different."

That won me a goofy grin and a sloppy doggy kiss. Duke was so happy, in fact, that when he followed me all the way down to the lair, in true dog fashion, he made an over-enthusiastic mistake. He trotted straight up to Festus, who was sitting on the hearth playing chess with Greer and licked the old cat full across the face.

"What the *hell!*" Festus roared, immediately slapping Duke's nose with claws extended.

Surprised and hurt by the reaction to his friendly overture, Duke retreated with a yelp and cowered at Greer's feet.

"Festus!" Greer said. "You scared him."

"He *licked* me!" Festus declared with angry indignation. "He hasn't *seen* scared yet."

"Oh, for heaven's sake," Greer said, "your fur will dry."

Duke looked up at her and whined. "Do not be upset," she

consoled him. "Festus speaks like that to everyone. Now, where did you come from?"

"He came with me," I said. "We need your help."

"Of course, "Greer said. She started to rise, then stopped and moved a piece on the board. "Checkmate."

"Whatever," Festus said, grooming furiously. "I'm too busy disinfecting my fur to play chess. Keep that damn dog away from me."

"That won't actually be a problem," I said, slipping the Amulet of the Phoenix off Duke's collar.

As she watched the dog fade to transparent gray, Greer said, "Ah, a spirit hound."

"I'm sorry," Festus grumbled, "did you say *spit* hound?"

Ignoring him, I ran down the situation for Greer who was immediately all business.

"Is there a way out of the store that does not require us to appear upstairs?"

"We can go through the cobbler shop next door and into the alley."

"Show me."

As we started out of the lair, Festus said, "Hey! What am I supposed to do with this *thing*?"

"His name is Duke," I shot back. "Play fetch with him. He loves to catch balls."

"You do know I'm a *cat*, right?"

Greer and I managed not to laugh until we were inside the small passage leading to Chase's basement. "Be grateful the poor creature is a ghost," Greer said. "Festus can do little to him save swear."

"You ever heard Festus swear?"

"Point well taken. We must hurry."

By the time we made it outside, the twilight hour was long past and full night had fallen. We stayed in the alley for an extra block and then doubled back to join up with Beau.

"Any trouble?" I asked, handing him the amulet.

"No, but there have been people passing by the entrance to the alley intermittently."

Greer reached into the pouch on her belt and pulled out a small bottle of what I could have sworn was glitter. Removing the lid, she shook a few of the sparkling flakes onto the palm of her hand and blew them behind us. They hung suspended in the air for a second, and then expanded across the alley creating an opaque barrier. Stepping a few feet past Beau, she repeated the maneuver.

"Fairy dust," she explained as she put the bottle away. "Anyone who glances down the alley will see only what they expect to see. Now, will you remove your spell please?"

The coherence of my spell impressed even me. The magic held perfectly until I waved my hand over the boy's body and said, "*Exsolvo*."

When Greer crouched to examine the corpse, she snapped her fingers to ignite a small illuminated ball that followed the movements of her hands. When the light fell on the puncture wounds in the boy's neck, for the first time I thought I might get sick. The dull red holes stood out in stark relief against the pallid, bluing skin.

"Exsanguinated," Greer muttered clinically. "As I would have expected. The bites are precise and even. This is not the work of new vampires. They have fed on the living before."

Then she did something that I'm ashamed to say surprised me. With infinite gentleness, Greer brushed her long, graceful fingers down over the boy's face to close his eyes. The gesture, filled with so much empathy, brought a lump to my throat, but this was not the moment to mourn the death of an innocent. There would be time for that later.

"Wouldn't we have heard reports of other killings?" I asked.

The hoarseness in my voice was not lost on Greer. She

stood up and caught hold of my hands. "There are many seen as disposable in this world. The homeless, transients, runaways. The ones who can disappear without a trace. It is a sad, but real fact."

One of many, I thought, before getting back to business. "Would the Strigoi Sisters kill often?"

"No," Greer said, lightly squeezing my arm before she removed her hand. "*Strigoi mort* do not feed daily, nor do they have to drain their victims. They could easily choose transients or homeless people as a source of food."

"Or," I hesitated, "do what you do?"

"Seduction is a long-standing method of acquiring a willing blood donor," Greer agreed, "but I was born as I am and modified my habits by choice. The *Strigoi mort* have baser instincts. They would have required instruction to refine their feeding patterns."

We had at least two candidates for Teacher of the Year—Anton Ionescu and Irenaeus Chesterfield.

"How will you get rid of the . . . of him?" I asked.

"The body cannot be found in this condition. You know that already or you would not have come to me. I must dispose of him where he will not be found."

I looked down at the boy. He would become just another name on a missing person list. Someone somewhere would spend years waiting for him, watching for him. If my magic had raised the Strigoi Sisters, his death was on me as well as on them.

"Do not think that way," Greer said as if she could read my mind. "You did not kill this boy."

"No, but my actions may have started the path that led to his death."

"Hear me," Greer said, "and accept what is a fundamental truth of the Fae. All magic has consequences. You cannot escape the effects of your actions, only seek to model them for the good."

"Tell him that," I said, staring at the dead boy again.

"Use his death to sharpen your choices, not to dull your resolve. Do not cheapen his sacrifice with weakness of purpose. They did this to make you fear your actions and doubt yourself. Will you give them that victory?"

I had a short answer for that question. Hell no.

But the idea of a "disposable" person didn't sit right with me. "I understand what you have to do, Greer, but isn't there any way we can make sure his family has a chance to bury him?"

She stared down at the body for a minute and then said, "Did you check his pockets for a cell phone?"

The question startled me. I hadn't touched the body at all. "No. Beau felt for a pulse, but otherwise we haven't done anything."

Greer reached into her pouch again and took out a pair of latex gloves. Snapping them on, she felt in the boy's clothes, finally reaching under the body and coming out with an iPhone.

She thumbed the screen on and spent a few minutes looking over the text messages. "This is one of the boys who shot the video of the baseball game?"

"Yes. I sold them both t-shirts the day it happened."

"Then I would assume his partner in the endeavor is this Lester person. Can you replicate the boy's manner of speaking?"

When I said I'd try, she handed me a pair of gloves and then gave me the phone. I read over the messages. "Sure. I think I can pull it off. What do you want me to tell Lester?"

"Indicate that Danny has acquired female companionship and will be in touch in a few days."

Danny. So that was his name.

Using my thumbs, I typed, "Bro, scored with a hot chick. Headed for the woods. Don't wait for me."

I sent the text and waited. Within seconds a reply came in. "Cool, dude. See you back in the city."

Greer nodded. "Perfect. I will see that the body is taken to this boy's natural haunts and that it is discovered in a likely location. It will take effort, but I believe the scene can be staged to suggest he was the victim of an assault. Do you wish to know further details?"

"Uh, no, and thank you."

It wasn't much, but it was all I could do for Danny. The rest I'd have to live with.

Chapter Twenty-Nine

Anton Ionescu stared out the window of his study at the sun rising over the mountains. The man standing behind him said impatiently, "Are you listening to me? This cannot continue."

Without taking his eyes off the dawn sky, Ionescu said, "I hear you Cezar. You are sure Seraphina and Ioana are responsible for this boy's death?"

"Of course, I'm sure. We haven't made the mistake of hunting the girls as a group again after the electrical mishaps on the square. I have two men on surveillance duty at the festival. Last night, Emil saw Seraphina approach the boy. As she led him toward the alley, Ioana joined them. Emil could not follow without attracting attention to himself, so he signaled Petre. By the time he reached the scene, both girls were draining the boy's blood. Petre called out to them to stop, but it was too late. They vanished, and the human fell to the ground dead."

Anton made an impatient sound. "And why didn't Petre dispose of the body?"

"Because that infernal ghost hound started howling and

Petre couldn't get him to stop. Petre could not risk being seen and attracting any attention to our family. He is known in the area as an electrician. That is why I selected him, so he would blend into the crowd."

Anton sighed. "Of course. I understand. Tell me again about this red-haired woman. You are certain she was Fae?"

"Yes, according to Petre, she veiled the scene with fairy dust. When the barrier dissolved, only the Hamilton girl and Longworth were left in the alley. The other woman and the body were gone."

"Thank you, Cezar. You may leave now."

"Anton, Seraphina and Ioana will kill again."

"I am aware of that, Cezar. Leave."

He listened as the door of the study opened and shut again. Only then did Ionescu lean his head against the cool glass of the window pane and close his eyes.

So, the Hamilton girl had help. He suspected the red-haired woman was the *baobhan sith* MacVicar who worked with the DGI. Chesterfield had files on all of them. Powerful wizard or not, did the man really think he could overcome the Mother Trees?

Anton Ionescu was not an unethical man. All his life he'd sought to abide by the rules of behavior Father Damian helped the Strigoi develop when he brought them to the New World and saved them from the bigoted vengeance of the Church. But that code of conduct failed to guide Anton when he lost his entire family and was left to raise his daughter and niece alone.

In the aftermath, Anton did what was required of him to prevent their resurrection as *Strigoi mort blasfematoare*. He drove the silver stakes in their hearts. He severed their heads from their bodies. But he only found the strength to do those things because he had a reason to live—two reasons. Seraphina and Ioana.

The girls were all that was left of joy in his world. He

spoiled them, indulging their whim to attend the human school to "fit in" even though the elders in the clan advised against it.

He knew Seraphina and Ioana would encounter the youngest Daughters of Knasgowa there, but what did he understand of the rivalries teenage girls develop? He'd laughed when Seraphina and Ioana explained at length the drama involved in the cheerleader tryouts. They were so young, so innocent to think that such things would retain relevance over the scope of a lifetime.

But then the morning of the car accident, collapsing to his knees on the cliff overlooking the mangled wreckage and the girls' broken bodies, Anton had sensed the lingering traces of magic in the air. The memory of Seraphina's voice rose through the cacophony in his head. "Kelly and Gemma swore they'd curse us so they could get on the squad, Daddy, and that's just not *fair*."

How many nights since had he walked the floor in this very room wondering if his leniency caused their deaths and debating the wisdom of the weakness that followed. By Strigoi custom, a private funeral was held, and then Anton was left alone in the family chapel to complete the death rituals. With shaking hands, tears streaming down his cheeks, he drove the stakes into Seraphina and Ioana's chests, but he could not bring himself to perform the beheading.

The night before the service, Anton had consoled himself reading Father Damien's private papers. In the darkest hours before dawn, an idea began to form in the grieving man's mind. If Damien's vision of curing the *Strigoi vui* of their hunger by finding an alternate food source could be realized, could there not also be a way to cure the *Strigoi mort blasfematoare*?

Now, looking back, Anton knew he'd been grasping at the thinnest of straws. Using the ritual sword, Anton cut a slice on his forearm, binding the cut with his handkerchief. Once hidden under the sleeve of his suit jacket, the bandage wasn't even visible. All he needed was enough blood on the blade to make it appear as if his job was done. Closing the casket lids, he summoned the pallbearers who carried the girls to their final resting place; a crypt in the private burial ground at the bottom edge of the Ionescu property.

There his daughter and niece stayed, slumbering in suspended animation while Ionescu searched for a way to awaken them safely. He chose to forego his immediate vengeance against the Daughters of Knasgowa, but as he watched Kelly Ryan and Gemma Campbell grow, hatred hardened his heart. Why were they allowed to live? To realize their dreams? To marry? To have children?

The bulk of his ire fell on Kelly. She seemed so contrite, so broken by what had happened. An innocent girl would not have reacted as she did. When he learned that Kelly was with child, anger swelled in Anton's heart. That was when he made a critical mistake. He confided in one of his clients, a Creavit wizard named Irenaeus Chesterfield.

"Why should you suffer this insult?" Chesterfield asked. "This witch caused the deaths of your daughter and niece. You are due your revenge. Curse them. It is within your power."

Under Chesterfield's goading, Anton gave in and issued the curse, only to relent in part when the aos si intervened and offered a deal that would spare the boy's life. Chesterfield seemed sympathetic, agreeing with Anton that his greater responsibility lay in preserving the peace with the Fae in Shevington for the sake of his clan.

The years passed, and Anton learned to live with the gaping hole in his soul. Then came the night, six months ago, when Chesterfield offered him a new hope. "Dear Anton, I have not lost sight of your lonely plight these many years. I believe I have found a way to cure your girls, but it requires the blood of the child who was sent into exile. The ritual must be performed before the second child, the girl called Jinx, attains her 30th birthday this December. It would appear that our interests converge. Perhaps we can work together to accomplish our individual goals?"

Chesterfield went on to explain that he required a living branch of the Mother Tree in Shevington for purposes he did not care to divulge. If Ionescu could find a way to get the boy, Connor, through the portal and ransom him for the branch, Chesterfield would use the boy's blood to cure the girls. "As an added caveat," Chesterfield offered, "you may then do as you please with the Hamilton woman."

It had all seemed so easy. Anton planned to leverage the legendary feud between the Pikes and the McGregors to get his hired kidnapper, Malcolm Ferguson, into the Valley. But yet again, his plans were thwarted by a Daughter of Knasgowa. Jinx raised the dead in the local cemetery by accident and the magic spilled over to the crypt where Seraphina and Ioana slept.

To Anton's horror, he answered a knock at his door one night and opened it to find the girls standing on his porch, confused and hungry. Not knowing what else to do, they'd come home. He'd tried to contain them, locking them in the guest house and feeding them the blood of stolen livestock, but as the girls' strength grew, so did their resolve to be free.

Everything unraveled in rapid succession. First Ferguson failed, and then the girls broke out of their makeshift prison. Anton had no choice but to confess everything to his trusted lieutenant, Cezar. After all, the clan was bound to honor Anton's curse, but his efforts to blame Seraphina and Ioana's current state on the Hamilton woman met with uneasy acceptance from his people.

They had lived in peace with the humans and Fae around Briar Hollow for more than 200 years. For the time being, his clan was helping Anton in his efforts to contain the girls, but if the corpses of drained victims began to pile up, that support would quickly evaporate.

Anton had no choice. He must now do what he had failed to do thirty years earlier. The girls must be put down. Cezar would help him, but only if Anton could offer a credible plan to accomplish the deed without calling attention to the Ionescu as a whole. That meant talking to Seraphina and Ioana.

Cezar and his men had already searched the crypt and found it empty. Anton suspected the girls had returned to the "hide out" they'd used as children for shelter; a shallow cave in the hills above the compound. Now was the time to go there, when most of his own people were asleep in their beds. Shrugging into a coat, Anton let himself out through the back gate of his property and began to climb into the woods.

His breath created clouds of vapor as he ascended the slope, following the winding course of a mountain creek to reach the outcropping of rocks where the cave lay hidden. As Anton approached the entrance, the hair on the back of his neck stood up. Although he had never fed on the energy of a living creature, Anton possessed the sharpened senses of his kind. He felt the girls long before Seraphina's voice spoke from the depths of the cave.

"You're not going to lock us up again, Daddy," she warned. "We won't let you."

"No, that's not why I'm here. I came to apologize for the way I've treated you. I understand now that you have ascended to the highest form our kind is capable of achieving. I let my fear rule me. I want to help you, to join with you, if only you will trust me again."

Slowly Seraphina, and then Ioana emerged from the cave, faces dark and suspicious. "Are you trying to trick us, Daddy?" Seraphina asked.

"I would never do such a thing," he said, allowing love to color his expression and willing his muscles not to clench at the sight of the murderous creature his daughter had become. "I truly am sorry, Seraphina."

He watched as a challenging gleam came into her eyes. "Then prove it. Let us make you one of us."

Swallowing the bile that rose in his throat, Anton said, "I want that more than anything, but I think I must stay in this weak form a little longer to put everything in place for your safety. Our people are foolish. They will fear me and turn against me if I ascend to your level now."

Seraphina seemed to consider that. "We still need proof that you are on our side. Help us with our plan."

"What can I do?"

"We have a surprise in store for Kelly and Gemma at the carnival Saturday night," Seraphina said. She grinned, revealing her fangs. "Be there on the square as night falls and we will tell you what you must do."

"I'll be there, honey," Anton said, adding hesitantly. "Maybe between now and then you should remain hidden?"

"Oh, we'll be safe, Daddy," Seraphina assured him. "We left a nice little calling card for the witches. We want them to stew in their own cauldron between now and Saturday night."

She began to giggle, and Ioana joined in. The cackling turned Anton's blood to ice, but he forced himself to smile.

"You'll be so proud of us, Daddy," Ioana said. "We're going to turn the streets of Briar Hollow red with blood. Have you ever tasted blood?"

"No," Anton said, "I haven't."

Ioana's eyes flattened into black pools.

"Oh, you will, and you'll like it."

Chapter Thirty

In the aftermath of Danny's death, we stepped up the GNATS surveillance. Tori and Chase spent a good hour punching buttons on one of the iPads and fiddling with wires, but when they were done, the display on the big screen TV was split into two rows of four boxes each.

One drone stayed on the lumberyard and only changed position to follow Scrap's truck wherever it went, which amounted to one destination—home. Thanks to the video feed, Tori had to watch as her father carried boxes of his possessions out of her childhood home. When I tried to talk to her about it, she shook her head, and whispered in a choked voice, "Don't, Jinksy. I gotta keep it together until this is over."

I was starting to get the uneasy feeling that no matter how well we resolved the crisis at hand, the issues in the Andrews house weren't going to be so easy to mend.

Three drones hovered over the Ionescu compound 24 hours a day. That left the bottom four video feeds on the screen for the GNATS cameras watching the square. The whole set-up gave the lair the feeling of a war room. Since I felt as if we were under siege that seemed appropriate.

Thursday passed peacefully. Things in town were gearing up for the two-day Halloween celebration starting Friday night. The citizens of Briar Hollow, blissfully unaware of what was going on right under their noses, were having a high old time.

Thankfully, none of the other ghost tours yielded any viral-quality evidence, although the group from Charlotte staking out the cemetery swore they captured "credible" electronic voice phenomenon.

Beau listened to the recording on the festival website and chuckled. At his feet, Duke cocked his head as if he recognized the voices as well.

"What do you hear?" I asked.

"The more strident of the two voices belongs to Miss Lou Ella, the hairdresser. She is arguing with Mrs. Walters, the lady in the blue gingham dress."

"About what?"

"I was only able to pick out a few words. but having mediated many of their spats, it would seem that Miss Lou Ella is quite taken by one of the young men on the ghost hunting team, which offends Mrs. Walters' sense of propriety."

"They know not to let things get out of hand again, right?"

"Yes, they have been duly cautioned."

"Okay, I'm going upstairs to check on things. Come get me if anything happens."

When I opened the basement door, I found Tori and the moms standing in a straight line staring at the front window. "What's going on?"

"*He's* what's going on," Tori answered, pointing to a man on the sidewalk staring into the store.

"What's he doing?"

"Just standing there," Tori said. "Your mother thinks he's one of the Ionescus."

A cold chill passed over me. "Are you sure, Mom?"

"Not really. Anton used to come to the football games to

watch Seraphina and Ioana cheer. He always had a man with him everyone said was his bodyguard. That was a long time ago, and he was a lot younger, but I think the man out there is the same guy."

"Well, there's only one way to find out."

Before they could stop me, I was out the door and in the man's face. "Something I can do for you, mister?"

The stranger regarded me impassively. "My name is Cezar Ionescu. My cousin Anton sent me to speak with you. Since your store is warded, I had no choice but to stand here until one of you came out. If you would be so kind as to take down the barrier, perhaps we could sit and have a civilized conversation."

"Yeah, not happening."

He regarded me with mock-innocent eyes. "Do you really wish to stand on the sidewalk here on the courthouse square and discuss vampires?"

He had me there.

"Stay here. I'll be right back."

I went inside the store.

"Is that him?" Mom asked.

"Yes. He says his name is Cezar Ionescu."

Tori rolled her eyes. "Of course it is, because nobody in Romania is named Tom, Dick, or Harry. What does Cezar want?"

"He wants me to let him into the store so we can talk."

Mom gasped. "You're not thinking about doing that, are you?"

"Of course not. I came back in to get my own bodyguards."

Tori frowned. "Greer and Lucas?"

"Exactly. Greer said they're here to work with me, so I'm going to give them something to do."

Stealing a look at the window, she said, "Cezar is still

watching. You should stay here and keep talking to the moms. Makes it look more like you're the boss lady in charge. I'll go get Greer and Lucas."

In a minute or two, the two DGI agents joined us. "Problem?" Lucas asked.

Nodding toward the window, I said, "That guy out there wants to talk. He's Anton Ionescu's cousin. You two feel like playing hired muscle?"

Greer reached into her seemingly bottomless leather pouch and brought out a pair of jet black sunglasses. She slipped them on, letting her face turn to ivory stone. "You mean in this fashion?"

"Exactly."

Lucas flipped open a pair of Ray Bans with one hand and slipped them on, assuming an equally impassive face. "Let's do this thing."

We walked outside, Lucas and Greer flanking me. Out of the corner of my eye, I saw Chase leaning casually against the wall of the cobbler shop. No one broke stride, but we all registered that we had a backup if we needed it.

"Okay," I told Cezar. "Now I'm ready to talk. Follow me."

I led them around the corner to the abandoned bus stop. As we went by the grocery store, a kid with an open package of Twinkies in his hand said, "Whoa! You guys coming as the *Men in Black* to the Halloween carnival?"

"Don't make me flashy thing you, kid," Lucas warned.

When we reached the bench, I inclined my head to Cezar. "Have a seat."

"Quaint," he said, taking out a handkerchief and dusting off the wood before he sat down.

Sitting opposite him, I said, "Okay. Talk." As I spoke, I let my eyes roam across the abandoned building across the street. I could make out Chase's dark shirt in the deep interior shadows.

"I understand that you have little reason to trust me,"

Cezar began. "Anton sent me. He would like to enlist your aid to stop Seraphina and Ioana."

That statement won him a skeptical, cocked eyebrow. "Really? He's the one who turned them loose on us in the first place."

"No," Cezar answered seriously, "he didn't. Anton never meant for them to rise in this form. He can no longer control the girls. They're planning to stage a bloodbath at the carnival. Anton knows that cannot be allowed to happen."

"Why should I believe you?"

"Miss Hamilton, did the aos si ever warn you about us?"

Reluctantly, I admitted Myrtle never mentioned the Strigoi as a threat.

"There's a reason for that. We want only to live in peace. After having been hunted by the Church for centuries, we have no desire to be targets of bigotry or hatred ever again. Anton let his love for the girls cloud his judgment. He did not bury them properly, but he could not have anticipated that your spell would run so badly amuck and resurrect them."

As much as I might have wanted to counter that, I couldn't. The idea might be hard for me to swallow, but my irresponsible use of magic was the undeniable wild card that set much of the current series of events in motion. Cezar saw what was going through my mind.

"You already know this, don't you?" he asked.

"Most of it, but you confirmed the theory for us."

"Anton thought they could be cured. Now he knows that isn't possible. We know you hid their latest kill. Help us to ensure there are no others."

"Not so fast. Did your cousin hire Malcolm Ferguson to come after us?"

Cezar's face registered surprise. "Not that I am aware of."

"Did it ever occur to you that your cousin might not be telling you the whole truth about his business?" Greer asked.

Cezar turned to look at her. "You are not a hired bodyguard."

"No," Greer said, slipping off her glasses. "I am not."

"What business has the baobhan sith here?" Cezar asked.

"None she cares discuss with you, *Strigoi vui*. Now answer my question."

Paling slightly, Cezar said, "It is quite possible I do not know the full scope of Anton's dealings with you, but he is telling the truth about the girls. He loves them, and he does not want them to live as they are now."

"Well, Cezar," I said, "here's the deal. Your cousin has a vendetta against my mother. He shattered my family, sent my brother into exile, and possibly turned a sociopathic murderer loose in my town. Sorry if I'm a pint low on trust for the guy."

"That is fair, but I have done none of those things to you. I speak not just for my cousin, but for the majority of the clan. We do not support Anton's curse against your mother, and we will not enforce it. If Anton makes a move against you, we will not assist him."

"Not assisting him isn't the same as helping us."

Cezar nodded in acknowledgment. "That is true, but would you rather face a single Strigoi or an entire clan of us?"

Okay, so I was looking at an offer that evened the odds and might give us a way to take out the Strigoi Sisters. It was worth hearing.

The plan Cezar sketched out for us was so crazy, it might work. To stake and behead Seraphina and Ioana without a lot of collateral damage, he suggested incapacitating them with electricity.

"Our people will be handling the ambulance. Rather than being taken to the hospital, the girls will be returned to their crypt and buried properly so that they are never a threat to you or us again."

"And all the witnesses on the square?"

Greer provided the answer. "You're planning to mesmerize all of them, aren't you?"

"Yes," Cezar said. "*Strigoi viu* will be stationed around the square. The people who attend the festival that evening will remember the light show only."

"Light show?" I said.

"My man Petre is an electrician. He will arrange to be working with the musical entertainment that night. He will direct the charge at Seraphina and Ioana."

That was the part I still couldn't quite believe.

"You are seriously planning on electrocuting them? With all those innocent bystanders potentially in the way?"

"Miss Hamilton," Cezar said, "if there is one thing we Strigoi know how to do, it's channel electricity with pinpoint accuracy. No one on the square will be harmed."

Lucas spoke up for the first time. "What role do you expect our people to play?"

"That's simple," Cezar said. "Bait."

Chapter Thirty-One

It probably won't come as a big shock to you that not everyone in the lair reacted well to the word "bait." Chase topped that list, bristling when Lucas said amiably, "Calm down, McGregor. It's a good plan."

Both men were standing near the fireplace. Chase wheeled on Lucas and for an instant, I thought they might come to blows. "I don't need you to tell me how to do my job. You are not charged with protecting the Daughters of Knasgowa."

Lucas didn't flinch. "Actually, I am, and so is Greer. We've been assigned to work with Jinx by the Mother Oak. If you don't like the arrangement, I suggest you take it up with her."

Before I could intervene, Greer did it for me. "Gentleman, I believe this situation calls for more focus and less time spent measuring your egos."

Chase turned angry eyes toward her. "Nobody asked your opinion, baobhan sith."

From the hearth, Festus said quietly, "Chase, either get your head in the game or get out."

"Dad . . . "

"I'm sorry, Chase," Festus said, "but I'm going to say what

everyone else here is dying to say. Get over yourself. You and Jinx were an item, and now you're not. You've had your pout. Now you're acting like a jealous jerk. Grow the hell up. Jinx needs a functioning team behind her. You and Lucas were friends when you were boys. I have no idea what happened between the two of you and I don't care. You're grown men. Act like it."

Lucas and Chase were friends once? That was an interesting tidbit to file away for later.

From where I stood, Lucas *was* acting like a grown man, and he confirmed that opinion when he immediately held his hand out to Chase.

"We're on the same side. When this is over, we can get drunk and settle our differences with our fists if we have to, but now is not the time."

The muscles in Chase's jaw flexed, but he shook Grayson's hand.

Then Lucas did something I liked. A lot.

"Don't you think you owe the lady an apology?" he asked Chase, nodding toward Greer.

The argument could have re-ignited if Greer hadn't taken control of the moment. "Who are you calling a lady?" she said, regarding both men with mock outrage.

Everyone laughed, and the level of tension in the room eased down a notch.

"I'm sorry, Greer," Chase said. "I was out of line."

"You're a McGregor. Sometimes you can't help yourself. Apology accepted."

After a few seconds of silence, I said, "Alrighty, then. Do we need to deal with anybody else's objection before we move on here?"

Dad held up his hand. "For the record, I don't like the idea of my wife and daughter being used like a worm on a hook. Or Gemma and Tori either for that matter."

"It's not as bad as you think," I said. "The plan really is a good one. It's not like we're going to be out there alone. Tori, can you enlarge one of the video feeds so we can get an overhead of the square?"

"Sure, no problem."

As I talked, Tori highlighted the areas around the courthouse where Cezar planned to position the Strigoi. "All we really have to do is be there. We don't know exactly what Seraphina and Ioana have in mind, but once they're on the lawn, they'll be surrounded by Cezar's people. We have the elder amulets, so we won't be affected during the mesmerization."

"How is the Petre guy going to direct the electricity?" Dad asked.

"To be honest, Dad, I really don't know. Cezar told us we have to keep the girls between the courthouse and the bandstand. That's where Petre will be working with the sound equipment."

"And the rest of us?" Beau asked.

"Will be right here in the store safely behind the wards," I said.

He started to protest, but I held up my hand to silence him. "No arguments. The only other people who are going to be out there on the square with us are Chase, Lucas, and Greer. Beau, you and Festus will be in charge here at the store. You can watch the whole thing over the GNATS drones. If anything goes wrong, get Barnaby and Moira here as quickly as possible."

I don't think he liked the assignment, but Beau is a good soldier. He simply nodded and said, "Understood."

So. We had our proverbial ducks lined up. Cezar knew exactly how the whole thing would play out. Anton was on board—and then the Strigoi Sisters threw a monkey wrench in everything.

Just after supper on Friday we were all down in the lair. Dad and Beau were manning the shop. I can tell you now it was that "calm before the storm" moment you always hear about, especially because black, scudding clouds filled the skies outside with thunder rumbling in the distance.

Without warning, Glory suddenly snatched up her megaphone and started screeching, "Red alert! Red alert! Main viewscreen! Red alert!"

Tori looked up from the herbs she was packaging. "Don't tell me we've got Klingons on top of everything else."

"Worse," I said, looking at the video feed, "the Strigoi Sisters are early."

Everyone moved to get a better view of the screen. The sun was starting to set, and the carnival goers were beginning to gather even with the threatening storm. Tori and I had promised Irma we'd come over later and take turns running the dunking booth and calling out the Bingo numbers if the event didn't get rained out.

Seraphina and Ioana stood in the center of the crowd appearing passably normal among the costumed festival goers. As we watched, Seraphina looked up and made eye contact with the drone's camera. Her scarlet lips drew back in a feral smile. Raising one hand, she curled her index finger in the sign for "come here."

"Can she really see the GNATS drone?" Tori asked in a hushed voice.

"She can," Greer said, "and she appears to be issuing an invitation."

"Well, we're not going to accept it, right?" Tori said.

A little girl dressed as Raggedy Ann ran past the Strigoi Sisters. Ioana casually put a foot out and tripped the child. The girl fell forward, landing hard on the grass and bursting into tears.

I watched in horror as Ioana immediately scooped the

child up and began talking to her soothingly, caressing the girl's cheek with her fingers. My stomach twisted in knots at the memory of Tori's description of those razor-sharp nails, but then Ioana took it a step farther. She ran her index finger over the girl's scraped knee coating the digit in blood. As we watched, she raised the finger to her lips and licked it clean, closing her eyes in pleasure at the taste. I wanted to throw up.

Seraphina, who watched the whole thing with an expression of obvious delight, turned her attention back to the camera and repeated her beckoning gesture. This time, however, she plainly mouthed the word, "Now."

"Okay," I said, "that's it. We roll. Chase, take Greer and Lucas through the cobbler shop and try to get around to the backside of the square without being seen. Mom, Gemma, Tori, you're with me. Everyone else stays here. I don't care what happens, do *not* leave this building. Festus, you're in charge."

"I can get a message through to the Registry," he said. "You want Barnaby and Moira here?"

"There's no time. This one is on us."

As we started up the stairs, I saw Mom and Gemma exchange a few words. I don't know what they said to each other, but Mom nodded, her expression resolute and fearless, as she fell into step behind me.

When we went into the shop, Beau and Dad knew instantly that something was wrong. There were a few people drinking coffee in the espresso bar, waiting to see if the storm would hit or not.

"Uh, hi," Dad said, "the four of you going over to the carnival?"

Mom went to him. "We are, and I want a hug before we go."

Dad opened his arms to her, but as he held her, his eyes grew wide. Mom was whispering in his ear telling him what was going on. When she released him, she said, "We'll be back in a little bit."

"Uh, yeah, sure, okay," Dad babbled. "Be careful . . . the . . . weather's looking bad out there."

At the door, I turned back and saw Dad go behind the counter to speak to Beau, who inclined his head to listen. After a few words, the colonel's head came up with a stricken look on his face. It was too late to stop us, and Beau knew it.

On the sidewalk out front, Gemma said, "How are we playing this?"

"I have no idea," I replied as we started across the street. "Wing it, I guess."

"We need to try to get Seraphina and Ioana away from the square," Mom said. "There are too many innocent people in the line of fire."

"How do you suggest we do that?" Tori asked.

"They want Kelly and me," Gemma said. "So we offer to go with them."

"Can't say I'm loving that option, Mom,"

"Me either, kiddo, but we may have no choice."

Seraphina and Ioana met us halfway across the lawn. Ioana was still holding the little girl, whose eyes were now wild with fright. Once again, the sounds around us faded, but not the way they had the first time we encountered the Strigoi Sisters. Out of the corner of my eye, I could still see people walk by and detect the faint pulsations of the music. The elder amulets were working.

"Hi!" Seraphina said brightly. "We've been *dying* to see you all again. Oh. Wait. We're already dead!"

Beside her, Ioana cackled insanely.

"Put the child down," I said. "This is between us."

"Oh," Ioana pouted, "I *like* her. She's my little doll, aren't you sweetheart?"

The girl looked at me with enormous blue eyes. "I want my mother, please," she whimpered.

"It's okay, honey," I said, "we'll get you back to her in just a minute."

Seraphina's lips curled. "You're not in charge here, witch."

"Fine. Let the girl go and you can be in charge all you want."

"Now, why," Seraphina said, "would I let our snack go toddling away when we'll only have to catch her all over again? Children are such tasty little sweetmeats."

Beside me, Mom stiffened, and I felt her power rise. She wanted a piece of this bitch as much as I did.

I honestly can't tell you what would have happened next if Anton Ionescu hadn't walked through the wavering field of energy around us and jammed what looked like a taser hard against Ioana's neck.

The jolt would have sent a human flying backward, but the weapon's charge reacted differently to the strigoi, bathing Anton and Ioana in a crackling web of energy. Thankfully, the initial blow startled Ioana enough that she dropped the little girl.

Mom was by me in a flash, gathering the child in her arms. When Seraphina lunged for them, my mother raised her hand and let loose with a wicked stream of blue fire. It hit Seraphina square in the chest. The Strigoi paused, but she didn't stop. If Gemma hadn't tackled her, Seraphina would have been on top of mom and the terrified girl.

That's when I saw Greer outside the thin envelope surrounding us. She stood against the wind that lifted and tossed her flaming hair as if it were a living creature. Her eyes burned with iridescent green flames that merged with the crimson fire pouring out of the ruby ring on her finger. Over the howl of the storm, the words of the incantation she chanted solidified and time literally stopped. She was giving us the cover we needed.

Rolling from Gemma's tackle, Seraphina collided with Anton, who clutched at her with his free hand. As his fingers closed around her arm, the field of electricity spread over her body as well. Through the static bursts, his eyes met mine. "Finish it, witch," he gasped. "I can't hold them much longer."

"I don't know how."

"Call down the lightning. It's the only way."

Above me jagged flashes of light branched through the roiling clouds. I felt Tori take my hand and then she reached for Gemma, who in turn clasped mom's hand. As one, we summoned our magic, channeling the power through our bodies and sending it up into the deepening heart of the storm.

The storm answered.

I felt more than saw the lightning strike. Before the world flashed white and hot around me, Seraphina and Ioana threw their heads back and screamed.

When my vision cleared, the Strigoi Sisters were gone, and Anton lay crumpled on the ground, his clothes smoking from the blast.

At first, I thought he was dead, but then he raised a blackened and charred hand, beckoning me to come to his side. Dropping to my knees next to the fallen man, I reached for his hand and then hesitated. His whole body was covered in burns. I was afraid to touch him.

"Are they dead?" he rasped, barely managing to squeeze the words out of his ruined lips.

"Yes. Now lie still until we can get you some help."

"There is no help for me. Promise me."

"What?"

"See that I am buried properly," he pleaded. "Please do not let me become a monster."

As gently as I could, I took his hand. "That won't happen," I told him as tears spilled out of my eyes. "I promise."

The dying man looked up at me. "I'm afraid," he said in a small voice.

"Shh," I said. "You're not alone. I'll stay with you."

I don't know if he heard me before he died. I hope so.

Epilogue

Greer did her job well. She stopped time and held it while we cleaned up the mess. Cezar Ionescu and his men arrived minutes after Anton died. They lifted their fallen chieftain onto their shoulders and carried him off the courthouse lawn like a warrior leaving the arena on his shield.

"He will be buried according to our customs," Cezar assured me.

"What was the weapon Anton used against the girls?" Tori asked.

"It is a modified form of taser. We use them as mobile feeding devices when we must be away from home."

"So Seraphina and Ioana are really dead?" Mom asked.

"Yes. The bolt of lightning incinerated them."

On my cue, Greer released the people at the festival, but not before she gently erased the little girl's memory, leaving nothing behind but the recollection of a scraped knee. As for the larger crowd, they remembered the storm, and some thought lightning might have struck the rod on the top of the courthouse, but no one knew a magical fight had taken place right under their noses.

Even though it was hard to get back into the spirit of things, we had to put on a good front through Halloween. Tori suggested we close the shop, and all attend the carnival in costume. "We seriously need to lighten up," she said.

No one argued with her.

Letting Darby in on the fun didn't pose a problem. He turned invisible and followed my dad around all night. Instead of a costume, dad put on his fishing waders and a cap overloaded with lures. When people asked, he told them he was that Jeremy Wade guy from *River Monsters*.

Beau went in uniform, with Rodney tucked inside the collar of his tunic. Mom and Gemma dressed up as Lucy and Ethel, which was too appropriate for words. Tori figured she was good with the hair, but she threw on a tiger-striped t-shirt for good measure. I embraced my inner truth and dressed as a witch.

In part, I selected the costume so Glory wouldn't be left out. When Chesterfield miniaturized her, he only gave her three magical powers: the ability to run the chessboard, fly on her broom, and plaster herself flat on the side of a coffee cup.

As it turned out, she could actually still manage the plastering thing on any surface, including the front of the pointy black witch's hat I wore to the festival.

Crowds of people packed the square. During the evening, Amity Prescott awarded the digital camera to Lester, the sole surviving Bigfoot hunter, in recognition of the still photo he submitted lifted from the baseball video. We knew it was Duke, with teeth bared charging the camera, but skeptics argued it was just dust blowing off of home plate.

Hilmer Eastwood won the contest for best decorated house for painstakingly setting out 100 tombstones in his front yard complete with mannequin hands reaching up out of the dirt.

Personally, I think it was the dry ice fog that pushed him past Etta Louise Morewood's display of giant spiders and their webs.

Much to Aggie's delight, a *Walking Dead* fan took top honors for his walker costume complete with disgustingly convincing disembowelment.

Irma couldn't have been happier with the success of the whole festival and was already talking excitedly about SpookCon2. Given what we'd been through that week, it was nice to see someone happy about how things worked out.

Don't get me wrong. I was glad we were free of the Strigoi Sisters, but I found myself genuinely grieving Anton Ionescu. Yes, he did awful things, but he did them from the depths of terrible grief and, twisted or not, from love.

That's exactly what I was thinking about as I sat at our table on the lawn listening to the music and watching the couples on the dance floor. As I let my gaze wander idly over the scene, I noticed a man in white tie and tails wearing a top hat. His face was covered with a *Phantom of the Opera* mask, and he had a girl on each arm. Both were dressed like Victorian-era streetwalkers, but their faces were covered by feathered Mardi Gras masks.

As the trio passed me, the man lifted his hat and bowed. "Good evening, are you enjoying the festivities?"

"Very much. And you?"

"Immensely," he answered as he strolled away.

My witch's hat was sitting on the table beside me so Glory could have a good view of the dance floor. Suddenly, the hat began to tremble violently.

Picking up my drink to disguise that I was talking to a piece of headgear, I said, "Glory, are you alright?"

"No," she said in a breathless, fearful whisper, "I'd know that voice anywhere."

"What voice? You mean that man who just spoke to me?"

"Yes. That was Mr. Chesterfield."

What the . . .

Turning quickly in my chair, I scanned the crowd to find the figure again. I finally spotted him in the pool of light cast by the streetlight on the corner. He and the women on his arm were walking away. As if he felt my gaze fall on him, the man turned and looked back toward the square. When he did, both women reached up and took off their masks. Even at that distance, I recognized them.

Seraphina and Ioana.

See what I mean about nothing ever being easy in my world?

A Word from Juliette

Thank you for reading *Witch on Second*. Now that you've reached the end of the book, I hope you'll want to continue the adventure with Jinx, Tori, and the gang in Briar Hollow and beyond.

The story develops through a page-turning series of urban fantasy novels that take the characters into new adventures and realms.

In the next story, *Witch on Third*, Jinx has plenty on her plate without a new evil trio in town. As the team works to counter Chesterfield's newest scheme, something happens in the Valley that changes everything for the Hamilton family.

Not certain you want to continue the journey? I've included the first chapter of *Witch on Third* to give you a sneak peak of the mystery, adventure, and hijinks lying ahead!

But first . . . Get Exclusive Jinx Hamilton Material

There are many things I love about being an author, but building a relationship with my readers is far and away the best.

Once a month I send out a newsletter with information on new releases, sneak peeks, and inside articles on Jinx Hamilton as well as other books and series I'm currently developing.

You can get all this and more by signing up here.

Witch on Third - Preview

The storm boiled up out of the north at dusk, splitting the skies over Briar Hollow, North Carolina with crackling tendrils of lightning. Seemingly oblivious to the fury raging over their heads, four women stood in the center of the town square with hands clasped. As one, they sent their magic skyward, finding and harnessing a single bolt to do their bidding.

In the intensity of that moment, they didn't know that smaller bolts also answered the call, crashing to earth on the slopes of the neighboring mountains. One of those strikes angled toward a lonely corner of the local cemetery. It sought out the weathervane crowning a forgotten crypt. At impact, the electricity engulfed the crumbling structure in a static web that found and flowed through the tiniest cracks.

As quickly as the crescendo built, the weather stilled. The clouds parted to reveal a full moon. A single beam of light falling through the high, round window atop the crypt wall illuminated a chessboard sitting on the floor.

The pieces carved to represent musical notations, cast long, distorted shadows in the dust. One by one, they fell to the side until only the white king stood upright. Then, as if lifted by an unseen hand, the lone chessman rose six inches in the air, hanging suspended for several seconds before descending with a resounding thud.

Miles away in Raleigh, a man looked up from the pages of his book and smiled. "Well," he said, "there you are."

***

Six weeks ago I made a promise to a dying man. I kept my word, even though he had no right to ask anything of me. Anton Ionescu cursed my mother, forced my infant brother into exile, and hired a hitman to go after me and everyone I love. Most folks would argue I didn't owe the man a blessed thing.

They'd be wrong.

Earlier that summer, thanks to an irresponsible bit of magic, I raised Anton's daughter and niece from their graves — as vampires. Anton died thinking they'd been freed from that curse. I thought the same thing until the next night at the Halloween carnival they strolled by my table on the courthouse lawn.

That appearance in itself created an obvious problem, but there's more. The two girls were arm in arm with a Creavit wizard named Irenaeus Chesterfield who has been working against my family for thirty years.

At the time, all I saw was a man in white tie with two women dressed as Victorian hookers. I thought they were going for a kind of Jack the Ripper/*Phantom of the Opera* costume vibe.

Then my costume had a violent reaction to the sighting.

It may not have been the most creative decision, but I went to the carnival as a witch. My Barbie-sized friend, Glory Green, came with me the only way she could without being obvious — plastered flat on the crown of my pointy hat. That, and the ability to fly on her broom, are Glory's only real powers.

So, to be perfectly accurate, Glory was the one who reacted violently. She began to shake so hard I had to put my hand on the hat to keep it from tumbling to the ground.

Chesterfield cursed Glory to live a miniature existence as a stereotypical green-faced witch. Then he sent her into the store I run with my best friend, Tori Andrews, to act as a spy. Glory is on our side now, but she lives in constant terror that Chesterfield will capture and punish her.

That night, however, the wizard and the two women with him didn't threaten Glory or me in any way. They were already past us when Glory told me the man was Chesterfield.

As I watched, the trio crossed the street and paused long enough to look at me and remove their masks. That's when I recognized Seraphina and Ioana. Before I could do much more than stare, the three of them disappeared into thin air.

Speaking in a low, soothing tone, I said, "They're gone, Glory. He's not going to hurt us."

"Not now," she croaked, "but he'll be back."

"He will, but after everything that's happened, don't you think we can let the enjoy the rest of the carnival before we break the bad news?"

The witch's hat grew still. "I owe you all everything," Glory said in a calmer voice. "I'm okay now."

Neither one of us believed that. I certainly wasn't "okay." Before Chesterfield and the girls showed up, I'd been lost in thought trying to assimilate the events of the last 24 hours. The point was to *act* okay.

From where I was sitting, I could see Mom and Gemma Andrews laughing together at the cake walk. Tori was volunteering in the face painting booth, and Colonel Beauregard T.

Longworth, stood in the shadow of the Confederate monument talking to a group of tourists.

We'd had a long week. Our most recent magic-related crisis coincided with the town's first annual paranormal festival. The event proved to be a huge success. The carnival amounted to a victory lap for the organizing committee and offered up some badly needed relaxation for my people. I didn't shatter that illusion until we all walked across the street to the store.

As I locked the front door, I glanced at my watch — just past midnight.

Dad yawned and stretched, announcing his intention to head straight to bed. I hated to do it, but I shook my head. "You can't. We all need to get down to the lair. Glory and I saw Chesterfield and the Strigoi Sisters this evening."

That's our nickname for Seraphina and Ioana. The Ionescu are a clan of transplanted Romanian *Strigoi viu* or, as I like to think of them, *Vampires Lite*. They feed on electricity, not blood. What happened to turn the girls into bloodsuckers? They weren't buried correctly after dying in a car crash — and I'm the one who woke them up. Go me.

Everyone froze in place. All the air seemed to leave the room. Mom ultimately broke the silence. "Are you sure?"

"Totally. Glory recognized Chesterfield, and I saw Seraphina and Ioana."

"So what do we do now?" Gemma asked.

"You all head downstairs," I said, taking out my phone. "I'm going to call Chase and Festus. I'll be down in a minute."

Even though he's my ex, Chase McGregor and I don't actually get to be completely "off." We still have to work together. He and his father, Festus, are werecats pledged to protect the witches in my family.

Chase answered on the first ring. "What is it? Did something happen tonight?"

When Chase told me he intended to skip the carnival, I

understood. Attending the same function in a small town when we were no longer together was still too awkward for him. Honestly, the last few months had been hard on Chase. When he guarded my Aunt Fiona, the work amounted to eating chocolate chip cookies and lending a hand with minor repairs around the shop. Then I took over — without a clue how to be part of the magical world — and everything became much more complicated.

Chase knows the hierarchy of things as well as anyone. Technically, he works for me, but in the first few months of my new life, I let him call a lot of the shots. As my confidence grew and I began to exercise my role as a leader, Chase wasn't ready for the change. Frankly, he acted like a jerk.

Finally, Festus set his son straight in front of everyone, a scene that made me feel genuinely bad for Chase. I know his heart is in the right place, and I know he's in love with me.

Unfortunately, there's a taboo against werecats and witches getting together. The magics are incompatible, and during our short relationship, we even had to face a crazy werecat half-breed, Malcolm Ferguson, who tried to kill us. Granted, he was a claw for hire in the employ of Anton Ionescu, but Malcolm brought loads of personal enthusiasm to the assignment.

Chase had been grappling with frustration, a wounded ego, and a hurting heart. But *he* made the decision about the breakup without even talking to me. I wanted to tackle those hurdles. He couldn't take the pressure.

The relationship drama coincided with major events that left me no time to sit around and moon over a broken heart, although there were plenty of crying nights. For whatever sympathy I might feel for him, Chase had to live with the consequences of his choices the same way I did and get on with life.

Truthfully, I hadn't even considered for me that might include another guy. Then Lucas Grayson showed up. And get this — he's assigned to protect me, too. He and Chase were bound to butt heads anyway, but there is a pre-existing tension between them I still don't understand.

Lucas works for the Division of Grid Integrity, an agency which serves the network of Mother Trees. (Don't worry if you don't know what that means. At the time, my understanding about the Grid was pretty sketchy, too. Just keep reading, and you'll learn at the same pace I did.)

Along with his partner, Greer MacVicar, Lucas has been running primary interference for me of late — and it doesn't take radar to see that the man is interested in me. If you'd asked me the night of the carnival, I would have said I *thought* I was interested in him, too, but that feeling came with a hearty dose of confusion.

At the same time that I was intrigued and flattered, I still missed Chase. But there's no sense in lying about it now. There is a real spark between Lucas and me.

But none of that changed the bottom line. We all had to function as a single team. I made it clear to Chase that my personal life was none of his business. Chesterfield and the Strigoi Sisters, however, *were* his business, which is why I called. Chase and Festus joined us in the lair in less than 5 minutes.

Chase's cobbler shop next door connects to our basement via a small passageway. The whole store sits atop a fairy mound that appears to be endless. When we go to Shevington, the Fae community that is Briar Hollow's direct counterpart in the magical Otherworld, the hike to the portal takes an hour. We've started using bikes to cut down on the travel time.

I think there's a similar passageway that runs next door to Amity Prescott's pottery shop and art gallery. We need to take a second here and talk about Amity.

She's also a witch and one of the few survivors of the now-defunct Briar Hollow coven. Oddly enough, however, Amity absented herself by choice from everything that happened around the paranormal festival and its aftermath.

At first her refusal to do more than help organize the event put me off. We needed all hands on deck. I said as much to Barnaby Shevington, the founder of the city that bears his name and its current (and only) lord high mayor. I recently discovered Barnaby is also my several times great-grandfather, but that's not something we'd discussed yet.

In response to my annoyance over Amity's absence, Barnaby said, "When her participation is needed, she will be there. Trust Amity's wisdom in this, and trust mine."

The answer didn't leave me much room to complain, but I will say for now that Barnaby was right. He usually is.

When Chase and Festus arrived, we all settled around the fire. Festus headed straight for his favorite spot on the hearth, which also happened to be right by Greer's chair. Because he has a lame hip, Festus lives his life primarily as a yellow housecat, but that doesn't dim his appreciation for a beautiful red-haired Scotswoman.

As we watched, Festus turned in three tight circles, put his back to the fire, cleared his throat, and proceeded to drop a bombshell. Earlier that evening, from his perch in the cobbler shop window, Festus watched everything that happened with Chesterfield and the Strigoi Sisters.

"Dad!" Chase protested. "Did it ever enter your mind to call me?"

Festus fixed his son with a perfectly impassive feline glare. "No, it did not. The Creavit scum didn't do anything. After the week we've had, I thought it could wait, and apparently so did Jinx."

"Hold on," I said, "you *recognized* Chesterfield?"

Festus turned his eyes toward me. An old anger stirred in their amber depths. "Of course, I recognized him. It's because of him I've been limping since 1936."

From one of the couches across the room, Gemma said, "You're certain you saw Seraphina and Ioana with Chesterfield?" She managed to stay calm, but the strained quality of the words and the pallor of her skin betrayed the depths of her fear.

"Yes," I said. "It was them."

"What if they go after Scrap again?"

A few days earlier Greer showed up at Andrews Lumber in neighboring Cotterville in time to keep the Strigoi Sisters from snacking on Tori's father, Howard "Scrap" Andrews.

Beside me, Tori started to her feet. "We have to find out if Dad is okay," she said, fighting to keep from sounding as panicked as she must have felt.

"Slow down," Greer said. "The GNATS drone is still watching your father. We would have known by now if anything had happened."

GNATS stands for "Group Network Aerial Transmission System." The tiny drones, each powered by a single grain of fairy dust, create the perfect juncture of magic and technology. No larger than the insect they're named after, the drones, under the command of Major Aspid "Ironweed" Istra of the Brown Mountain Fairy Guard, are our remote eyes.

"Can you show us?" Gemma asked, sounding steadier. "I'd be happier if I could see for myself that Scrap is safe."

"Sure," Chase said, hitting the button to lower the big screen TV from its recessed niche above the fireplace. As the set came into place, he punched commands into his iPad to transfer the drone's video feed to the larger display.

Gemma instantly sat up. "That's not our house. There must be some mistake."

Chase studied the tablet in his hands. "There's no mistake," he said gently. "Scrap moved his things out of your house this afternoon. He's staying at Mrs. Llewellyn's Boarding House on Oak Street in Cotterville."

No one said anything. Gemma deflated, sinking back into the sofa. Mom put an arm around her shoulder. They'd gone to the carnival dressed as Lucy and Ethel. Mom wore a blue dress with big white polka dots and colored her dark hair flaming red with washout dye. Gemma engineered a credible imitation of Ethel's blonde permanent with my curling iron. Like their television idols, the two women had been best friends for as long as I could remember

"At least he's safe, Gem," Mom said. "You two will get this all sorted out."

"All this" referred to the state of the Andrews' marriage. Mom had the good sense to tell my Dad about the magical world before they married. Even though Fae politics forced them to send their only son into exile as an infant, Dad accepted that being a witch was part of my mother's identity. For years she turned her back on magic, but now that she's back in the game — largely because of me — he supports that choice, too.

Gemma, on the other hand, never told her husband about her life as a witch and alchemist. When he found out, he didn't take the news well — and then pretty much lost his mind after a face-to-face counter with the Strigoi Sisters. Scrap's rejection extended to his daughter, which had left Tori, a true Southern daddy's girl, devastated. Mother and daughter were holding it together in the name of taking care of business, but barely.

Blinking back tears, Gemma said, "I'd still like to see for myself that Scrap is safe. Can the drone do that?"

Chase typed in a request to GNATS Ops Command. As we watched, the image of the boarding house grew larger. When the porch loomed into view, the pilot maneuvered along the left side of the house. He reached a cracked window, slipped through, and brought the surveillance craft to a level near the ceiling.

The camera trained on Scrap sound asleep in bed. From

the way his mouth opened and closed rhythmically, we could tell he was snoring. That put a tremulous smile on Gemma's face.

"I don't even need sound to know he's raising the roof," she said in a choked voice. "I've been listening to that man snore for 35 years. Will the drone keep watching him?"

"For as long as we need it to," Chase assured her. "We'll clear it with Barnaby, but I know he'll say yes."

"I appreciate that," Gemma said, still staring at the screen. "I'm mad enough at that man to wring his damned neck, but that doesn't mean I want anything to happen to him."

Thank God my mother laughed first, which gave the rest of us permission to do the same. "He's your husband," Mom said, "if he's going to get killed, you definitely get first dibs on doing the murder."

That's when Dad chimed in. He's been playing straight man for them forever. "Can I point out that as the only married man in the room, this conversation is starting to make me nervous?"

Beau chortled. "I, too, once had a wife and I feared her wrath far more than any horror of the battlefield."

"Ditto," Festus said, raising his paw in agreement. "My Jenny knew how to put her claws out. She had a damned good aim, and I've got the scars on my backside to prove it."

He was sitting on the hearth between Lucas and Greer. Since I didn't know a lot about Lucas, I noticed that he grinned at the banter, but didn't say anything. I took that to mean he'd never been married. Even though we'd just met, I already understood that sometimes Lucas gives away a great deal more about himself when he says nothing.

"Quit your bellyaching, you scoundrels," Greer teased, making her eyes flash. "You're all lucky those good women agreed to marry the likes of any of you in the first place."

"Here, here," Beau agreed. "You could not be more

correct, dear lady."

Dad caught Mom's free hand. "I never said I wasn't lucky, just that I want to stay on your good side."

"You don't have anything to worry about," Mom said, pausing for the perfect amount of time before adding, "for now."

At that, all the men in the room roared with laughter. "She's got you there, Jeff," Festus said, looking fondly at my mother. "That's a Ryan woman for you."

In his long career, Festus has guarded both my mother, and my grandmother, Kathleen Allen Ryan. And honestly? I think he fell in love with both of them.

The good-natured teasing at the expense of the men present helped Gemma to regain her composure. When she asked the next, and perhaps most important question yet, her voice sounded strong and confidant.

"Let's get back to business. How did Seraphina and Ioana survive us dropping a lightning bolt on their heads?"

Chase answered. "Good question. We kept the drones in place over the square tonight for good measure. First, let's all take a look at what Jinx and Dad saw."

He started to change the display, but Gemma stopped him. She had a strange look on her face.

"Before you switch the video," she said, "could you ask the drone pilot to zoom in on the dresser by Scrap's bed?"

"Sure," Chase said, tapping on the screen.

As we watched, the camera panned over the top of the piece of furniture revealing a set of keys, a wristwatch, a wallet, and a bottle of *Obsession* perfume.

"Thank you," Gemma said briskly. "That's all I wanted to see."

I looked at Tori and raised an eyebrow in question. She shook her head. It wasn't until later, when we had a moment alone, that she told me Gemma doesn't wear *Obsession*.

Also by Juliette Harper

In the Jinx Hamilton Series:

ALL Books Available in KindleUnlimited!

Witch on Third

The books opens on the the last night of Briar Hollow's first annual paranormal festival. With Chase still stinging from the breakup and Lucas Grayson more than a little interested, Jinx has plenty on her plate without a new evil trio in town. As the team works to counter Chesterfield's newest scheme, something happens in the Valley that changes everything for the Hamilton family.

Buy Witch on Third

In the Jinx Hamilton/ Wrecking Crew Novellas:

Moonstone

Werecat Festus McGregor leads his Recovery of Magical Objects Squad on a mission to retrieve the Moonstone Spoon from the penthouse of eccentric financier and collector Wardlaw Magwilde. Festus has the operation planned to the last detail until a wereparrot and a member of his own team throw a monkey wrench in the works -- but thankfully no actual monkeys.

Join Festus, Rube and the rest of the raccoons in this fun-filled novella from the bestselling author of the Jinx Hamilton series. Filled with hysterical Fae acronyms and overlapping agency jurisdictions, Moonstone is an escapist romp you won't want to put down.

Buy Moonstone

Merstone

A werecat and a raccoon walk into a dragon's lair . . .

Join ROMO agent and werecat Festus McGregor in this second installment of the Jinx Hamilton/ Wrecking Crew novellas. Agreeing to an off-the-books mission with wereparrot Jilly Pepperdine, Festus and Rube find themselves on the Isle of Wight in search of an ancient lodestone with the power to enslave shifters.

The perfect match of whimsical fun and fantastical adventure, enjoy the latest novella from bestselling author Juliette Harper. An escapist romp in the Fae world where magic, artifacts, and laughter abound!

Buy Merstone

The Selby Jensen Paranormal Mysteries

Descendants of the Rose

Selby Jensen's business card reads "Private Investigator," but that seriously downplays her occupation. Let's hear it in her own words:

"You want to know what I do for a living? I rip souls out. Cut heads off. Put silver bullets where silver bullets need putting. You think there aren't any monsters? . . . I have some disturbing news for you. You might want to sit down. Monsters walk among us. I'm looking for one in particular. In the meantime? I'm keeping the rest of them from eating people like you."

Juliette Harper, author of The Jinx Hamilton Novels, creates a cast of characters, most of whom have one thing in common; they don't have a pulse. The dead are doing just fine by Selby, who is determined never to lose someone she loves again, but then a force of love more powerful than her grief changes that plan.

Join Selby Jensen as she and her team track down a shadowy figure tied to a murder at a girls' school. What none of them realize, however, is that in solving this case, they will enter a longer battle against a larger evil.

Buy Descendants of the Rose

The Study Club Mysteries

You Can't Get Blood Out of Shag Carpet

Wanda Jean Milton discovers her husband, local exterminator Hilton Milton, dead on her new shag carpet with an Old Hickory carving knife sticking out of his chest.

Beside herself over how she'll remove the stain, and grief-stricken over Hilton's demise, Wanda Jean finds herself the prime suspect. But she is also a member of "the" local Study Club, a bastion of independent Texas feminism 1960s style.

Club President Clara Wyler has no intention of allowing a member to be a murder suspect. Aided by her younger sister and County Clerk, Mae Ella Gormley; Sugar Watson, the proprietress of Sugar's Style and Spray; and Wilma Schneider, Army MASH veteran and local RN, the Club women set out to clear Wanda Jean's name — never guessing the local dirt they'll uncover.

Buy You Can't Get Blood Out of Shag Carpet

About the Author

"It's kind of fun to do the impossible." Walt Disney said that, and the two halves of Juliette Harper believe it wholeheartedly. Together, Massachusetts-based Patricia Pauletti, and Texan Rana K. Williamson combine their writing talents as Juliette. "She" loves to create strong female characters and place them in interesting, challenging, painful, and often comical situations. Refusing to be bound by genre, Juliette's primary interest lies in telling good stories. Patti, who fell in love with writing when she won her first 8th grade poetry contest, has a background in music, with a love of art and design. Rana, a former journalist and university history instructor, is happiest with a camera in hand and a cat or two at home.

For more information . . .
www.JulietteHarper.com
admin@julietteharper.com

By Juliette Harper
Copyright 2016, Juliette Harper

Skye House Publishing, LLC

License Notes

eBooks are not transferable. All rights are reserved. No part of this book may be used or reproduced in any manner without written permission, except in the case of brief quotations embodied in critical articles and reviews. The unauthorized reproduction or distribution of this copyrighted work is illegal. No part of this book may be scanned, uploaded, or distributed via the Internet or any other means, electronic or print, without the author's permission.

This is a work of fiction. Names, characters, businesses, places, events, and incidents are either the products of the author's imagination or used in a fictitious manner. Any resemblance to actual persons, living or dead, or actual events is purely coincidental.

EBOOK ISBN: 978-1-943516-74-2

PRINT ISBN: 978-1-943516-75-9

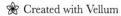 Created with Vellum

Made in the USA
Columbia, SC
12 October 2020